An Unexpected Party

First published 2023 by
FREMANTLE PRESS in association with Get YA Words Out

Fremantle Press Inc. trading as Fremantle Press
PO Box 158, North Fremantle, Western Australia, 6159
fremantlepress.com.au

Fremantle Press respectfully acknowledges the Whadjuk people of the
Noongar nation as the traditional owners and custodians of the land
where we work in Walyalup.

Cover art by Sarah Winifred Searle.
Cover design by Rebecca Mills.
Printed and bound by IPG.

 A catalogue record for this
book is available from the
National Library of Australia

ISBN 9781760992699 (paperback)
ISBN 9781760992705 (ebook)

Fremantle Press is supported by the State Government through the
Department of Local Government, Sport and Cultural Industries.

An Unexpected Party

EDITED BY SETH MALACARI

Get YA Words OUT

FREMANTLE PRESS

CONTENT WARNING

The following stories contain potentially triggering content. The editor has endeavored to keep all explicit forms of transphobia and homophobia, including slurs, out of this book, though some themes of queerphobia and dealing with this are present. Potential triggers within this anthology include violence, assault, misgendering, death, grief, mentions of drowning, police brutality, swearing, gore, blood, hospital settings, murder, emotional abuse by a parent, body horror, vomiting and supernatural themes.

These stories are predominately science fiction, fantasy, speculative fiction, dystopian, or light horror. They contain depictions of mythical and supernatural beings.

If you need support, please contact QLife: qlife.org.au.

CONTENTS

INTRODUCTION

Seth Malacari

There are two versions of the queer experience in mainstream media: rainbows and pride parades, or violence and death. These extreme ends of the queer spectrum do exist, but most of us live somewhere in between. I am a bisexual non-binary trans man. That makes me sound quite cool, but I'm really just a (literal) dad who on Saturday nights can be found curled up on my couch with some take-out, binge watching reality TV. I love my dog, the beach, hiking in the forest and hanging out with my family and friends. Society seems to have a hard time wrapping its head around queer people like me. I'm visible in the trans community, but when I'm at the shops doing my groceries I'm just some guy. I live a decent life, though I recognise much of this comes from holding a certain amount of privilege as a white male who passes as cis and had access to tertiary education. My family supports me and I have a loving partner. In mainstream media, people like me are rarely seen.

As a kid growing up in Boorloo in the 90s I didn't even know trans masculinity existed. The history of trans representation in the media has largely been that of trans women: trans women as jokes, trans women as objects of disgust, trans women as victims, or trans women as criminal men in drag. That was the extent of my knowledge of the trans experience as a kid. Trans men were rarely portrayed, though the few examples in mainstream (American) film or television, such as Brandon Teena, Max Sweeney or Viola/Sebastian Hastings reinforced the same ideas: to be trans is to be hated, feared, or laughed at. There was no such thing as trans joy on our screens or in our books, and there were certainly very few trans people who were given the platform to suggest otherwise. Couple this with the AIDS pandemic of the 1980s that wiped out a generation of trans and queer voices — people who today should be elders and mentors, people who should be in positions of power in publishing houses, on the boards of arts organisations or sitting in government — and what we are left with is a void. Trans representation in so-called Australia is simply not good enough. This is part of the reason I failed to recognise myself as trans until well into adulthood. What would my life have been like if positive, nuanced, and diverse trans characters existed in mainstream media as I was growing up?

Queer YA fiction in Australia has come a long way in the last decade. There are more queer books being published than ever before, some of those books win awards, and a rare few get made into movies and TV shows. What is 'queer' though? When we say queer we mean the whole LGBTQIA+ spectrum and all the intersectionalities of that. When we look at the queer YA books being published, one thing becomes obvious: Australia still has a diversity problem. Contemporary gay and lesbian stories are more abundant than ever (though nowhere near the numbers of heterosexual YA being pumped out every day), and many even have happy endings. Gay and lesbian youth, particularly white ones, can find multiple examples of themselves in literature today. These stories are important. Gay and lesbian teens deserve to see themselves in literature. But what about everyone else? In early 2022 an Instagram post went viral that listed all the Australian YA books with a trans or gender diverse main character. There were only seven of them. Five were by Alison Evans. We love Alison Evans, but it is completely unreasonable for one person to carry the weight of representing all gender diverse experiences. So where are all the trans stories? Where is the rest of the LGBTQIA+ representation?

This anthology was born out of the pure rage of not seeing the stories I wanted to read being published. I don't mind the odd contemporary, but I grew up on monster stories, problematic classic sci-fi and feminist fantasy. Give me sentient robot clones and Earthsea wizards over meet-cutes any day. I wanted stories about all that juicy middle ground of the queer experience. I wanted stories of friendship, family, and finding yourself (but with magic and ghosts and stuff). I wanted stories by people who have been denied a voice for too long. That is why this anthology contains only emerging writers, those who have not had a full length novel traditionally published before. Eighteen (nineteen including myself) new queer voices who have now been given a chance to be heard, to be recognised and to push the boundaries of what Queer YA in Australia is. Many of them are under thirty. There wasn't an age restriction, but it has been incredible to see so much young talent emerging.

This book features many trans and gender diverse voices, asexual, aromantic, bisexual and unapologetically queer voices.

The writers are as diverse as their stories. We are intersectional. We use pronouns how we want to. We challenge stereotypes. We write weird stuff. The stories range across genres, but mostly fall into the SFF categories. Some are funny, some are bittersweet, some are shocking, some are hopeful. And yet, we haven't covered it all. Not every queer identity is here. Not every intersection is explored. I hope this book leads to greater opportunities for queer writers in mainstream publishing so that eventually all queer people can find multiple examples of themselves in literature.

If you are a queer person reading this, I hope you find a hint of yourself amongst these pages. For everyone else, take note: the queer experience is more than just rainbows, 'equal love' and death. The queer experience is every minute of every day for us. It is the mundane and the magical. The inbetween. The unexpected.

Trans lives matter. Queer lives matter.

In solidarity,

Seth Malacari (he/they)

An unexpected Party

SIXTEEN CANDLES (BUT WITH DEMONS)

Shaeden Berry

It was 7pm on the 19th of September and Tal had turned sixteen nineteen hours ago. but his family and friends had completely forgotten. No one could deny the parallels between his life and the iconic 1984 comedy *Sixteen Candles* wherein Molly Ringwald's Samantha Baker was left bereft after her parents forgot her sixteenth birthday. The only difference Tal could see was that he had infinitely better hair than Molly — although he would have killed for those lips.

Tal liked to think he was a lovable person. He liked to think he was a good son and brother to his single mother and younger sister. Kind, considerate, occasionally grumpy — but who isn't when you're a raging ball of hormones and your little sister likes to hide under your bed to eavesdrop on your conversations and then promptly blab to your mum that 'Tal's art teacher ran him over with a truck!' This was incorrect. He'd said he'd *wanted* his art teacher to run him over with a truck, which was an entirely different thing.

But anyway. He was a good brother (mostly), and a caring friend (at least to Rowena, his best friend). And yet his sixteenth birthday, the big 1–6, and he was alone in his house, abandoned by his mother and sister for a sleepover and forgotten by his own friends who hadn't so much as texted or called. He had purposefully not planned a birthday party because he expected Rowena to organise a surprise party — he'd dropped enough hints — and yet, nothing.

Dramatically, Tal collapsed spread-eagled on his back to glare moodily at the ceiling. With the darkness of night edging out the sun, similarly grey thoughts started to slither their way into his consciousness. Maybe he wasn't a good son? Maybe he was a terrible friend? After all, for everyone to completely forget his birthday surely that had to mean something was inherently flawed in his personality? Tal closed his eyes. He was teetering on the verge of thinking very bad thoughts about himself and he very firmly told himself to stop it.

He returned his focus to righteous fury again. How dare everyone make him think he was some sort of hideous person when he wasn't even that bad. He could be so much worse.

It would serve them right if this moment — this moment of abandonment in his time of need — was his turning point. This would be the scene in the documentary of his dastardly life when they would be shaking their heads, crying silent tears in their interview. 'He just changed after that moment and it was all our fault!' His villain origin story.

Only he didn't actually want to hurt anyone or do anything bad. Maybe he could just scare them a little. Rowena had told him about a boy named Dayton who'd been missing from school for a week because he was undergoing intense counselling. 'They found all these Satanic symbols in his closet and apparently he'd written plans to sacrifice a goat,' she'd told him. Tal had asked where, in the middle of suburbia, he would even get a goat, and Rowena had shrugged and suggested, 'eBay?'

Tal decided he would channel his inner Dayton. He'd draw symbols all over his closet, leave it just slightly ajar enough for his mother to see and then reap the benefits of the guilt when he told her he'd only done it in a fit of loneliness after she'd neglected him on his birthday. Passive-aggressive perfection.

He googled 'dark scary-looking symbols' and took chalk from his sister's playroom, because he wanted the symbols to be easily removable, and then got to work drawing them. He chose the prettiest and more ornate symbols because he was good at drawing and why not show that off a bit, and then added a few Latin words for good measure. Things that said 'demon' and 'conjure' and 'dark forces'.

He added the last dot, the final flourish, sat back on his haunches and said, 'Perfe—'

There was a flash of red, a burst of heat across his face and something knocked him backwards onto the ground with a terrible thump. Darkness tumbled across his vision, thick black smoke filling the air. He scrabbled at the floor in panic.

'WHO DARES CONJURE ME?'

Tal launched himself to his feet and flung himself away from the closet towards the door to his bedroom. Only in the archway did he stop and chance a look backwards. A very tall figure in black robes was standing in his closet. Tal emitted some sort of strangled noise that sounded like *eep* before he ran down the hallway.

He could've sworn he heard someone say behind him, 'Hey, wait, I haven't finished!'

He ran downstairs with the wild idea in his head that he would grab the landline and dial 911 when, at the bottom, he realised two things: he was in Australia, and 911 was not the correct number and also, it was 2022, they didn't have a landline, because no one had a landline, because everyone had mobile phones. Like the one he'd left on the floor upstairs.

There was a creak on the stairs behind him. Tal spun around. The tall figure was standing there. They were translucently pale, draped in robes and had eyes that were completely black, like two pieces of coal shoved into their face. And they had horns.

'I died,' Tal said aloud.

'Oh, cool,' said the horned-figure. 'Listen, you realise you didn't let me finish my spiel, right? Kinda rude.'

'Sorry?'

'You should be. It's a really good speech. I've tweaked it and everything. Really dramatic. But, your loss. Also, I don't think you're dead. Dead people can't conjure demons.'

'Demons?' Tal echoed. He needed to sit down.

'Well, yeah. What did you think you were summoning? Or were you trying for the ghost of a relative because I have to tell you, you were way off with your symbols if that was your aim.' They leant forward conspiratorially. 'Ouija boards. That's the ghost portal. That's how you get the dead relatives.'

'I—I don't want dead relatives.'

The creature straightened up. 'Ah, so you did mean to summon a demon then.'

'No!' Tal blurted. 'God, no! I didn't — did you say demon?'

Tal put his fingers to his temple, screwed his eyes shut and tried to think. He'd obviously hit his head and passed out.

This was a twisted coma dream. Or the sheer loneliness of his forgotten birthday had caused his brain to create an imaginary friend. Something poked him on the nose. His eyes flew open. The demon was peering intensely at him.

'Are you alright?' the demon asked. 'You've gone quite pale.'

The skin of the demon was so translucent Tal could see black lines spread like spiderwebs shifting beneath their skin. But sure, *he* was pale.

'I don't know what's going on,' he said.

The demon rocked back on their heels. 'Well, let me catch you up. You summoned a demon, rudely interrupted their introductory speech and now you have me until midnight tonight to do your bidding. Which, incidentally, I'm curious about. What deeds will you have me perform?'

'Deeds?'

'Yeah, deeds. You know, jobs. Tasks. I'm yours to command.' The demon clapped their hands together. 'So, let's get to it. Why did you summon me?'

'Because everyone forgot my birthday and I wanted to make them feel bad,' said Tal to his own feet.

The demon frowned. 'By summoning a demon?'

'I told you, I didn't mean to summon anything.'

The demon ignored this. They rubbed their chin with a clawed hand. Tal swallowed.

'So, I guess …' the demon started slowly, 'you want me to wreak havoc, rain hellfire on their homes, tear them limb from limb and shatter their bones?'

'What? No! They're my friends and family. Why would I want that?'

The demon was starting to look cross. Tal felt this was unfair because if anyone was in a frustrating and absurd situation warranting getting upset, it was him.

'What do you want me to do then?' said the demon, with a small stamp of their foot.

'I don't know,' Tal said, as he threw his hands in the air.

'You're the worst summoner.'

Tal breathed out through his mouth. 'I'm not—' he started, then stopped and rubbed his face in frustration.

The demon watched him intently. Whilst Tal's fear had subsided somewhat, the soulless voids staring at him were still incredibly unnerving. He gestured toward the lounge room.

'Can you just sit over there and …' he racked his brain for how to keep the demon out of trouble for the next few hours until midnight when they would, apparently, vanish, '… and not do anything.'

'For five hours?' The demon closed their eyes briefly and Tal thought they looked like they were counting to ten. 'Look, kid, I don't think you're quite getting this. I'm a demon. You can't just waste an opportunity like this.'

'Fine,' Tal sighed. 'What do people normally do with you?'

The demon opened their mouth.

'That doesn't include raining hellfire on everyone,' Tal hurried to add.

The demon closed their mouth. For a moment the demon gnawed their lip, then finally confessed, 'You're the first person who's ever summoned me.'

'What?' Tal blinked.

Demons, it seemed, could not blush, but this one still

managed to look incredibly embarrassed.

'Well, the thing is, I'm only a new demon.'

'A new demon?' Tal repeated. 'What does that even mean?'

'It means just that. I woke up a demon only a few hundred years ago and I've never, you know, been called out to do anything. Until now.'

Tal contemplated this. 'Woke up where?'

The demon fixed him with a stare. 'Can't tell you that. Trade secrets. Strictly forbidden.'

'By who?'

The demon planted their hands on their hips. It reminded Tal of his mother. 'Stop avoiding the question. What are you going to have me do?'

Tal sighed and walked into the lounge to finally enact the dramatic flop atop the cushions that he'd been dying to do for the past five minutes.

'I don't have anything for you to do,' he told the demon. 'It's my birthday. I'm all alone and everyone has forgotten about me.'

Saying the words gave birth to another fresh wave of hurt, and he turned his head slightly, trying to hide the way his jaw tightened with the effort of not crying. There was a moment of excruciating silence before the demon spoke.

'What would you usually do on your birthday?'

Tal shrugged. 'Eat cake, I guess?'

The demon nodded slowly, and then looked around the lounge room. 'Right,' they said. 'Let's make a cake then.'

'Okay. Wait, what?'

'Make a cake,' the demon repeated.

'You're a demon. Demons don't bake cakes.'

'Demons do whatever their master commands. Including baking cakes.' They turned and set off from the room.

Tal struggled upwards to his feet. 'Where are you going? Are you seriously going to bake a cake?'

The question seemed to be answered when Tal entered the kitchen and found the demon rifling through the cupboards, pulling out pots and pans at random and placing them on the counter.

'Okay, here's the thing,' they said, holding a rice cooker in one hand and a kettle in the other, 'I don't actually know how to bake a cake.'

For the first time that day Tal felt a little bubble of laughter in his throat. 'That is incredibly unsurprising.'

'I just need instructions,' the demon hastened to say, 'then I'll be up and running.'

Tal hesitated, then he headed to the stack of recipe books his mother kept slotted between the microwave and the pantry. He tugged out a cake recipe book, *Women's Weekly Kid's Birthday Cakes*, and started to flick through.

'Here, we'll choose one from this,' he told the demon, who came to stand alongside him. 'I think there's some cocoa powder in the pantry. Maybe a chocolate cake?'

The demon seemed spectacularly disappointed by his choice, but when Tal pointed out the time constraints, and then finally told them they could decorate the cake with sprinkles and chocolate M&Ms, they got on board with the idea. For a supernatural being that had so far indicated an alarming predilection for raining hellfire on humanity, they seemed quite excited at the entire premise of cake construction.

What ensued was possibly the strangest hour of Tal's life. He perched himself on a stool at the kitchen bench and read aloud the instructions. The demon proceeded to efficiently, and with vigor, carry out everything that Tal told him to. The sight of clawed fingers carefully holding a mixing bowl as the electric mixer spun the ingredients into a smooth batter was one Tal was sure he would remember for a good few years to come.

When the cake was baked, cooled and iced, the demon used M&M's to write Tal's age on the top. They ran out of space though so instead there was nothing but a big '1' and a lot of sprinkles. With a flourish they cut him a slice, presented it on a platter and watched intensely while Tal ate it. The demon practically vibrated with anticipation. Tal made sure to make appreciative noises, nodding his head.

'Delicious,' he said, which wasn't entirely untrue.

'Of course it is.' The demon tapped their claws on the kitchen table. 'Now what?' 'Presents?' Tal ventured, then shook his head, ready to abandon the idea.

'Presents, right!' the demon enthused. 'No problem. How do you make a present then?'

'That's not … look, I don't really have anything on my wish list that we can make. It's mostly, you know, things.'

'Things?' the demon repeated.

'Like a new iPad,' Tal explained.

The demon looked around the kitchen. 'This 'iPad': where would you get it?' they asked, peering intently as if an electronic tablet was going to tumble its way out of the pantry any second.

'There's no iPad here,' Tal told them. 'Look, forget the presents.'

The demon frowned. 'We are not forgetting presents. If we

can't make them, what about something you want to do instead?'

Tal thought for a moment. 'Well, I'd like to learn how to drive a car.'

The demon pointed a triumphant claw at him. 'Excellent, let's do that then.'

'You didn't even know how to bake a cake, how are you going to teach me to drive a car?'

The demon was already headed out of the kitchen. 'Minor details. Besides, this is all about the experience. Now, where do you keep the cars? Upstairs?'

'Up—' Tal spluttered as he rose to follow the demon. 'Do you even know what a car is?'

The demon shifted their walking direction from the staircase to the front door. 'So, not upstairs. Where then?'

'My mum took the car. There's only her work vehicle parked in the driveway but we can't take that.'

The demon was already out the front door. Tal stood for a moment, considered not following, but then thought of his mum taking his sister to a sleepover — a sleepover! — on *his* birthday. He grabbed the car keys from the side table.

The demon's idea of teaching Tal to drive was to clamber their hulking form into the passenger seat, wait for Tal to get himself settled in the driver's seat and then shout, 'Okay, now drive!'

Tal had watched his mum drive enough times, and that one time when he was ten he'd reversed the car out of the driveway with her help, so surely he could manage this.

It took a total of half an hour to go less than a kilometre down the street because Tal refused to let the car get above ten kilometres per hour and braked heavily several times when he saw shadows that he swore were cats, small children, dogs or deadly pinecones. Nonetheless, when they finally returned home Tal couldn't help the flush of triumph that raced through him.

'I drove!' he said, all but levitating from the car with excitement.

The demon clapped a hand on his shoulder. 'If that's what you want to call it, sure. So what now, birthday boy?'

Tal walked into the lounge to flop himself onto the couch. 'I don't know. I think that's probably it.'

The demon frowned. 'Really? A cake and slow driving? That's all a birthday is? Seems kinda dull to me.'

'Well, people have parties as well. Usually with friends and family. If they remember.' Tal dug a fingernail into the couch, scratched the fabric, and tried to play off the bitterness that had crept into his voice. 'But whatever, that's not really important.'

'You gotta stop with the 'no' and the 'not really'. Remember me? Supernatural creature? Your literal bidding is my command. You want a party, we have a party. Also, what's a party?'

A short snort of laughter escaped Tal. 'Okay, sure. I mean, a party is just a gathering, I guess, with snacks, music, activities.'

The demon brightened. 'Oh, right, like a sacrificial ritual?'

'I mean, sure?' Tal offered, eyebrow raised. 'Minus the sacrifice.'

'Boring,' the demon rolled their eyes. 'But fine. Right — snacks. Kitchen? See, I'm learning. I'm getting the hang of this.'

'You're a regular party-planner,' Tal deadpanned.

'Thanks!' The demon seemed unaffected by his sarcasm, and bounded to the kitchen. 'What snacks do you want? What about this stuff? Is this stuff snacks?'

Tal entered the kitchen. The demon spun around from where they'd been exploring the pantry and extended a tin of beetroot.

'No. I think there's a packet of chips in there though?'

The demon put the beetroot back in the pantry, pulled out a bag of chips and shook it with a doubtful expression on their face.

'Just this? We need more snacks than that. What else?'

'Well,' Tal laughed to himself, 'we could make fairy bread?'

The demon's face darkened. 'Fairies?' They growled as if they were a dog.

Tal stared at them. 'What the hell was that?'

The demon stared back. They sat there staring for over a minute.

Tal gave up. 'The jar of sprinkles is back in the pantry,' he said.

The demon took the jar of sprinkles out and Tal fetched the bread and the butter from the fridge and plonked them onto the chopping board. The demon seemed doubtful when Tal explained how to make fairy bread and less enamoured by the human race at the conclusion of their making. Tal didn't blame them. It was hard not to look at fairy bread and feel just a little dubious about humanity afterwards. But it sure did taste amazing.

The demon used a claw to poke at some stray sprinkles on the chopping board. 'Now we get the people over,' they said.

Tal inhaled sharply mid-mouthful. Sprinkles shot to the back of his throat and he choked. 'What? What people?'

'Your friends and family.'

'I already told you. They forgot my birthday. That's why we're in this whole situation in the first place.'

'So remind them,' the demon said, like it was that simple. 'It's simple.'

'It's almost eleven at night.' Tal put his half-eaten fairy bread slice to one side. He wasn't hungry anymore. 'It's too late to be inviting anyone over.'

'They had all day to come over on their terms,' the demon said. 'Who cares if it's inconvenient to them now?'

Tal shook his head stubbornly. 'I'm not inviting people over. Besides, what are you supposed to do while they're here?'

'I could provide the music.'

'You can sing?'

'I can wail,' the demon said proudly.

Tal shuddered. 'No thank you. And anyway, I meant, what would you do while they're here because you look — well, like a demon. They're likely to call the police or something.'

'So I dress as a human,' the demon said. 'They won't know the difference.'

Tal eyed their horns. 'I think they will.'

'Has anyone ever told you you're really negative?'

The fact that a demon — a supernatural creature aligned to the dark side of life — viewed his energy as negative hit a nerve. Tal led the demon upstairs into his mum's room, because he was not sacrificing his own clothes to be torn by horns, and besides his mum had (against his sartorial advice, he might add), a big collection of hats. He found the floppiest, widest-brimmed hat and gave it to the demon, then scrounged around to produce a fabric floral face-mask. The effect, when Tal stepped back to look, was of a demonic creature with a floppy hat and a face mask on.

That is to say, it was not a particularly effective disguise.

The demon looked in the mirror. 'I look *just* like a human! Whoa!'

'You look like three Kobolds in a trench-coat.'

'A what?'

'It's a *Dungeons and Dragons* … never mind.' Tal stopped his explanation and admitted to himself he was slightly terrified that the demon might react to the term 'dragon' the same as they had 'fairy'.

Tal watched in fascination as the demon twirled in front of the mirror, absolutely delighted by what they saw.

'It's uncanny!' They dropped their tone into a weird, oddly gruff voice, 'Hello there fellow humans!' They returned to their normal voice. 'How was that? Just like a human right?'

'Well, for one thing, we don't call each other 'fellow humans'', said Tal.

The demon seemed unaffected by Tal's criticism. 'So are we summoning friends now?'

Tal sighed and turned to leave his mum's room, wandering back to his own. His phone was still on the floor. He picked it up. He could feel the demon looming behind him as he opened Rowena's number on his contact list. He hesitated, huffed, then went to sit on his bed, putting the phone to one side.

'We're not calling anyone,' he said. 'It's stupid and pointless.'

'Okay,' the demon said, and Tal was momentarily surprised at the easy acquiesce before the demon took two steps forward, grabbed the phone, and pressed the screen multiple times until the unmistakable sounds of ringing emitted from the speaker.

Tal's mouth hung open. 'Are you actually kidding me?'

The ringing stopped. Rowena's voice came through the line. 'Tal? What the hell, it's like eleven o'clock.'

'Give me that!' Tal leapt to his feet, grabbed the phone from the demon's claws.

'Give you what?' said Rowena.

'I– sorry, that was. You know what, never mind, sorry.' Tal backed away from the demon and glowered at them.

'Are you okay?' asked Rowena. 'Why are you calling so late?'

'No reason. It's fine. Um, hi, how are you?'

'I mean, I'm tired and in the middle of studying.'

The words were pointed. Tal bit his lip, and then turned his back to the demon.

'Right,' he said. 'Just, you know. Anything you want to mention? Maybe?'

'What?' Rowena sounded confused.

Tal's shoulders sagged, the last shred of hope leaving his body.

'Tal, I really need to go,' said Rowena.

'Okay, no worries.'

'You sure you're okay?'

'Fine and dandy,' said Tal.

There was silence on the other end of the line. Then Rowena said, 'Okay, well if you say so. See you on Monday at school.'

The phone made a *bloop* sound as the call disconnected. Tal's face burned, his throat burned, his eyes burned and he stared hard at a spot on the wall, a tiny fleck of black on the white surface, because if he focused hard enough, long enough, he could ignore the way his body felt like crumpling into a heap and crying.

Tal heard the demon shuffle closer. 'Sorry,' they said quietly.

Tal wasn't sure if they were apologising for calling Rowena, for pushing so hard, or for the bigger picture of Tal's hurt, but it genuinely felt nice, because Tal didn't think demons apologised very often.

'It's okay,' he said, and he was relieved that his voice didn't shake.

'Is now a good time to wail?'

Tal snorted a startled laugh. 'I– yeah, I think we'll pass on the music part of the party. I don't feel much like dancing anyway.'

The demon twisted the face mask in their claws, the fabric tearing at the seams. Tal had successfully made a demon feel awkward with his terrible social situation, and he wasn't sure whether to be sad or proud.

'So what do you want to do then?' the demon asked finally. They took off the floppy hat and laid it on the bed. 'What party activities are up next?'

Tal mulled the question for a moment. 'How about we watch *Sixteen Candles*?'

The demon nodded. 'I have no idea what that is, but bring it on.'

There was an odd sense of companionship as they both settled on the couch and Tal lined up the movie. At fifteen minutes to midnight he picked up the remote and pressed pause.

'Thank you,' he said, 'for tonight. For everything.'

'You do realise I had to do your bidding,' the demon pointed out.

Tal shrugged. 'I know, but still. You didn't have to enjoy it. And you did. I think.'

'I did,' the demon confirmed quietly. 'Listen, about your friends and family and this whole birthday thing. The thing is, humans, you're all flawed. All of you. Some more than others.'

'Inspiring so far,' said Tal.

The demon flapped their claws. 'Let me finish. Humans — they basically suck, to varying degrees.'

'Bloody hell.' Tal didn't know whether to be offended or not.

'There's a point to this, okay? I'm trying to say that humans do bad things. But there's a difference between doing bad things because you're a flawed human, and doing malicious things. People do bad things, but they don't necessarily do it to hurt you. So, this whole situation: your friends, your family, forgetting. It's bad, they did a bad thing, but it's not personal. It's not malicious.'

Tal took a moment to fully absorb the words. He fiddled with the TV remote. He could feel tears building.

'I'm not saying it's okay what they did,' the demon continued. 'I'm not even saying that you need to forgive them immediately, or even at all. Maybe this is where you decide what you put up with in the future and what you don't. But don't let it get to you. You got a lot of years ahead of you. This is just a blip. Four hundred years from now you won't even remember this birthday.'

'In four hundred years I'll be dead, but that's ... actually good advice?' He couldn't help the questioning inflection at the end of his sentence. The demon didn't seem to notice.

'And, look, if it was malicious and not just selfish, silly human stuff, if they ignored you on purpose,' the demon continued, warming to their topic, 'then—'

'They're not my true friends,' Tal finished.

'—rain hellfire and shatter their bones!'

'Ah,' Tal said, 'and we're back to demon advice.'

The demon grinned, big and wide, exposing rows of pointy, fanged teeth. Tal couldn't help but grin back.

'How about if they forget again next year,' said Tal, 'we do this again.'

The demon laughed and a part of Tal wanted them to respond to the invitation, to confirm that they could come back, but they just gave Tal's shoulder a good-natured clap.

'Thanks for the good night,' they said. 'How about you put the movie back on?'

'Okay,' he said, and clicked play.

He tried to focus on the television screen, but his gaze kept flicking to look out of the corner of his eye at the demon, back and forth, as the time ticked closer to midnight. Until, in one glance, the demon was gone. It was abrupt enough that Tal jolted where he sat, his heart doing a little leap from his chest to his throat. He had expected something more — smoke, a bang, a huge black creature dragging the demon screaming into the beyond — but the demon had simply vanished.

And all that was left was a slight indent in the cushion where they had sat, and a sense that the room felt slightly lonelier, slightly emptier, yet it was undoubtedly the best birthday Tal had ever had.

SHELLSHOCKED

Aidan Demmers

Framed against the glittering vault of open space, the Starscraper looks like a nutri-bar that's been chewed up, spat out, left to moulder for ten years, then picked up by a neon-obsessed four-year-old for their first ever Arts 'n Space-Crafts.

'Damn, that thing is ugly,' says Nancy 7.

In the shadowy reflection of the viewport, she sees Jana shoot her an unimpressed look.

'Get those paws off the glass,' Jana says. 'You'll smear it.'

Nancy tears her eyes from the sickening sight of the Corpo ship, and puts her hands up in surrender.

'Yes, ma'am.'

In the dark of the viewing room, the only illumination comes from the Starscraper's lurid neon lights. They flicker across Jana's face — in red, purple, green — catching upon her large black eyes, thin silver nose-ring, and the curve at the very corner of her mouth.

Their captain's voice breaks the moment, crackling through the faulty intercom.

'Nancy, Sanjana,' Ngaire says. 'As you may have noticed, we are approaching target. Please make your way to Command.'

'Copy that,' Jana says, and arches a brow up at Nancy.

Grinning back down at her, Nancy cracks her knuckles.

'Let's go fry that spaceworm.'

After ten minutes of running through The Plan for the billionth time, and fifteen minutes of lecturing about safety and subtlety and other s-words that slip in one of Nancy's ears and straight out the other, Ngaire lets Nancy and Jana leave the Command room. On the way out, they trade cheerful *see-ya-laters* with the rest of the crew, and receive a couple of goodies from Ellie, the ship's slightly unhinged mechanic. Finally, it's just the two of them suiting up by the starboard airlock.

Well, Jana suits up. Nancy scrapes her rough white hair back into a tie, checks the battery of her two-handed plas-blade, and makes fun of Jana's suit.

'Having fun in that fishbowl?' she asks, rapping a knuckle against Jana's helmet, a sphere of silver-sheened astroglass connected to Jana's stylish crimson spacesuit by curling pipes.

Jana raises one of her tiny laser-spitters in overt threat.

'Having fun with those hands?'

'Children,' Ngaire says, voice transmitted straight into their skulls by expensive mission-grade transmitters, 'stay on task.'

'Yes, ma'am,' they reply in unison, before exchanging a smirk.

The walk to the Starscraper is uneventful, until one of Nancy's propulsion boots fizzles out halfway between the two ships. Nancy punches it and curses. The sound is lost to the vacuum of space, but the vibration of her throat is picked up by the transmitters.

'Foul-mouth,' Jana says, as she sweeps past, glowing like an ember in the light of the stars.

'Priss,' Nancy says, hitting her boot again. It sputters back to life, and she jets after Jana, wincing at the flash of the Starscraper's lights.

Within seconds, they reach one of the ship's external hatches. Up close, it's even more disgusting — the polycrete is stained and blotched, pitted by debris. Nancy wrestles one of Ellie's toys from her breast pocket, and presses it to a panel by the hatch.

'That thing better work,' Jana mutters.

Over the comms, Ellie squawks, offended. 'Of course it'll work!' he says. 'When have I ever let you down?'

'If you really want me to answer that, I have a list,' says Jana.

The device flashes hot-pink, and the hatch judders open.

'Well, whaddya know,' Nancy says. The device detaches itself from the panel, and whirs back to her hand, like a space-proof metal insect.

'Told you!' says Ellie.

'Yeah, yeah,' Jana says, a little too quickly. Eyeing the device, she pulls herself into the ship. Nancy tucks it back into her jacket, and follows.

The hatch shuts behind them. Sound returns to the world, as air hisses into the cramped space, an off-tone beep announcing full pressurisation. Nancy's boots lower her to the floor, gravity dragging at her spine. Her left ear pops. She smacks at the other until it follows suit, while Jana tugs off her helmet and ruffles a hand through her silky undercut.

'This place stinks,' Jana says, wrinkling her nose as she peers around the room. 'I don't want to know how many spores I'm breathing in right now.'

Unsurprisingly, the airlock smacks of Corpo cheapness. It's fitted all in mottled grey, and its stark strip-lights buzz like dying blowflies. They leach everything of colour, draining the warmth from Jana's dark brown complexion, and turning Nancy's own blue skin an unappealing shade of snot.

Jana slants a look at Nancy.

'Help me with my suit, would you?'

'Gladly.'

Nancy moves to Jana's back, and sets about disassembling the sleek red panels that kept all her precious human liquids from boiling. Of course, Jana could do it herself with the touch of a button — but both of them know that isn't the point.

'Remember what we discussed,' Ngaire says, an edge to her tone. 'I want you in and out as quickly as possible.'

'Yeah, less flirting, more robbing!' Ellie says. 'I wanna find out how well my Terminites work.'

Jana rolls her eyes, as Nancy hands her the last pieces of the suit. She shoves them into her oversized shoulder-bag. Underneath, like Nancy, she wears the uniform of a Corpo security guard — grey and bulky and completed by the ridiculous little cap she pulls on to hide her hairstyle. Corpos aren't allowed to have undercuts. Or piercings, tattoos, or blue skin, but the hope is nobody will get close enough to notice.

'So you've given up pretending to be competent, Ellie?' Jana asks.

Ellie squawks again, but Ngaire interrupts him.

'Stay on task, and get this over with.'

'Gotcha, Captain,' Nancy says.

Suck-up, Jana mouths.

Nancy winks at her, and pulls out Ellie's stupidly-named Terminite. It darts up from her hand, flitting over to the internal door. Jana steps out of its path, laser-spitter raised as if she's ready to shoot it from the air.

'You just love that cute little mite, don't you?' Nancy asks, without even trying to hide her grin.

This gets her a glare, the spitter's snub nose turning her way.

'Keep that thing away from me,' Jana says.

Nancy snickers as the mite flashes pink again, and the valve groans open.

'Whatever you want, sweetheart.'

The mite leads them through the Starscraper's creaking maze of corridors. As usual, the cubicle workers in the open-plan sections pay them no attention, too busy tapping at their screens and feverishly trying to meet impossible KPIs.

Making it to the data centre is almost too easy. It's only guarded by DNA recognition, which the mite fools in seconds. The interior looks exactly like any other Corpo centre they've broken into: ranks of rickety servers, wheezing away in the heavy cold dark, red wires spilling from them like human intestines. The mite goes where it needs to, flanked by its five duplicates, which Nancy releases to Jana's evident distaste. They're all controlled by the little box in her chest pocket, thankfully, 'cause neither Nancy or Jana could code a toothbrush, and Ellie won't step foot on Corpo ships.

'You look good in that outfit,' Nancy says, reaching to flick at the brim of Jana's cap. 'Such a cute little fascist.'

'Shut it.' Jana tugs her hat back down, purple-painted lips

curving. 'You just look like a half-dead Tank-Bear, as always.'

'Oh, you're calling me big?' Nancy asks, and flexes.

Jana smacks Nancy's bicep, smile growing.

Their comms buzz with Ellie's exaggerated groan.

'Ugh. Ngaire, chuck me into the nearest black hole, I can't listen to this anymore.'

'Keep working,' Ngaire replies, tone calm in a way that warns of an hour-long post-mission lecture. 'And cut the chatter, please.'

'Aye-aye,' Jana says, and makes an obscene gesture when Nancy smirks. They pass the time with elaborate nonverbal insults, until Ellie gives a triumphant cackle.

'All ours, baby!'

'Nice work, Elliot. Ladies, get out of there.'

The first mite flutters back over, leaving its duplicates to burrow into the servers. Jana's hand drifts to the holster at her hip. 'With pleasure,' she says.

They stride back through the musty hallways, more serious now they're on a timer. From experience, it takes the overworked techies about fifteen minutes to notice the stacking server errors. Plenty of time to get back to the ship, and put a few parsecs between them and the Starscraper, if nothing gets in their way.

Their first warning comes when the mite starts flashing yellow and buzzing around Jana's head. She curses, swatting at it.

'Ellie, your stupid bug's malfunctioning.'

'Huh? What's it doing?'

'It's gone yellow,' says Nancy. 'And … frantic.'

'Oh, shit,' Ellie says. 'That's the seccy alarm. You've got company.'

Nancy's hand goes to the hilt tucked into her belt. 'I thought the mite was leading us away from the patrol routes?'

'Well, someone's gone off-route.' His voice is taut with frustration. There's only so much he can help from back at the ship — the one thing Corpos don't skimp on is remote shielding. 'I don't know where they're coming from, but—'

'Get to cover,' Ngaire cuts in, but Nancy's been scanning their immediate surroundings, and it's nothing but bare polycrete.

'There isn't any,' Jana says. Her dark eyes slip over to Nancy's, and they exchange a nod.

Nancy leans against the slimy wall. She pulls out a pack of stim-cigs, as the mite flutters back to hide in her pocket, alarm received.

'Time to act natural.' She offers a cig to Jana, before flicking one out for herself.

Hiding her trigger hand behind her waist, Jana takes a puff.

'Ugh. Bubblegum, really?'

'What's wrong with bubblegum?'

'Nothing, if you've got the taste buds of a Spit Grubbish.'

Footsteps sound down the corridor — two sets, coming from the left. Without a word, they swap positions, so Nancy's back is to the approaching seccies, hiding her blue face.

'Still better than grape,' Nancy replies.

'Screw you,' Jana says, as the seccies round the corner. Nancy can't see them, but she does see Jana give a very macho chin-jerk, before her gaze slides would-be-casually back to Nancy. 'Grape's delicious.'

The steps pause, just behind Nancy.

'You girls on your ten?'

It's exactly the voice Nancy would've expected. Too loud and too deep, clearly practised to be as gruff as humanly possible.

'Yep.' Jana exhales another curling cloud. 'Making the most of it.'

'Feel that, bro,' says the second seccy, who's managed to become even gruffer than the first. 'Never seem long enough, do they?'

The purple glow of the cig catches in Jana's eyes, which are shadowed by the cap's low brim, and as scorching as the plasma-oceans of Nancy's home planet. Calling her bro was a mistake — both too familiar and too masculine for Jana, who the world mistook for a boy, until she set things right at the age of seventeen.

'So true, *bro*,' she says, baring her crooked canines in a grin.

'What're y'all up to?' Nancy asks, turning her head a little towards the seccies. While they'd definitely deserve a sting from Jana's spitter, Ngaire probably wouldn't be too happy about it. 'This ain't the regulation patrol route.'

'Oh, ain't it?' Gruff asks, casually.

'Why you asking?' Gruffer asks, even more casually. 'Gonna report us?'

Shit. For a moment, Nancy forgot about the fragility of the seccy ego.

'Nope. None of my business.'

Too little, too late.

'Oi,' says Gruff. 'Why won't you look over here?'

Nancy gives Jana an apologetic grimace.

Jana rolls her eyes.

'You ignoring us?' Gruffer asks.

A hand lands on Nancy's shoulder.

'Well, well,' Gruff says, 'that skin sure ain't regulation.'

Jana sucks up the last of her cig, and flicks the casing away.

'Please be careful,' Ngaire sighs.

The hand on Nancy's shoulder tugs. She follows it, pivoting on her heel, and sees just a flash of Gruff's face — clean-shaven and pale beneath a too-low cap — before her arm swings out, following her momentum, and hits the centre of that bulky chest.

Gruff goes flying, smashing into the bend in the corridor twenty metres down with an unfortunate *crunch*. The world turns lurid red, a klaxon screeching through the silence: the Man Down alarm, triggered by a change in any seccy's monitored vitals.

It is, unfortunately, a very familiar sound.

Nancy turns back just as Gruffer crumples to the floor, bulky gun clattering across the stained polycrete. Jana lowers her spitter, the tiny weapon glowing.

'Two down, six hundred to go,' she says, alarm lights glittering off her grin.

'Get out of there,' Ngaire says, 'or I'm coming in to get you.'

Nancy winces.

'Yes, Captain.'

In the swamping red of the corridors, the mite winks yellow.

Before Nancy can so much as switch on her plas-blade, Jana sends a hail of laser beams bouncing around the corner. Sequential thuds announce the success of her move, and she spins her twin autobeam pistols with a self-satisfied grin.

'Show-off,' Nancy says. 'How many guns did you even bring?'

Jana pats her bulging shoulder-bag. 'Only a couple.'

'Well, you're the one who's gotta carry 'em,' Nancy says, and jogs around the corner.

Jana follows with a rattle of guns.

'Like you're any different. How many blades have you got stowed away in those pockets, hm?'

'Wouldn't you like to know,' Nancy says, stepping through the tangle of incapacitated seccies.

Jana clicks her tongue. Beneath it, Nancy hears another click, like an echo. She turns. Movement at the corner of her eye, one of the bodies shifting, a glint in a black-gloved hand.

Jana starts to speak. 'Maybe I—'

'Down!' Nancy snaps, shoving Jana back. Jana goes stumbling with a gasp, as something flashes through the air, sparking red in the lights. Some part of Nancy recognises it immediately. She hurls her body forward, curling around it and slamming to the ground.

She goes down hard, the thing digging into her stomach. She feels it vibrate against her hip, hears Jana shout, sees a spidering crack in the polycrete before her eyes.

Then:

The world is grey, and silent. She feels light, like she's back in zero-grav, like she could drift kilometres with a single flex of her pinkie.

Her pinkie won't move.

Her eyes are open, but she can't see anything. Only the grey. Blinking takes so much effort, and her lashes cling to each other, so she has to force her eyes back open.

Red bleeds into her vision.

Jana?

Nancy tries to open her mouth. Something gushes out of it, spilling from the corner of her lips, pooling warm against her cheek.

She's lying on her side. She feels so light.

Something before her eyes, flickering blue.

She blinks again, forcing her lashes apart, some tearing free.

The mite — Ellie's Terminite.

She can still taste her cig's synthetic sweetness. Can still feel Jana's shoulder beneath her hand. Can still feel the grenade purring against her hip.

Nancy forces out a breath, hears a strange bubbling hiss.

'Jana,' she says, but it sounds awful, weak, wheezing, too much like …

'Nancy!'

Movement in front of her, something warm touching her face. After a dazed moment, it resolves into Jana's hand, pressing against her cheek.

'Oh, shit,' Jana says. Her breath brushes Nancy's lashes. All Nancy can see is her uniform, dark Corpo-grey drenched in scarlet light. 'Oh, Nance.'

Nancy's hip buzzes. But she can't feel anything else below her ribs — can't feel her stomach, or legs, or feet — can only feel an emptiness, an absence, and an awful thin *leaking*.

'Nance,' Jana says again, her voice painfully gentle. 'This one's done, darling. We have to go.'

Nancy breathes out. More liquid trickles from her.

Jana's thumb strokes beneath her eye.

'Come on. I'll get us out of here, trust me.'

Nancy knows what she means. And that is worse than the

absence, worse than the leaking — so much worse.

'No,' Nancy says.

'No? Is it broken?' Jana's voice is sharp with worry. 'I'll do it. Tell me how to fix it, tell me—'

'No!'

Nancy grits her teeth, her mind jolted into clarity.

'Just leave me,' she says, through the fluid burning in her throat. 'Go.'

'I'm not leaving without you.'

The alarm's still flashing, and they're still stuck in a Corpo ship, alone, with hundreds of guards after them, but Nancy can hear that Jana means it, that she'll kneel here until they're found, if Nancy doesn't give in.

Nancy can't let that happen.

'Fine,' she whispers.

Jana exhales, her breath hitching. 'Tell me what to do.'

'Open my shirt. I'll do the rest.'

Jana fumbles against Nancy's neck, undoing her buttons. Jana's never so uncoordinated — always sure, always graceful. Feeling her fingers shake makes something inside Nancy twist.

'Not the context I imagined saying that in,' she croaks, and forces her mouth to curve. Only half of it obeys, but it's enough to make Jana huff, her hands clenching in Nancy's shirt.

'Say it again later, then,' she replies. 'When we're back on the ship, and Ngaire's done lecturing us.'

'Yes, ma'am.'

With that, Nancy withdraws from her Shell.

It's been five years since she last did it, but it's not something she could ever forget. The sensation of leaving her body — her skin, her eyes, her muscles and bones and breath — for the tiny little *thing* encased within it, in the warm black pressure of her home-world's atmosphere, will never leave her. However much she might wish it to.

In the space of her body's chest cavity, Nancy curls into herself. She can taste the metal surrounding her, its coppery tang sinking into her flesh. Can taste, beneath it, the familiar brine of her homeworld, infused into the ammonia-rich space.

Hesitant with the absence of sight or limbs, she pushes part of her body out into a tendril, dragging it along the bitter metal until it meets the release button. A sharp hiss, and she's assailed by the sudden change in air pressure; feels herself swell like a lung, bloating into something even more shapeless. The odours of the world pour in: prickling smoke, and clinging blood, and Jana — the scent of her skin and sweat and hair oil, her anxiety and grief and relief.

'There you are.' Jana's voice, murmuring through Nancy's skin. The air shifts, the complex column of burnt-sweet scents that is Jana moving closer. Nancy feels her hands approach, and recoils a little, shrinking back into the shadow of her Shell.

Nancy knows what she resembles. She's seen holos of her species through the eyes of her Shell. Knows she looks and smells and feels like a fruit left to rot for weeks upon weeks, gone soft and grey and reeking.

Jana's fingers scoop beneath her. Nancy tastes their salt and lavender hand-cream, feels them twitch at the greasy sensation of her flesh. As she is lifted from her cavity, she breathes in the cold stillness of the seven dead seccies, the vinegary fluids of her destroyed Shell, and the cloying sweetness of Jana's distaste.

None of her crewmates have ever seen her true form, though they were all aware her Shell was only that. She knew they'd never be able to treat her the same way, if they saw this part of her. And she can't blame them for it. Especially Jana — Jana, who's so neat and clean, who can't stand mess or dirt or small disgusting things.

'Here,' Jana says, cupping Nancy before her chest. 'Is this alright?'

Nancy's distracted by a shrill zipping, at a pitch her Shell wouldn't have been able to hear. Ellie's mite, still functioning, which means its control box is still intact. They'll need it to get out, and they'll need to keep it safe, so the other mites can finish their job.

She'll have to speak.

She doesn't want to.

She has to.

Resigned, Nancy puffs herself up, then contracts, forcing out what passes for her voice in this thin blend of oxygen and nitrogen — a faint wheeze, tiny and pathetic.

The box. Chest pocket.

It takes a moment, but Jana's translator must still be working.

'Okay,' she says. 'Is there … anything else I should take?'

Nancy doubts much of her stuff survived the blast, if it was strong enough to blow her Shell in two.

She just wants this over. Wants to be back on the ship, in the reserve Shell stowed in her room. Wants to stop speaking, stop shivering, stop tasting the evidence of Jana's revulsion.

No.

Jana nods, and reaches down to retrieve the control box, tucking it into her belt. Nancy hears her transmitter buzz, vibrating with Ngaire's voice.

'Sanjana, Nancy, update. Are you two almost out?'

'Captain,' Jana says, and hesitates. 'We got hit by a bomb. Nancy took the worst of it, protected me, but she ...'

Her voice wobbles. For a moment, her stress and sadness wash over Nancy, overwhelming her disgust.

'Shit,' Ellie whispers.

'Tell me,' Ngaire says, voice unnaturally flat.

Jana's hand tightens briefly around Nancy.

'She's okay. Her body — her Shell — it's destroyed, but I got her out. I have her.'

There's a long silence, before Ngaire speaks.

'Keep moving. I'm coming in.'

Nancy responds immediately.

No!

She can't take it. Jana alone is bad enough. The thought of Ngaire, her Captain, her friend, seeing her like this — she can't take it.

'No,' Jana says. 'Ngaire, I can do this. The mite's still working, and I remember where we are. We're almost out.'

Another silence.

Nancy trembles.

'Alright,' Ngaire says, heavily. 'Be careful. And get back to me, both of you.'

'Yes — yes, Captain.'

The mite whines about Jana's head. Her revulsion is suffocating, seeping from her palm and into Nancy's skin.

Jana exhales a long breath.

'I'll get us out of here,' she says, voice strengthening. 'Trust me, Nance.'

And, above all else, Nancy does.

Without Nancy goading her into showing off, Jana is a lot more stealthy. She empties her bag of guns, leaving them with Nancy's broken Shell, and takes only her suit and her spitter. She moves slowly through the corridors, taking stock of crannies and storage closets on her way. Whenever the mite flashes a warning, she doubles back to squeeze herself into a space Nancy's Shell could never have fit into, filling it with her sharp-citrus determination. Nancy keeps herself as still and small as possible, reluctant to remind Jana of her existence.

In one closet, crammed in beside a pile of defunct cleaner bots, waiting for a pack of seccies to stop arguing in the middle of the corridor, Jana speaks.

'So,' she whispers, beneath the sound of one seccy insisting they're being raided by space pirates, 'what are we?'

Nancy has no idea what she means.

What?

'I mean—' Jana pauses, something that tastes oddly like embarrassment itching at Nancy's flesh. 'Like, are we girlfriends? Partners?'

At first, Nancy has absolutely no response to that.

Then, she hears a shrill, hitching rasp, and realises it's herself, laughing.

You're asking that now?

'Why, is it a bad time?' Jana asks, half-seriously.

Outside the closet, another seccy calls the first a pulsar-brain, and announces the ship is obviously being infiltrated by spies from a rival company.

Within the closet, Nancy inhales dust and mould and congealed hydraulic fluid, apprehension and discomfort and distaste.

You're disgusted by me, she says. *I can smell it.*

Jana stays quiet for a long time, longer than her translator would need to decipher Nancy's wheezing. Nancy listens to the seccies bicker — another raising Fair Work as their assailant — and starts to regret being so blunt.

Look, don't worry about it. Let's just get out of here, and we can talk when I'm—

'It's my problem,' Jana says.

Nancy pauses. Jana's scent is going acrid, going angry.

'It's my problem,' she repeats. 'If I'm—if I feel that way. It's my fault, not yours.'

Her voice is rising, and the seccies' argument is dying down. Panicked, Nancy shushes her.

Okay, Jana, just—

'There's nothing wrong with you!'

Nancy holds back another laugh, worried about provoking Jana further.

Seriously, it's alright. She wishes she had a hand to put on Jana's shoulder, eyes to meet hers with. Realises, too late, that she's put out a little tendril, touching Jana's callused palm, and quickly retracts it. *I know what I look like. You don't have to force yourself.*

Jana lets out a sharp breath. Raises her hand, until Nancy must be right before her eyes — her beautiful, brown-black eyes,

47

bright and blistering as Nancy's plas-blades.

Then she brings Nancy closer, and kisses her, pressing her lips briefly to Nancy's flesh.

'I'll force myself all I want,' she says, as the taste of her grape lipstick sinks through Nancy's skin, curdling into an emotion so overwhelming that Nancy can't move, can't speak, can only curl down into herself, as Jana pushes open the closet door, raises her spitter, and prepares to get them out.

Nancy 8 runs a hand down her arm.

It's completely smooth, without scars, or burns, or tattoos — none of the signs of life she'd accumulated over five years in her last Shell. This body is a blank canvas, perfect in every way.

Perfect for a new start.

Some part of her had always known Jana would see her real body, eventually. Nancy had joked and argued and flirted, while knowing it would all come to an end.

She'd known. But some small part of her had hoped it wouldn't happen — a part she only discovered upon its death, which has left her listless, waiting for the inevitable.

After alighting back on the ship, Jana had hurried through the waiting crew, her hands clasped around Nancy's body, hiding it from sight. She'd gone straight to Nancy's quarters, opening up her reserve Shell and placing her inside, before going to report to Ngaire.

And here Nancy waits, in her undecorated room, in her undecorated body.

The door chimes. It slides open a second later. Nancy's room doesn't lock against Jana; she's been here too many times.

Jana hasn't even changed out of the seccy uniform. She's ditched the hat and jacket, though, so she's just in the heavy pants and grey tank. Her short hair is slicked back with sweat, and the moment she sees Nancy, her entire body relaxes.

Nancy swallows something jagged.

'Hi,' Jana says. 'You're okay.'

'Thanks to you.' Nancy tries to smile, but knows it comes out half-hearted. 'Did you get lectured?'

'Nah. Ngaire's saving it till we're both there, so she doesn't have to give it twice.'

Jana steps closer, gaze skipping down Nancy's figure. It's strange, to no longer sense her emotions — though judging by how Jana ducks her head, Nancy knows what she'd smell. Nancy wanted to check out her new body, so she's wearing nothing but a pair of skin-shorts, and Jana's always had trouble looking away from her muscles. Nancy's known for a long time that Jana finds her body attractive.

This body.

Her Shell.

'I'm sorry for kissing you without asking,' Jana says, suddenly.

Nancy very carefully doesn't think about that moment. She shrugs one shoulder, and leans against her bunk.

'No worries.'

'I—' Jana folds her arms, purple-painted nails digging into her defined bicep. 'I don't like how you talked about yourself, Nance. And you never answered my question.'

Nancy scratches at her neck, gaze drifting to her room's tiny viewport. It's completely black, an inky hole in the warm amber space.

'Jana,' she says. 'I don't want you to force yourself.'

Even if Jana meant what she said earlier, Nancy can't accept it. She can't accept such a fragile relationship. Can't accept Jana being with her while being disgusted by her, being with her while knowing what she really is.

'Don't these things always take effort?' Jana asks.

'I guess, but—'

'What, you never have to force yourself to like me? Not even a bit?'

Nancy frowns. 'No, of course I don't.'

This makes Jana scoff, so acerbically that Nancy looks back to her. She's pissed, *really* pissed, in a way Nancy hasn't seen in years, not since Nancy first joined the crew, and kept offending everyone because she hadn't figured out human interaction yet.

'Bullshit,' Jana says. 'There's no way you find me perfect and desirable all the time. I have crooked teeth and a monobrow and I sweat too much. I might not be able to *smell* it, but I know I annoy you, when I get too pedantic about holo-game rules, or cleaning the fridge, or leaving your hair everywhere, or—'

'I—'

'And that's okay,' Jana continues, loudly. 'We're all ugly and annoying sometimes, you know? Are you gonna look me in the eyes and tell me I'm perfect?'

She stares straight at Nancy, challenging.

'Because if you do — I don't want that. I'm a sapient, just like you, and we're all complicated and stupid and unattractive. And we love each other despite it. That's the point.'

Nancy looks at Jana's mouth, and remembers it pressing to her flesh. That same strange emotion rises through her again, twisted and sickening and unnameable, like disgust but not, like longing but not.

'I'm not sure I can,' she says, voice coming out small, uncertain, weak. 'I don't know if I can accept you knowing … what I am. I don't know if I can stand it.'

Jana's expression softens. She takes another step closer, until even Nancy's Shell can smell her.

'Yeah, you clearly have some serious self-esteem issues you need to work on.' She holds out one hand. 'But so do I. And we can try and figure it all out together, if you want.'

Nancy looks down at the offered hand.

It's small, littered with peeling calluses, and intricate, flowing tattoos, and dark liquids of various origin.

This hand has touched her flesh. Held her revolting little body, flinched from the texture of her skin, shielded her from seccies and the eyes of her crew.

It's Jana's.

Nancy reaches out, and takes it.

'Yes, ma'am,' she says.

THE EXCURSION

Seth Malacari

The red and blue lights of the ambulance bounced through the karri trees. The people on the shore stood huddled together, slick with water. They hung their sunburnt arms around each other's shoulders. Some of them were crying. Others held their phones out, recording every second. The body lay on the blazing concrete slab, its face covered by a blue striped towel. The air was thick with summer afternoon heat. No breeze disturbed the surface of the lake, but every so often something splashed, like a rock was being tossed in. The ambulance made its way down the winding gravel path, tyres crunching, followed by a police car. In the limp trees above the crowd, the magpie-larks sang their two-note tune. The cicadas chirped manically in the surrounding bush. The police siren wailed once, and then shut off. The whole place smelled like sunscreen: like coconut and beach days.

The first paramedic to reach the body lifted the towel, glanced at the face beneath and then covered it back up. She turned to her partner, who was walking over with the rest of the kit, boots crunching the dried leaves underfoot. The first paramedic shook her head.

A police officer stepped out of their vehicle, dressed in black, blonde hair in a tight bun. They flashed their badge at the crowd, though it hardly seemed necessary. The paramedic stood up and wiped the back of her hand across her forehead.

'Detective,' she said, 'it's them.'

Two hours earlier

Giacomo sat on the jetty overhanging Honeymoon Pool, feet dangling in the water, watching his friends swim. They had an assortment of inflatables of all colours and shapes and were taking turns pushing each other off them. He watched as his best friend, Isla, launched herself off the jetty and splashed into the centre of the fray. Ice cold water sprayed onto his legs.

Isla surfaced and looked over at Giacomo. 'Are you seriously not coming in, Jack?' she called.

'Nah, I'm good,' he said, tugging his t-shirt closer. 'It's nice out here.'

Isla swam closer. 'Bullshit,' she said, dragging herself up onto the jetty to sit beside him. 'I can see the sweat dripping down your forehead. Just come in. You've got your swim binder on, right?'

Giacomo wiped at his forehead. It was a scorcher and the lack of wind didn't help. Even in the shade of the peppermint trees he could feel himself burning. 'Yeah,' he said. 'I just don't feel like swimming.'

'You can keep your shirt on, if it helps. Some of the other guys do, see?' She pointed to a group of boys taking turns to swing from a rope into the water, half with their shirts on. 'Or take it off. You don't have to have a flat chest to be a guy, you know.'

Giacomo bumped Isla with his shoulder. 'Thanks. It's not that, though.'

'Then what's your problem?'

He leaned down to whisper in her ear. 'I got my period.'

Isla's laugh was not what you would describe as discreet. Several people looked over at them.

'Oi!' Giacomo reached down and flicked water at her. 'Shut it!'

'Mate, why didn't you say so before? I have spare tampons in my bag if you need one.'

Giacomo followed Isla over to the buses. There were three of them lined up across the car park, orange dust stuck to their undersides. The lake was a two-hour drive from the city. No aircon. The window by Giacomo's head had only half opened. He wondered if it was because some kid had jumped out at one point. To pass the time he played a game where he imagined running alongside the bus and leaping over every tree. When he got bored of that, he imagined he had a big machete sticking out of the side of the bus and cut all the trees down.

'Do you need something?' Mx Dramoni asked, looking up from their book. They were sitting in a fold-out chair by the buses, with their prosthetic leg blocking the door like some guardian of the lunchboxes.

'Tampon,' said Isla.

Mx Dramoni nodded, swung their leg out of the way, and pressed the switch to open the door of the middle bus. 'Be quick about it.'

Giacomo waited outside as Isla ducked in to retrieve her bag.

'You know, Jack,' said Mx Dramoni, taking in Giacomo's dry clothing, 'this is one of the last inland swimming holes left in the south-west. We were lucky to get a pass to come here. You should swim, before it dries up like all the rest.'

Giacomo looked over at Mx Dramoni. They taught Outdoor Ed, and while Giacomo didn't mind sitting in a park on occasion, he really hated the great outdoors. The bugs. The heat. The dirt. He liked being inside.

'Yeah, cool,' he said, hands in his shorts' pockets. He was saved from discussing nature anymore by Isla lobbing a full packet of tampons at his head. 'That should last ya!'

'Cheers. Be back in a sec,' he said, heading for the male toilets.

Now that he was out of excuses, Giacomo let Isla drag him toward the lake. Mr Thompson, the sport teacher, stood waist deep in the water with his shirt off. 'Not bad for a school day, eh, Jacky-boy!' said Mr Thompson, his voice far too loud considering the proximity to Giacomo's left ear. 'Bloody beautiful,' he continued, without waiting for Giacomo to reply.

'Please don't turn into a Thompson,' Isla said to Giacomo as they waded out toward their friends.

'Sorry, it's already been decided. I'm peaking in high school and joining a straight pride group.'

Isla wrinkled her nose. 'Do you think he's actually in a straight pride group?'

'Probably,' shrugged Giacomo.

'Really glad I'm bisexual,' said Isla.

'Same.'

Giacomo stared down into the tannin-soaked water of the

lake. The sun sparkled off the surface like a thousand shards of glass. As he looked into the water he saw a flash of silver; a big fish shooting past. Giacomo didn't love fish, especially the big ones. They had weird eyes and weird mouths. He hated when his dad used to make him go fishing and he'd have to watch the fish they caught desperately gulping the air while his dad pulled the hook out of them. He never said anything though. He didn't want his dad to stop inviting him.

Beneath his feet a fine silt cushioned his toes, which he found gross. The fragrant branches of the peppermint trees hung down all around the pool, making it seem like a secret oasis. To the right was a small waterfall, barely a trickle, where the pool flowed over the rocks into the lower section. To the left was a creek that disappeared around a bend into thick scrubland. There was a metal chain-link fence across the creek and a rusty old sign nailed to it, warning that the land beyond was private property and trespassers would be prosecuted.

Isla dived in head first. Giacomo took a slower approach, sinking up to his shoulders and frog-kicking toward the group. He left his t-shirt on, the black fabric sticking to him in places he'd prefer it didn't.

'Here he is!' cheered Kaito as Giacomo made his way over to where his friends lounged on a giant inflatable pink donut.

'Here, Jack, take my spot,' said Deepa, as she slid off into the water.

He clambered onto the donut and dangled his hands over the side, grateful to be out of the water. He liked swimming in pools, but this was different. Not being able to see the bottom made his stomach turn. Above him, the blue sky was barely visible through the canopy. The lattice of leaves made criss-cross patterns on everyone's faces. He laid his head back and closed his eyes. He could hear his classmates' laughter, and the faint sounds of the music coming from the portable speaker on the shore. He could feel the sun drying out his shirt already.

'You playing softball this season?' asked Isla, climbing up on the donut beside him and nearly toppling them both off.

Giacomo shrugged. 'I dunno. I don't want to join a new team.'

'Just ask if you can stay in ours.'

'Already did. Girls only.'

'The boys team is good though. They actually win sometimes,' Isla laughed.

'Hey, we won that one time!'

'Yeah, because the other team forfeited.'

Giacomo let out a sigh. 'It just sucks, having to leave. You're my teammates. Plus, what if I'm not as good as the other guys? I don't want to be the worst on the team.'

Isla reached over and put her hands on his shoulders. 'Giacomo D'Angelo, listen to me. You were the worst player on our team,' she grinned.

He faked outrage and wobbled the donut, sending Isla over the edge. She'd kept hold of his shoulders though, and took him down with her. They landed in the water with a splat.

Mr Thompson blew the red whistle he kept strung about his neck. 'Settle down, you two!'

'How much longer until we can leave?' asked Giacomo, slicking back his shoulder-length hair.

Isla rolled her eyes.

'Jack. Isla. Come with us,' said Kaito, waving a hand at them.

'Where are we going?' asked Isla.

Deepa held a finger to her lips, her dark hair knotted high above her head. 'Quick, while Thompson's not looking.'

Giacomo glanced over to the shore and saw Mr Thompson was no longer there. He followed the others as they swam toward the chain-link fence.

The four of them positioned themselves on the far bank, hidden from view behind a rock, examining the fence. They figured they had about ten minutes before someone noticed they were gone. There were a hundred kids on this field trip, and only three teachers. The maths on that one seemed off to Giacomo, but he didn't question his public school's budget.

'I don't think we should do this,' said Isla. She was wringing her singlet in her hands, drops of water splashing onto her glittery painted toenails.

'Scared of a fence?' teased Giacomo.

'No, but I am scared of getting lost and the bus leaving without us and having to live in the bush forever,' she said.

'Good point,' said Giacomo. He didn't want to live in the bush. He'd miss his mum's lasagne too much. The very thought made his stomach growl.

Kaito and Deepa rolled their eyes in unison. 'We won't go far,' said Kaito.

'Just around that bend,' said Deepa, pointing up the creek to where it curved out of sight.

'Deepa thinks the merfolk live here,' Kaito said with a smirk. 'Wants to find herself a mermaid girlfriend.'

'Well they might!' she said.

'I thought they only lived in the ocean?' said Giacomo, suddenly empathising with Isla's fear of the fence. The merfolk creeped him out. They were too much like fish for his liking.

Kaito re-tied their long hair into a bun, preparing to scale the fence. 'Deepa reckons they're moving inland now, because of the food shortages.'

'And why exactly do we want to go looking for them?' said Giacomo, creeping further away from the fence.

'Science,' said Deepa, eyes ablaze. 'To know the truth. The media keeps reporting that the fish stocks are fine, but I know that's bullshit. If we can find evidence of the merfolk moving inland, maybe we can raise awareness.'

'Evidence how? You planning to capture one?' asked Giacomo, his eyebrow raised.

'No, I'm just going to film one,' said Deepa, digging into the pocket of her boardshorts and retrieving her mini GoPro.

'Stay here if you want,' said Kaito. 'We're going in.'

Isla and Giacomo looked at each other. 'I'll go if you go,' said Giacomo.

'Deal,' said Isla, holding out her pinky finger. Giacomo linked his with hers.

The four of them looked back toward the shore. No sign of the teachers.

All together, they climbed over the fence.

The world on this side of the fence looked completely different to the lake side. The water here was shallower, and though it ran steadily downstream toward the lake, it was slow and thick. Giacomo thought it felt like walking through slime, but without the stickiness. The creek bed was made up of golden pebbles, worn smooth. At its deepest, the water went up to their waists. On the banks, acacia scrub replaced the peppermint trees and the land seemed sucked of colour. Above them, the sky burned a bright white. They walked in a line up the creek. Deepa first, camera held aloft, then Kaito, then Isla, then Giacomo. Giacomo didn't like being last. He felt eyes on his back, but when he turned he only saw a glimpse of the fence before they rounded the bend.

The creek widened slightly, creating a shallow pool, like the kind they have at aquatic centres for the toddlers to splash in. Giacomo thought this seemed like a good place to turn around.

'Should we head back?' he said.

Deepa picked up a rock from the creek bed and threw it before her. It made a plink as it landed, concentric circles radiating out. She walked toward where it had landed. 'I just don't think it's deep enough here for—'

Deepa was gone. One moment she was there, the next she had disappeared under the surface.

'Deepa!' Kaito called out. They rushed forward, but were quickly pulled back. Isla had them by the back of their shorts.

'Wait!' she warned. 'Jack, get a stick.'

Giacomo edged his way toward the bank and ripped a branch from a yellow wattle, disturbing the bees collecting pollen. He passed the branch to Isla. She grabbed it, and edged her way forward using the branch to gauge the depth of the water. When they reached the spot where Deepa had been, the stick could no longer reach the bottom. They peered over the drop off. Nothing but darkness below. It made Giacomo feel dizzy.

'I have to go down there,' said Kaito, preparing to dive.

'Wait, look,' said Isla.

Bubbles broke the surface. A ghostly figure rose from the darkness. A head appeared before them. This head did not belong to Deepa. It had silver hair, dark eyes and too many teeth. Kaito stumbled back into Isla. Giacomo stood frozen, every part of him screamed to run, but his body refused to move. The shark-like creature rose higher out of the water. In its arms it held Deepa. Her eyes were shut and her body hung limp. The mercreature opened its mouth but the sounds that came out were unrecognisable.

'Put her down!' yelled Kaito, grabbing the branch from Isla and waving it at the mercreature.

The creature showed its teeth and hissed. There was no mistaking that sound. It meant back off. Then it laid Deepa onto the edge of the creek and dove back under. Its tail was huge, like a sail, and shimmered like aluminium dust in the sunlight.

Giacomo and Isla rushed to Deepa. Giacomo checked her vitals. No breath, but her heart was beating. He breathed into her lungs. It took several tries before she gasped and coughed up water. Giacomo rolled her onto the side.

'We need to call an ambulance,' he said to Isla and Kaito.

'We need to fucking kill that thing!' said Kaito, still brandishing the branch.

'No,' said Deepa, softly. 'Don't hurt it.'

Kaito hesitated, then let the branch fall from their hand into the water. Giacomo watched as it travelled slowly along with the current, back toward the fence.

'What happened down there?' asked Isla, crouching down beside Deepa.

'Give her some space,' said Giacomo. 'She could still have water on her lungs.'

Deepa struggled her way to a seated position, resting against Giacomo. Her voice croaked. 'I just … slipped. It was so deep. There were merpeople down there. Dozens. I couldn't see well, but I think … I don't think they liked me filming. They took my camera. One of them bit me,' she said, showing a crescent-shaped bite mark on her calf. 'That one that brought me up — it kind of beat them off. It saved me.'

'Why?' Giacomo asked. 'Why did it save you?'

Deepa shrugged, and gazed over toward the deep part of the creek. 'I don't know. It seemed … human.'

'They're not human, they're monsters!' said Kaito. 'They tried to kill you.'

'You're wrong,' said Deepa. 'I scared them is all. Invaded their privacy. They're like us. I know it.'

'We should get out of here,' said Isla. 'They might come back.'

Giacomo and Kaito carried Deepa between them back toward the lake. They'd wrapped Giacomo's shirt around Deepa's wound, but drops of blood fell into the creek as they walked. Isla followed behind, glancing back every so often. She was certain she could hear the splash of something following them.

At the fence, Mr Thompson was waiting. 'Found them!' he yelled over his shoulder. 'You four are in so much—' he stopped and pointed at Deepa. 'What happened to her?'

'We need an ambulance,' said Giacomo.

They got Deepa back over the fence, Kaito supporting her

from below, Giacomo guiding her gently over the top. Mr Thompson stood in the water staring at them, but not helping.

'Are you just gunna stand there,' asked Isla, as she swung her legs over the fence, 'or are you actually going to do something?'

Mr Thompson did not reply. He was looking beyond her, up the creek. He raised a hand and pointed. His mouth opened, but no sound came out.

Isla, from her position atop the fence, turned to look.

'Run!' she yelled.

Mr Thompson raised his red whistle and blew it three sharp times, cheeks puffed up like a squirrel. As the merfolk reached the fence and pressed up against it with their scaly grey-blue bodies, Thompson managed to find his voice. He turned toward the lake. 'Everybody! Out of the water!' he yelled frantically, waving his arms overhead.

Kaito helped Deepa up onto the shore, resting her against a ghost gum. Giacomo was still standing in the water, reaching out for Isla. On the other side of the fence, the merfolk were a mass of slithering bodies below her.

'Jump!' he begged.

'I can't!'

'You have to!'

Isla looked down at the hoard of merfolk straining at the fence. It was not a strong fence. Already it swayed under the pressure, and soon it would topple completely. She closed her eyes, prayed to a god she didn't believe in, and jumped. She landed awkwardly, her ankle rolling sideways. Giacomo scooped her up under the armpits and dragged her out of the water. He was sweating heavily. His stomach churned. He leant against the tree and threw up.

In the lake, unaware of the churning mass of merfolk about to bear down on them, kids were trickling into shore, some rushed out, some swam as lazily as possible. Thompson still stood in front of the fence, whistle hanging limply from his lip, transfixed.

For a moment, the world froze. Nothing moved. Nobody spoke. Not a sound was heard, no flies buzzed, no leaves rustled. This moment of stillness hung there for what seemed an eternity, until it was broken by the deafening screech of the chain-link fence collapsing. The world began to spin again. Hundreds of cockatoos squawked from the trees. The music on the speaker boomed louder than ever. Every kid began to run in a hundred different directions, all swirling before Giacomo's eyes. He clung to Isla as they watched Mr Thompson be swept away in the surge. Giacomo tried to call out, but he had no voice. He felt like one of those fish he'd caught long ago, gaping pathetically at the air.

Dorsal fins sliced through the water like wire through clay. Mr Thompson's body momentarily flew into the air, before being snatched up by gnashing teeth. Tails clashed in the air. The lake began to boil over. Giacomo had seen something like this before. He'd been out on his dad's boat and they'd come across a dead seal. Sharks had only just arrived on the scene. In a few seconds the water had gone from calm to chaos. A feeding frenzy.

Then, as quickly as it had started, it stopped. The merfolk turned and headed back up the creek. The lake smoothed itself over. The last mercreature to leave stopped at the fallen fence. It was the same one who had rescued Deepa, silver hair slicked back now. It stared directly at Deepa, its eyes hollow, its mouth a hard line. Deepa reached out a hand toward the creature.

'Wait,' she called.

The mercreature turned and fled.

The four of them — Deepa leaning on Kaito, and Isla leaning on Giacomo — slowly made their way around the lake toward the buses. Giacomo reminded himself that this sort of shit is why he didn't go out in nature.

'We have to do something,' Deepa said as they stumbled along the path. 'They'll kill them. We need to protect them.'

'You saw them! How are we supposed to do anything? They've eaten all the fish and now they want to eat us,' Kaito puffed. They were exhausted. They didn't want to do anything else. They just wanted to go home.

'That's not true. I think they just got spooked when I fell in. We were trespassing after all. And then, I don't know why they attacked Thompson. I don't think they meant it in an evil way. I think they were just hungry, and my blood stirred them up, and maybe … maybe …'

Isla put a hand on Deepa's arm. 'It's okay. We can figure it out. Do some research when we get back. They've never killed any humans before, right?'

'Not that we know of,' said Kaito, eyeing off the lake.

Isla paused and let out a groan. 'Jack, do you have it in you to carry me? I can't keep walking.'

Giacomo didn't have it in him, but he knelt down in the dust and let Isla climb on his back anyway. The trans-masculine urge to carry things.

'Let's just get back to the bus,' he said, though his mind raced with ideas. He would figure out a way to help. He just didn't know how yet.

Everyone was crowded around the buses when they arrived. Someone had carried Mr Thompson's body in and laid a towel over it. The inflatables that had survived the attack floated listlessly in the water still. The music had been switched off. Mx Dramoni was pacing back and forth along the concrete platform. They had a clipboard in hand, ticking off names.

'Jack D'Angelo? Has anyone seen Jack? Or Isla?'

'We're here,' said Giacomo, setting Isla down on the picnic bench, his muscles screaming. 'Kaito and Deepa, too. Deepa's hurt. So is Isla. They need an ambulance.'

Dramoni glanced over at the body lying only a few metres away. Blood was trickling out across the concrete, a deep red that matched Mr Thompson's shorts. Dramoni audibly gulped.

'It's on its way.'

'Now,' said the detective, after the paramedics had bandaged Deepa's wound and attended to Isla's sprained ankle, 'one of you needs to explain exactly what happened here.' The detective stood before the four of them, notebook flipped open. Two other uniformed officers walked amongst the crowd, confiscating phones. Deepa went to open her mouth first, but Giacomo cut her off.

'It was a shark,' he said. It was an easy decision for him to make. He took care of his friends first, himself second. That's what he had always done, even if it wasn't always the healthiest option. If Deepa wanted to protect the merfolk, he would protect the merfolk, even if they scared the shit out of him. He just hoped nobody had been quick enough to capture the attack on film. Though, even if they had, he doubted the footage would be clear enough to tell the difference.

The detective raised an eyebrow. 'You're sure? The merfolk can look similar to sharks, especially underwater.'

'I'm sure,' said Giacomo, nodding a little too enthusiastically. 'My dad's a fisherman, so I've seen loads of merfolk. And sharks. These were definitely sharks.'

'Lots of sharks,' added Isla.

Giacomo kicked Kaito's shoe. 'Oh right, yeah, big ones,' said Kaito, widening their arms to indicate just how big they were.

'And you?' said the detective, eyes boring into Deepa. 'Did a shark do this? Tell me the truth now.'

Deepa looked down at her bandaged leg. She thought of the face of the mercreature who had saved her. She heard Thompson's whistle echoing in her mind. She thought of what the government might do to the merfolk if they believed them to be killers. They'd hunt them down, one by one. But she hated to lie. She prided herself on always being honest. She valued the truth. She stared at her feet: muddy and bruised. Giacomo nudged her with his knee. She took a deep breath.

'Yes,' she said. 'It was a shark.'

The detective sighed and flipped their notebook shut. 'I'll be in touch with your parents,' they said, before marching back toward their car.

'Do you think they bought it?' asked Isla.

'Definitely,' said Giacomo.

'Absolutely not,' said Deepa, at the same time.

'So, what now?' asked Kaito.

The four of them sat, staring out across the lake. Their classmates had started boarding the buses. The paramedics had zipped up the bag that contained Thompson's body and loaded it into their van. The sun was slowly dropping down toward the western horizon.

'Look,' whispered Deepa, pointing toward the fallen fence.

The mercreature, Deepa's saviour, was watching them, half hidden underwater, like a crocodile awaiting its next meal.

'What's it doing?' asked Kaito.

'Listening to us, probably. Merfolk have exceptional hearing,' said Deepa.

Then, as if to prove this point, the mercreature rose up and put its hand to its mouth, palm facing inwards, webbed fingers closed, then moved its arm out quickly again toward them. It repeated this action twice.

'What does that mean?' asked Isla.

Giacomo recognised the action as a sign he learned from an AUSLAN course. 'Thank you,' he said. 'It's saying thank you.'

HARMLESS

Jesse Galea

In the same year that the world's population starts spontaneously developing mild supernatural abilities, the highlight of my year is sneaking out of school today. Partly because the *X-Men* franchise lied to me about how superpowers behave — they're more underwhelming than anything else — and partly because I needed to get away from Tegan Dunne.

She's been haunting me all morning. Not physically. I don't know what my power is yet, but I don't think it's seeing ghosts. No, her words are haunting me. What she said yesterday keeps looping around inside my head, faster and faster. As much as I tell myself to get over it: I can't.

I slump further down in the passenger seat of Ethan's car, letting my head rest on the window. Maybe the vibrations of the glass can shake the echo of Tegan's words from my skull.

'Don't tell me you're still being a sad sack,' Ethan says, smiling so I know they're not being serious.

They can get away with saying shit like this because we've been friends since before our first attempts at puberty and I know they not-so-secretly care about me. They cared enough to orchestrate today's adventure. Didn't ask any questions and made a plan to get us both out of school with the lowest possible risk. I'm scared of getting in trouble, which is obvious considering it's taken me until Year Eleven to break any major school rules. And I didn't even skip an entire school day, only the last two periods of English to avoid Tegan.

'So what if I am?' I ask, not moving away from the window. I know it's overdramatic, but sometimes I deserve to indulge in my overdramatic tendencies.

'C'mon, Cove,' they say, 'aren't you curious about where we're going?'

They've caught me in a classic stubbornness trap. If I say no, they won't tell me anything even though I'm dying to know. But if I admit it, that means they've won the conversation. Rationally, I understand it's probably not good or healthy to want to win conversations. Emotionally, I'm too stubborn and competitive for that knowledge to change anything.

To avoid losing, I say nothing. Ethan laughs.

'If I didn't know you before this year,' they say, 'I'd put money on your power being the inability to give in.'

'Who says it's not?' I ask.

'Me. This isn't a new development.'

They're not wrong.

I go back to staring out the window. Every time we pass someone I look for signs of their superpower. It's more a caution than curiosity, a habit I picked up from my mum.

Mum discovered her ability to teleport during one of my driving lessons, dematerialising while I concentrated on not crunching the gears. When I clocked her disappearance I pulled over, turned off the car and promptly freaked out.

It could've been worse. Turns out Mum can only teleport to the deli on the corner of our street. Now she refuses to drive and I've all but given up on getting my licence. If she had her way I'd probably never leave the house.

Ethan pulls the car into a familiar carpark and I groan. Even though I've never been here, I recognise it. It's the backdrop to countless videos of people from school either celebrating or crying. Mostly crying. Though in the videos it isn't this run down. Ethan carefully avoids potholes before parking in front of the only building around that doesn't have a For Sale sign in the window.

We're at The Arcade.

'Couldn't we go to an actual arcade?' I ask. 'A lowercase-a arcade with air hockey and claw machines?'

The Arcade popped up at the beginning of the year, a few weeks after people started reporting weird shit happening to them. It was meant to be a place to come and discover your powers. Despite how massively popular it had been, it rarely worked. Powers are too specific and niche to be uncovered in places like this so it was always filled with desperate people waiting to be disappointed.

'We're killing time,' Ethan says, getting out of the car. 'I have other plans, but they're not until later. Besides, it's criminal that you haven't been here before.'

I shrug. 'This place opened at the height of Mum's anti-driving thing.'

Inside The Arcade, it's like a low-budget science museum with the aesthetic of a laser tag arena from the 1990s. There's a lot of chrome and metallic decorations that I'm guessing are meant to look futuristic rather than cheap and gimmicky.

Scattered throughout the building are plaques detailing how people discovered their powers, next to an activity designed to replicate that experience. I've heard it's pretty rare for more than one person to have the same power though.

'This always trips me out,' Ethan says, looking at a plaque with their sister's face on it. A series of pedestals stretch out beside it, each displaying an unlabelled muesli bar beneath protective glass. They're dusty — do the employees not switch them out once they've expired? No wonder this place tanked.

I'm a nut detector, the plaque reads. I snort.

'You have the sense of humour of a ten-year-old,' Ethan says, but they're dreaming if they think I don't recognise the face they pull when they're trying not to laugh too.

Ethan told me Paige's origin story back when it first happened. She got headaches around food sometimes and her housemate made a spreadsheet to track her reactions and find the cause. Whenever Paige is within a metre of tree nuts, she gets a headache that gets worse the closer she gets to the offending food. She's not even allergic to nuts.

'Would you want a plaque?' Ethan asks. Their voice is carefully neutral.

'Even if I wanted to, I can't,' I say.

'Yeah, but like, if you found your power. Would you?'

'No,' I say. Then, gesturing to Paige's plaque, 'What happens if your sister eats a peanut?'

'Nothing would happen,' Ethan says. 'Peanuts are legumes. Technically.'

'Nerd.'

I used to agree with Ethan. Superpowers were cool, of course I wanted to find mine. I never went to The Arcade but that didn't stop me from running my own experiments. Every morning at school, I'd swap notes with Ethan. We'd tell each other what we'd tried and I'd pretend not to feel the disappointment stabbing my chest deeper with each unsuccessful day.

I was simultaneously dreading finding my power before Ethan in case they were upset, and trying to bite back my jealous side if they found theirs first. It stopped being about powers and started being about winning. There was no way to explain to Ethan without sounding like the worst friend in the world: hoping they'd fail so I wouldn't feel like a failure.

As weeks passed, I found excuses. School was ramping up, due dates looming, and powers weren't as exciting anymore. Eventually, we got bored and stopped trying. When Ethan brought it up later, I played it off as an ADHD thing. It wasn't hard to believe. With most stuff I'm interested in, I'll be super dedicated and put in loads of effort at the start, and then abruptly stop caring once it stops being shiny and new. Even my collection of identity crises.

Sexuality crisis? I'll think about it again when I find someone I want to date.

Gender crisis? I know what I want my transition to look like; I don't need specific labels.

Power crisis? It took months of deliberately not looking for it, but I don't care anymore. I'm doing fine without it. If I discover it, cool. If I don't, that's also cool.

Usually, nothing gets to me. Which is why it doesn't make sense that I can't get Tegan Dunne out of my head. It shouldn't get to me. I shouldn't be this angry about it.

'Hey, Cove,' Ethan says, 'we don't have to stay here if you aren't feeling it.'

We're standing a careful distance apart in front of a wall covered in windows. Each window opens and closes at random intervals. As far as powers go, the ability to lock a window — exclusively when it's four centimetres open — isn't the worst one I've heard.

'I'm feeling it.' Does it still count as lying when you're not sure if you're telling the truth?

'Seriously though, why did you want to skip today?' they ask. 'Did something happen?'

'No, nothing bad happened.'

Ethan clearly doesn't believe me, but they don't push it. I don't know if I'm disappointed.

Later, Ethan drives us to their sister's apartment. With each step we take towards the apartment's door, my pulse sounds louder inside my skull. I thought we'd be going back to Ethan's place like we usually do after school. I wasn't prepared to be social.

Someone I don't recognise answers the door. Did Ethan get the address wrong? Or is this part of their plan: shock Cove into forgetting about whatever's stressing them out by throwing him at an intimidating-looking stranger.

Then, the intimidating-looking stranger says, 'Paige's sibling, right?' and I remember housemates exist. Paige appears a moment later, opening the door wider so we can come in. She introduces us to her housemate, but I put too much effort into looking like I was listening instead of actually listening to their name.

'Are you two excited for tonight?' Paige asks.

'Oi, shut it,' Ethan says. 'I haven't told him yet.'

'Gotcha,' she says. 'I won't spoil it for them.'

I wish she would.

Conversation happens around me. Despite trying to pay attention, I end up zoning out for most of it. I'm genuinely trying, but it's hard. I've run out of meds and I keep forgetting to ask Mum to book another psych appointment to get a new script.

Teachers are starting to notice I've been *unlike myself* recently. They always phrase it like that, as if the medicated version of myself is my true self or something. When I first got diagnosed and told the school about it so they wouldn't confiscate my meds, some teachers were awful. Not outright rude or anything, but annoying. Some of them tried to tell me that ADHD is my superpower.

I can't stand people who say that. First of all: it's not true. It's also patronising as hell. Do they think I'm ashamed of how my brain works? Because I'm not. They don't need to repackage my own brain to sell it back to me.

Whenever I complain about it to Ethan, they have the same response: 'They mean well.' I think that's why I haven't told them what Tegan said after our speeches in English. Because she meant well.

Tegan's speech was fine. Like, logically, it was fine. We had to pick an issue that affects high school students and write a speech as if we were talking to the principal, trying to convince her to agree with whatever we were saying. Most people talked about how the canteen is too expensive, which is true. It got grating after the fifth person's speech though.

Tegan's topic was how the school can better support its LGBTQIA+ students, but it was pretty surface level. She only talked about things like anti-bullying campaigns and having pride flags around the place. I know that stuff is important, but it's the most basic of basic. The first page of the Google search results. Plus, the school already does that. We're constantly having assemblies about bullying and some teachers have pride flags on their doors or pride pins on their lanyards. Tegan didn't even put her pronouns in her slideshow, but made sure to mention that she's only an ally.

My topic was similar-ish. Not to be too much of a stereotype of myself, but I talked about trans and non-binary students. Specifically, how we should have more than one gender-neutral bathroom — which shouldn't be rebrands of our few accessible bathrooms — and how the school's online system should recognise chosen names. The way it is now, I have to walk to the other side of the world to pee and I get deadnamed every time I check assignment due dates.

It took so much effort to not sound angry during my speech. Maybe I should've. Maybe I'd be less angry now if I let it out earlier.

In the apartment, someone says my name. I do my best impression of someone who's been paying attention this whole time.

'Yeah?' I say. Nailed it.

Paige's housemate is sitting beside me on the couch, holding a pair of half unlaced platform Doc Martens. I have no idea where Ethan is, but their designated spot on the couch is empty.

The housemate pulls out the rest of the Docs' bootlaces and unwinds a new pair of laces. The new laces are black with white text that reads HE/HIM over and over. The housemate starts feeding them through the boots' eyelets.

'If you want, I can tell you what's happening tonight,' he says. 'While the other two aren't here.'

'Why?' I ask.

'This isn't a dig at you, but I can tell you're not keen on being out of the loop,' he says. 'I'm a mood ring. Still haven't figured out exactly how it works, but sometimes my nails react to peoples' emotions.'

He keeps lacing his Docs, giving me flashes of his nails as he moves. I thought they were painted, like that iridescent nail polish that shifts colours in the light, but the colours are physically moving. A swirling mess of dark blue with flecks of burnt orange. What do those colours mean? Does Paige know how to read his colour-code? Does Ethan? Is he broadcasting my emotional state to the whole world?

'I don't know what the colours mean,' he says. 'I promise, I can't read your mind or anything.'

'Then how?'

'Because you're about to tear a hole in that blanket.'

I look down. Without my permission, my hands have been clawing at the knitted throw blanket draped over my end of the couch. I push it away from me.

'Sorry,' I say.

But the nameless housemate isn't listening. He's left his boots by the couch while he's over by the bookcase, rummaging through a storage box. He pulls out something small and chucks it to me. It's a surprisingly heavy and wobbly metal cube that gently *clinks* when I move it.

'Try that,' he says. 'I had a chainmail phase a while ago. It makes for a decent fidget toy.'

'A chainmail phase?'

'Yeah, I got bored when I was meant to be doing uni work. Anyway, do you want me to tell you the plan for tonight?'

Why is it so embarrassing to admit I want to know? Every time I have to tell someone what I want or what I'm feeling, I struggle. From experience, if I say what I want, there's only two ways this conversation can go.

In Option A, I say I want to know the plan. He tells me and acts like it isn't a big deal, which makes me feel pathetic for making it such an ordeal in my head. Result: I feel like shit.

In Option B, I say I want to know the plan. He tells me, but this time, he can tell I was uncomfortable admitting it, so he reassures me, tells me it's okay, that I'm allowed to ask for the things I want. All the things I already know and understand logically but can't make my brain believe. Result: I feel like shit and now he feels sorry for me.

Probably left too long of an awkward gap for Option A, but I go for it anyway.

'Yeah, what's the plan?' I ask. My fingernails dig into the edges of the chainmail cube.

'We're going to an all-ages variety show in the city. Mostly drag performances, but not exclusively.'

'Oh,' I say. 'Cool.'

And, in theory, it does sound cool. I've never seen drag in-person since most shows are for over-18s, but I've watched enough clips to get the vibe. Glitter and rainbows and lip-synching to upbeat pop songs. Colourful wigs and outfits and a rowdy-but-harmless crowd.

But.

'It's okay if you don't think it's cool,' he says. 'Not your scene?'

He's smiling a little. I can't tell if he's patronising me or humouring me. If there's a difference.

'No, it sounds fun. I just don't want to bring the mood down. Not really feeling the spirit of Pride or whatever.'

'That's totally okay and I get it,' he says, 'but it won't be—'

He's interrupted by the front door opening.

'I'm back,' Ethan says, carrying a reusable bag. 'Sorry it took so long; I found a cat and had to stop to befriend them.'

'Completely understandable,' the housemate says.

'Here,' Ethan says, handing the bag to me. 'Stuff to get changed into. I didn't know how you'd be feeling, so I brought a ton of outfits. Masc, fem, whatever you're vibing with. Mac, when do we need to leave?'

'Soon. Maybe fifteen minutes?' the housemate says. Mac says. Thank you, Ethan. You're a legend.

Inside the bag, aside from clothes I recognise from Ethan's wardrobe, is the binder I accidentally left at their place the last time I slept over. I couldn't bind to school today since I had double-period Phys Ed and knowing Ethan planned for that further supports their legend status.

Now, maybe, hopefully, tonight won't suck.

Tonight already sucks.

After we arrived, Paige and Mac disappeared to get a drink,

and left me and Ethan saving our spot in line before the doors open. And in front of us, maybe five people ahead, is Tegan. Right when I was starting to feel better. The universe hates me. I hate it back.

'Dude, what's up?' Ethan asks. 'You look like you're in physical pain.'

'I'm fine,' I say, staring straight ahead.

The line is pretty spread out and the collective volume of people talking is loud enough that I doubt anyone could easily eavesdrop on us, but I still don't want to risk it. I'm not going to be that guy that causes a scene in public. At least Tegan hasn't noticed our presence.

'Are you sure?' they ask. 'I won't judge you if that's what you're worried about.'

'If that's what I'm worried about?' I say, skin prickling. The person in front of us turns around, then quickly faces ahead again. Great. So much for avoiding embarrassing public confrontations. I lower my voice. 'What does that mean?'

'I'm sorry,' Ethan says. They place their hand on my wrist in what I assume is meant to be a comforting gesture. I resist the urge to twist away from them. 'That came out wrong. I want to help, but it's hard when I have no idea what you need.'

'I already told you. I'm fine, alright? Nothing bad happened. Would you get over it already?'

I'm no expert, but I imagine my fine-ness would've been more convincing if I wasn't half-yelling by the end of my sentence, voice cracking. Around us, the line is dead silent. Fantastic.

For a moment, Ethan doesn't say anything. Their grip on my arm loosens slightly and I try to suppress the twinge of disappointment low in my stomach. But I can't suppress the jump in my traitorous pulse, and Ethan, whose fingers are wrapped around my wrist, must feel it too because they don't let go of me, not completely.

'You said that before, but that's not what I asked,' Ethan says. 'I asked if something happened. Not if something *bad* happened.'

My shoulders sag. They're still holding onto me, but something's shifted and I don't hate it anymore.

'I don't know how to explain in a way that makes sense,' I say.

'It doesn't have to make sense,' Ethan says.

'You know how we had those speeches in English yesterday?'

'Shit, were people transphobic about it?'

'No, people were fine. Mr Hollis was almost uncomfortably enthusiastic about it. But you know Tegan? She came up to me afterwards.'

Ethan inhales and I know they're ready to be defensive — or aggressive — on my behalf.

'She didn't say anything mean,' I say. 'I think. But it got to me for some reason. I don't know, I'm probably reading into it too much.'

'What'd she say?'

I work myself up to it. Even inside my head, Tegan's words sound inconsequential. Polite, even.

'She said I was well-spoken. And I know that's not bad because other people told me they thought I did a great job and I sounded confident and I clearly cared about the topic …'

'Are you sure she meant it in a mean way?' Ethan asks. 'She's the most genuinely nice person I know. She probably meant it as a compliment.'

And that's exactly why I didn't want to tell them.

'That's not the point,' I say.

Someone taps me on the shoulder and I jump. I didn't hear anyone approaching. When I look, Tegan is right beside me, saying something I can't hear. Actually, I can't hear anything apart from the increasingly loud thudding of my heartbeat in my head.

'Oh, hang on,' Ethan says.

Ethan's hand drops back to their side and the noise of the people around us crashes back into us. Almost literally. I startle at the sudden noise, stumbling, but Ethan grabs me before I can fall. As soon as they touch me, the noise vanishes again. It's completely silent. No chatter, no distant traffic, no kids being loud and annoying. An unnatural silence. A supernatural silence.

'Holy shit. Is that you?' I look back and forth between Ethan's hand, still holding my forearm, and their face. They're looking at the ground as if they're embarrassed, but they can't hide their grin. I put my anger aside for now. 'How? Since when? Why didn't you tell me?'

'Since this morning,' they say. 'I wanted to wait until I knew you were alright. I didn't mean to steal your moment like this, I swear.'

I'm still upset with them, but I'm mature enough to ignore my stuff to be happy for them. It's not because I'm afraid of the possibility of Ethan telling me that I'm irrational and wrong for being angry at Tegan. They wouldn't do that, not if I explained it properly. I know that. Right?

They let go of me and everything comes back. This time,

everything comes in the form of Tegan saying, 'Are you two okay?'

'We're okay,' Ethan says, turning to her. They sound hesitant, as if they're looking for proof that Tegan is anything but sincere. 'New power.'

'That's amazing, Ethan!' she says, and they smile back. 'Wait, I didn't interrupt anything, did I? Sorry, I just saw you and wanted to ask if you'd want to sit with me up the front? I was meant to come with some friends but all three of them cancelled last minute, so I'm here by myself.'

'That sounds—' starts Ethan.

'We can't,' I say. I was shooting for apologetic but, judging by Ethan's frown, didn't quite make it. 'There's four of us. There won't be enough room. Sorry.'

'Mac isn't sitting with us,' Ethan says to me.

'Why not?' I ask, but Ethan ignores me.

'And our seats are really far back,' they say. 'Don't you want to get a better view?'

I know what they're really asking. They're asking if I can get over my issues with Tegan for an hour. Never mind that Ethan planned today to make me feel better, and now they want me to sit next to the reason I've been feeling bad.

'We'd love to sit up front, are you kidding?' Paige says as she joins us in the line, drink in hand.

Something inside me wilts. If Ethan doesn't understand my reluctance, Paige definitely won't, especially with how easily she starts talking to Tegan as if they're best friends and not strangers.

The line shuffles forward and I don't move until Ethan grabs my arm and gently tugs me along. The world is quiet as we go inside a small room full of chairs facing a raised stage. Tegan says something inaudible to Paige and leads us to the front.

I end up two seats away from Tegan, who's sitting between Paige and Ethan. We're in the second row, slightly to the left of the stage. I briefly consider telling Ethan I need to go to the bathroom and then going to our original seats instead, but I'm not going to tell the old lesbian couple sitting beside me to move for me to get past. Especially since their existence as a lesbian couple roughly the age of my grandparents makes me feel a lot of feelings that I don't know how to explain.

Instead, I close my eyes and listen to my breathing, my heartbeat, the rustling of my shirt as my shoulders rise and fall. It doesn't work to make me calm or relaxed or less angry. If anything, it focuses my anger.

When I open my eyes again, the room is full. Something powerful radiates from the audience and beats in time with my pulse. Next to me, Ethan's head is slightly tilted like they're trying to work out what song is playing through the overhead speakers.

I don't wait for them to look at me. I'm done with waiting for other people to move first. It's my turn.

'It's not about what she said,' I say, gripping Ethan's arm and blocking out everything else.

They look at me, confused. I don't wait for them to speak.

'It's not about what Tegan said,' I repeat, louder, speaking over the noise of my heart pounding against my chest. 'It's about how it made me feel. I know she didn't mean it but it hurt like she did.'

'Are you—?'

'I'm not done,' I say. 'Being called well-spoken felt super backhanded. Like she was complimenting me by insulting other, angrier trans people. Saying I did a good job because I didn't make her feel defensive. And I couldn't say anything at the time because then I'd be fulfilling the stereotype of a sensitive, angry trans person.'

My hands are shaking.

'And when I told you, you said exactly that. She's nice, she didn't mean it, she meant well. Implying I'm the problem because I created an issue where there wasn't one.'

'Shit, Cove, I'm sorry,' Ethan says, wincing.

'I'm just … so angry,' I say, deflating. 'So much of the time. I need someone on my side, and I want that someone to be you.'

Ethan doesn't say anything for a moment but I can tell they're taking what I said seriously.

'I want to be on your side,' they say. 'I'm sorry I haven't been. And not that it's an excuse or anything, but I've been distracted with power stuff today. It's rough, trying not to accidentally touch anyone in case it scares them or something.'

They're perched awkwardly on the front of their seat, almost huddled into themself. I didn't think anything of it before, but I guess it's the only way they can sit without brushing up against me or Tegan on their other side.

I start to apologise, but Ethan cuts me off.

'I didn't tell you to make you feel bad,' they say. 'I wanted you to know so we can be on each other's side. And now we are.'

We sit in a power-induced silence until the lights dim around us, signalling the show is about to start.

'Can you hear that?' Ethan asks quietly.

I listen, but Ethan's still touching me so all I can hear is my breathing, my heartbeat, the rustling of my shirt. When I shake my head, they shuffle away and the sound of my breathing and rustling of my shirt disappears in the excited murmuring of the audience.

But my heartbeat stays, solid and strong. And *audible*, like a human metronome. After those months of worrying about whether Ethan or I would discover our power first, of course we'd find them on the same day. It was never going to be any other way.

Paige and Tegan look over at me to find the source of the noise and Paige grins and turns back to the front once she realises it's me. Tegan keeps staring but my heart beats loud, angry, and strong until she looks away.

Someone walks onstage and the audience almost drowns out the sound of my heart, but it's still there, underneath everything. I look up to see Mac swagger up to the mic in his HE/HIM platform Docs and intense makeup.

He stands tall at the microphone, mouth moving. It takes me too long to realise Ethan is excitedly holding onto me, cutting off Mac's speech. But even without hearing his words, I feel them in the flicker of his nails and the look in his eyes, the way he's standing and the way I can't look away.

Under the spotlight, his nails spark yellow and purple, pink and blue. They pulse in time with my heart and I realise I'm still angry. Maybe I never stopped. But it doesn't bother me as much as it did before, when I thought anger was something I shouldn't let other people see. When I thought it was a bad thing.

I let Ethan see my anger and the world didn't end.

After the show, maybe I'll let Tegan see it too.

VIOLET GRIM AND THE IN-BETWEEN PLACE

L.E. Austin

When the ghost in Violet Grim's kitchen poured the last of her cornflakes into his mouth, followed by the remnants of her oat milk, she wanted to tell him that he didn't have a functioning digestive system and maybe he should leave the overpriced cereal for those in the world who actually drew breath. Instead, Violet Grim — said drawer of breath — chose the high road and instead lobbed her soggy, lukewarm peppermint tea bag across the kitchen counter at his cheek.

'I know you're trying to aggravate me,' said Eddie the Cornflake Bandit, upturning his nose, 'but peppermint has wonderful skin benefits, so now I'm going to eat your cereal and unclog my pores.'

The fork she'd been using to eat her eggs started to look like a good weapon, but before she gouged his eyes out, Violet repeated the words that had been drilled into her since birth.

You should never tell a ghost that they're dead.

When you passed the In-Between Places — a bus stop crowded with apparitions that never boarded or a café with a faulty neon sign and a string of baristas who haunted it — you weren't supposed to stare and you weren't supposed to ask.

Eddie, who had no notion of the second death he had narrowly avoided, flung himself onto the couch and took up his guitar, plucking out a barely in-tune melody. Violet noted the sleeves of his denim jacket, a touch more frayed than yesterday, and the darkness pooling beneath his eyes. She guessed it was nearly time for him to move on.

Beside him, Penny, another ghost, was hunched in the armchair. She was dressed in a light blue nightgown and knitting furiously while her eyes were glued to the hair dryer infomercial playing on the TV. Every so often she glanced around, as though someone had made a noise, then returned to her activity.

Violet's phone pinged, indicating she was about to be late for her third shift in a row. 'I'm off,' she announced. 'See you guys tonight.'

As she tried to get up, the leg of her chair suddenly snapped beneath her. *Not again.* First, her bathroom mirror had cracked, and now the beloved chair she'd found at a garage sale was nearing the end of its days. In the last few months, the apartment had really started to show its age. Glancing at the small space of wall above the stove, her eyes traced the thin crack that had appeared yesterday morning. During the night, it had evidently snuck a few more centimetres up the wall. There were other things, too. Flaking plaster in the living room, strange groaning noises from the pipes in the laundry, and an odd-smelling mould collecting at the corners of the carpet. Violet had contacted the building manager several times to see to the disrepair, but the only response she'd received was a brief email explaining that someone would be along to check it out soon.

'Don't forget your lunch!' A door swung open and Violet's

third ghostly roommate, Layla, danced out of her bedroom in a highlighter-yellow top and booty shorts, a pop track blasting from her headphones. The dainty red pendant she always wore swung from her neck in time with her steady jog as she yanked open the fridge and pulled out a lunch bag, tossing it gracefully over the counter. Violet caught it with one hand and opened the front door with the other, throwing a final look over her shoulder.

The apartment was small, just her room, Layla's, and the guest room where Eddie, Penny and any other visitors bunked down. It smelled like burned coffee, Layla played her music too loud at night and the infomercials were on 24/7 at Penny's insistence. Not to mention Eddie always left empty milk cartons in the fridge. Still, it was a home of sorts, shabbiness and all. Violet waved to everyone on her way out, but couldn't quite bring herself to smile like she usually did. Today, her mind was on the crack on the wall, and the feeling of foreboding that came with it.

'Are you sure you don't remember the title or the author?'

Mr Coleman, a library regular on the high end of eighty, waited patiently on the other side of the information desk while Violet tracked the loading bar's steady crawl to the catalogue.

'The cover was red,' he said with conviction.

She smiled tightly.

Ten minutes later, Mr Coleman waddled out the doors, clutching the first red book she'd pulled off the shelf, a satisfied smile on his face.

'I had the most disastrous thought,' Margo, her co-worker, said as she eyed his exit warily, a pile of freshly returned books balanced in her arms. 'What if, when it's his time, he ends up in your In-Between Place?'

Violet's apartment block was built on top of the library. Convenient for commute purposes, but the elderly regulars tended to show up at her door every now and then.

'Wouldn't be so bad,' she decided eventually. 'Asking for vague books is really no different to Penny asking about her cat every other day.'

'Still no sign of it?'

'She insists that it came with her, but nobody else has seen it. Sometimes she looks around like she can hear it. How do you even find a ghost-cat?'

'You should check under the couch for ghost-cat poop.' Margo tipped the books into a waiting trolley. 'I know money for a uni student is tight, but I could not handle living in an In-Between Place. Too creepy.'

'The ghosts are nice.'

'What about that musical theatre kid last year?'

'Oh no, she was unbearable! How many renditions of 'Let it Go' do we really need?'

'Speaking of dead people.' Margo leaned her hip against the trolley and jerked her chin. 'Silver hair, two o'clock.'

The stranger perusing the shelves was hard to miss. Her eyeliner alone could cut a person through, however, most eye-catching of all was her jacket: a patchwork masterpiece of pink, yellow and blue, sewn together in rainbow thread. Violet guessed it was either handmade or the luckiest op-shop find in history.

Violet glanced down at her own thrifted sweater, achingly beige with embroidered buttercups patterning the hems. Pinned to her chest was her work badge with a glittery bi-flag sticker and her she/her pronouns scribbled on in Sharpie. She was decidedly not on this girl's level of cool.

The silver-haired girl was considering one of the books on the top shelf when Violet shuffled up behind her. Instead of facing her, the girl tilted her head — god, that was such a power move — and scrutinised her. 'Violet Grim?'

She nodded, throat dry. 'May I help you?' *Translation, I will literally step on myself to help you.*

The silver-haired girl hummed, running a shiny black nail along the spine of a leather-bound text, tipping it gently into her hands. 'You live in the In-Between Place upstairs, right?'

'Yes.' Violet wracked her brains to think where she might have seen this person before. She was sure she would have remembered a girl so strikingly gorgeous. There was also something not quite right about her. Margo said she was a ghost, and most people were pretty good at deciphering the living from the dead. Humans were *here* and ghosts were *there*, but this woman felt … neither.

'How do you know my name?' Violet asked.

The girl hummed again, the sound caressing Violet's ears like silk sliding over skin. 'Not many humans live in the In-Between.'

Violet watched her thumb through the pages of the book thoughtfully. 'It was the only place I could afford,' she found herself saying. 'On-campus accommodation is way out of my budget.'

'What's your major?'

'Creative writing.' Violet bit the inside of her cheek. She didn't even know this girl's name, why did she suddenly want to tell her everything about her life? She blinked hard, swallowing. 'Sorry, do we share a class or something?'

'Or something.' The girl smiled faintly, then put the book back on the shelf, in the correct spot. 'I'm Darcy.'

'Violet. Sorry, you already knew that, apparently.' She stuck out her hand before she could say anything else ridiculous.

Darcy's hand was freezing. Goosebumps raced up Violet's arms. It was decided then: there was no way she was human, not with that body temperature. However, she was far too present to be a ghost.

What is she?

And most importantly, was Violet allowed to shoot her shot with a girl who may or may not be dead?

'So …' She drew out the word, letting it fall between them. 'Is there something I can do for you?'

'I hope so.' Darcy — who may or may not be dead — released her hand, but her fingers lingered on the hem of Violet's sleeve, tracing the buttercup petals. Violet fought to stay still. 'I'm looking for someone I think you might know. I'm, well, sort of like a private investigator.'

'Sort of like?'

Darcy's voice dropped to a lower, almost sultry octave. 'There's an ex that has something I need.'

The way Darcy spoke — making each word sound like a delicious morsel that nobody would ever be worthy of tasting — almost lulled Violet into believing her. It took her a second to hear the slight quiver of a lie. In fact, upon closer inspection, Darcy's entire form seemed thinly coated in a layer of untruth, like seeing her from behind fogged glass. She was there, but she was not there. A truth but a lie.

Ghosts weren't dangerous like they were in movies. They didn't remember anything about their life before and they wouldn't haunt your dolls or try to possess you. But now Violet was certain that Darcy wasn't a ghost. And she was even more certain that she shouldn't be attracted to her.

Darcy watched her carefully. Her eyes, the unsettling shade of midnight blue, caught every micro-expression on Violet's face. Violet's breath froze somewhere in her chest, like this girl had reached out and stolen it. She was almost convinced that Darcy could see every lie she'd ever told, every mistake she'd made, everything. She was struggling to regain her breath when she realised Darcy was holding out a photograph. When she looked down, it took every muscle in her body to keep her expression neutral.

Shit.

Darcy's ex lived in her apartment.

'Sorry,' she said, shaking her head, 'I don't recognise her.' The lie immediately tasted bitter. The photograph of Layla stared up at them both. She looked different there, as a human. She dangled shiny car keys in front of the camera, and behind her was a bright yellow Beetle. A date was scrawled at the bottom. Five years ago.

Darcy was in the picture too, lips pressed to Layla's cheek, looking exactly the same with her silver hair and patched jacket. Only one detail had changed. There was a small, ruby red pendant dangling from picture-Darcy's neck. The girl she saw now wasn't wearing any jewellery. The hairs on her arms prickled. She'd seen that necklace before. Violet's stomach turned, and she felt a little better about lying.

After staring at her for a second too long, Darcy pulled out a notepad and pen and scribbled something down. 'Just in case you see her, give her this, would you?'

The paper in Violet's pocket burned hot as she sat at the kitchen counter. She stared into the teacup steaming softly between her fingers. The crack on the wall seemed to goad her.

'You okay?' Layla pulled her headphones down with one hand, a protein smoothie in the other. An evenly dispersed layer of berries, milk and peanut butter covered the kitchen counter. 'Did you get Mr Coleman again?'

'No, I mean yes, but that's not …' Her mind felt strung in several impractical directions, enticed by thoughts of silver hair and patched jackets and buttercups.

Her roommate waited expectantly, the pendant around her neck almost gleaming in the harsh overhead lighting. Violet gripped the teacup, praying she wasn't about to rip a hole in space and time. 'Layla, have you ever been in love?'

The silence that followed reminded her of the moment before a school exam, the panic of turning over the paper and seeing everything she hadn't studied for. Layla's brow furrowed, and a shadow moved slowly across her face. Around them, the apartment groaned softly.

Layla blinked once. Twice. 'What do you mean?'

'Did you … date? Before?'

'Before?' She rolled the word around in her mouth, considering it. Her hand, almost imperceptibly, fluttered to her collarbone. 'I suppose I must have.'

She didn't elaborate, and Violet cursed herself for even bringing it up. What did she expect? That Layla would suddenly recall her past and spill the beans on Darcy? She was probably breaking all sorts of sacred ghost laws just by considering the possibility. Violet was truly the worst roommate ever. When Violet didn't say anything else, Layla gave her a long, quizzical look, before shaking her head and putting her headphones on. Deafening music crackled out, and she danced back to her room.

Violet worried her bottom lip. She should have told Layla about Darcy and the note. It was only right. The business between her roommate and the silver-haired girl was nothing to do with her and she shouldn't be interfering.

Then again, Violet didn't know anything about Darcy. She hadn't even given Violet a last name, if she even had one. And if Layla had taken that pendant from her, so what? What was so important about it that Darcy had resorted to stalking a dead person?

Violet got up abruptly and, before she could change her mind, tossed her tea bag into the bin along with Darcy's note. She felt somewhat better, though guilt still nibbled at her, and the words were branded into her brain.

Hey Angel,
Nice place you got. If I were you, I'd never want to leave.
See you soon.
Turns out, my heart wasn't yours to keep.

Mood souring, Violet joined Penny on the couch. The wisened ghost was working away at a tri-coloured scarf with pink, orange and white woven in stripes. An elderly man on the TV looked rather smiley while he discussed erectile dysfunction. After a moment, Violet frowned. Pink and white were being methodically added to the project, but Penny's favourite ball of aggressively orange wool was nowhere to be seen in the living room.

'Where's your orange wool?'

'Cat got it,' Penny huffed, jabbing a knitting needle at the couch. Violet didn't need to check underneath to know there was nothing there. Aside from herself, Penny and Layla, the apartment was empty.

She sat up.

The apartment was empty.

'Where's Eddie?' she said.

Penny huffed again, giving her a pointed look.

Oh.

She got up and went to the guest bedroom, stepping over the patches of mould that seemed to be sprouting up everywhere. The guitar was gone, his dirty boots weren't upturned by the door. His bed was neatly made, something she had never witnessed in the entirety of his stay. Violet opened the fridge and let out a choked, short-lived laugh. The empty carton of oat milk sat waiting in the side door. She smiled to herself, then tossed it in the bin.

She froze.

Inside the rubbish bin, Darcy's note was gone.

A rustling sound drew her attention. She glanced up, just in time to see Layla's eyes boring into hers before she slammed the bedroom door shut.

Violet Grim was halfway through making her morning cup of tea when she realised that Darcy was sitting on her couch. Her booted feet were crossed on the coffee table and her beautiful jacket lay over the armchair next to Penny, who was furiously avoiding eye contact.

Violet promptly dropped her freshly-purchased milk carton, sending oat milk cascading across the kitchen counter.

'Morning.' Darcy tipped two fingers in a salute that made Violet forget how much she hated guests putting their feet on her coffee table.

'Hi!' she blurted out, righting the carton and mopping up the mess with a cloth, hoping Darcy couldn't see her hands shaking. She was used to sudden appearances in the apartment, but when those appearances were not of the newly-dead ghost sort, it was a little odd. A cool pair of hands stilled hers over the cloth.

'Here,' Darcy murmured in that rich, chocolatey voice of hers, 'allow me.'

Darcy wiped up the milk in neat strokes, but her eyes weren't focused on the task. They were flickering to something over Violet's shoulder. She willed herself not to follow. Layla's bedroom door had been closed all morning, and the absence of her music set the apartment on edge. Even Penny had muted the television, as if sensing a disturbance in the air.

'Day off?' Darcy squeezed the cloth into the sink and sauntered around Violet to wash her hands, her palm pressed gently against Violet's hip, moving her ever-so-slightly out of the way.

Violet suppressed a shiver, then swiftly caught hold of herself. Darcy was in her apartment. She knew Violet had lied about knowing Layla. Of course she did, because Darcy was something else entirely, not ghost, not human, and somehow Violet had become wrapped up in a situation she wasn't sure she wanted to understand.

She realised a little too late that Darcy had asked her a question. 'Oh!' She flapped her hands, grabbing the rest of the milk and dashing it into her English Breakfast. 'Yes, day off. I don't work Fridays.'

'Lucky me,' Darcy murmured in a tone that set Violet's heart thumping. Tiny flakes of wall plaster flitted down around them like a sun shower. Darcy placed both hands on either side of her and leaned forward, pressing Violet back into the counter. The kitchen lights flickered and buzzed. 'Now, aren't you going to ask me what I'm doing here?'

Violet hadn't planned on broaching the subject so soon, but she also hadn't planned on being flirted with that morning by a very attractive girl who had broken into her apartment, so all bets were off. That was, if Darcy was even flirting with her. Was she? Bisexual panic gripped her, layered with her own poor self-esteem. It was definitely the gorgeous patched jacket distracting her.

'I—I don't know who you are,' she stuttered, clenching her fingers into fists, partly out of anger and partly to stop herself reaching out to see if Darcy's hair was as soft as it looked, 'but just because this is an In-Between Place doesn't mean you can traipse in and out when you please.' She really hoped that sounded intimidating.

A knowing gleam winked in Darcy's eyes. 'Is that the tone you should be taking with your landlord?'

'Landlord? You said you were a private investigator.'

'Call me an entrepreneur. I need to have a word with one of my tenants, but you already know that, don't you?'

Violet gulped. She knew when to concede defeat. She ducked out of Darcy's arms, putting some much needed distance between them. God, what she would have given for Eddie to interrupt with a stupid joke just to cut the tension. 'You're right. I wasn't exactly telling the truth when I said I didn't know Layla, but—'

'Layla?' Darcy chuckled darkly. 'I suspected she'd changed her name to evade me. When she was human, she went by Leah, but Layla's just as cute.'

Violet ignored the fresh stab of envy. 'How do you know her?'

'I told you. She's got something of mine and I'd like it back.'

'Who are you? Really.'

'Someone who's trying to save your life.' Darcy eyed Layla's door once more, drumming her fingers on the counter. 'Tell me, have you noticed things getting a little worse for wear around here?'

Behind them, the crack released a light puff of wall dust, hammering the point home. Darcy pinned her with a meaningful look.

Violet crossed her arms. 'What's that got to do with anything?'

'Ever wonder why? In-Between Places are timeless, they don't wear down like everywhere else — you must know this.'

Violet shook her head, the sense of foreboding that had been building since yesterday finally reaching its peak.

'How long has Layla been here?' Darcy asked.

Violet stared at her roommate's door. Her memory was hazy. A while, definitely, but not that long. Right? Now that she thought about it, had Layla already been in the apartment when she moved in? In two strides, Darcy was at Layla's door. She rested her palm flat against the wood and the hinges creaked in response.

'Do you know what happens when a ghost refuses to move on from an In-Between Place?'

When Violet didn't answer, the apartment took over, letting out an almighty bellow. Beneath their feet, the floor began to tremble, the crack shot up the wall and along the ceiling. In the living room, Penny shrieked and threw her half-knitted scarf over her head.

'It's been five years. This place can't maintain the energy to keep Layla here.' Darcy held her ground while Violet grabbed the kitchen counter for balance. 'Eventually, it's going to collapse and everything in it will be destroyed.' Her gaze darkened. 'Including you.'

Penny clung to her armchair, knitting needles clutched in her fingers. In the guest room, a lightbulb shattered. The floor maintained its steady rumble, the walls howled and split, identical cracks spider-webbing the roof.

Violet swayed dangerously. 'What do we do?'

Darcy raised her brows intently, then knocked on Layla's door. At once, the apartment stilled, like it was taking a breath. Layla's door creaked open, and out emerged a ghost who was so far removed from the one Violet had grown used to.

Her skin had turned papery white, almost translucent. Her eyes were sunk deep into her head and her hair hung limp and lifeless around her shoulders. There was no music coming out of her headphones. Even the pendant she wore looked too big for her body.

'So,' Layla muttered, eyeing Darcy up and down, 'you found me.'

The apartment took up its cacophony again. The shudders sent paintings tumbling off the walls, the TV crashed onto the floor. Penny rocked ceaselessly in the armchair, eyes wide and alarmed.

Darcy, however, leaned against the door frame, oblivious to the mayhem. 'Hello again, Angel.'

Layla sucked in a breath. 'Hello again, Death.'

Death? Violet hoped she'd misheard. 'Somebody explain what's going on. Now!'

Darcy — Death — had the audacity to smile. 'Well, when two girls fall in love—'

'That's not what I meant!' Violet snapped, nearly knocked off her feet by another shockwave. 'You're the Grim Reaper? As in the literal ruler of the dead and the Afterworld. And you're in my house.' She stared at her roommate. 'And you! You *dated* her?'

'We had a deal.' Layla gripped the door for support, though, in all the chaos, it barely clung to its hinges. 'Darcy agreed to let me keep my memories while I was in the In-Between, and stay the hell away from me.'

'Believe me, it was not out of benevolence.' Darcy eyed Layla reproachfully. 'I'll be taking my heart back now.'

'Your heart?' Violet watched as Layla's hand closed protectively around her pendant.

Darcy's gaze followed hers. 'I should never have given it to you. I was a fool to believe you wouldn't use it against me someday.'

Layla rolled her eyes. 'Can you blame me? You gave me the

one thing that would allow me to control you.'

'Because I loved you!'

'I had just died driving that stupid car that you bought me,' Layla pointed out. 'I was frightened. Nobody knows what happens in the After, not even ghosts. What if we never remember our lives at all? What if it's just darkness? I'd rather stay In-Between than risk whatever's beyond, and I couldn't take the chance of you showing up and forcing me to move on.'

'You know I can't tell you about the After. You just have to trust me.' Darcy held out a hand, beckoning. 'Come with me.'

'No!' Layla yelled, shifting away. 'I still have your heart, you have to do what I say.'

'That's why I'm here,' Darcy replied quietly. 'I've moved on, Angel. My heart doesn't belong to you anymore. It's time for you to move on too.'

Layla stepped back into her room. 'I can't.'

Violet opened her mouth, but right at that moment, there was an ear-splitting boom as part of the ceiling caved. She had just enough time to fling her arms over her head before plaster rained down on top of them. They were running out of time.

'I'll go with you.' A voice came from behind. All three heads swivelled to find the source.

Penny stood in the kitchen, nightdress covered in dust and debris. She'd wrapped her incomplete scarf around her neck, still attached to the knitting needles. Her expression was nervous, but determined. Violet's eyes widened. A scruffy cat blinked slowly back at her, its little black head nestled in Penny's shoulder. Despite the place falling down around them, it looked reasonably unbothered, and possibly a tad confused as to why everyone was yelling. The old woman approached them.

'We can do it together. Here.' She shoved the cat into Layla's arms, who held it stiffly, shock written plainly on her face.

'You don't have to,' Darcy explained to Penny. 'You still have time.'

The old woman shook her head. 'I'll go with Layla. We'll find out what's on the other side together.' She stroked the cat's head, then ran her crooked fingers along Layla's cheek, catching a tear on the way. 'And if there's darkness, at least we'll have a friend.'

'I don't—' Layla choked, burying her face in the cat's fur. It purred, nuzzling her neck. 'I don't know what to do.'

'Say goodbye,' Penny said firmly, 'then take the hand of Death with me.'

Layla nodded. Her hand hovered over Darcy's. Her gaze met Violet's, two lifetimes of pain and grief hidden behind them. 'Goodbye, Violet.'

'Good—'

Layla and Penny gripped Darcy's hands and the apartment exploded into blinding light.

Violet Grim sat at the kitchen counter, munching on her cornflakes. She stared at the wall above the stove, checking for signs of wear, but only a pristine white surface stared back at her. The carpet was mould-free, the whole place smelled faintly of fresh paint and, if she really concentrated, burned coffee.

Layla's bedroom lay vacant. It was a second guest room now, like it was always supposed to be, but Violet would forever think of it as Layla's room.

Her phone pinged. Late for work again. She gulped her last

spoonful and headed for the door. Before she got there, however, something urged her to pause. A tug of intuition maybe, or a lingering memory. She doubled back, opened the fridge, and got out her lunch bag.

When she opened the front door, a familiar face waited for her.

'Hey, Buttercup.'

'Death,' she replied, not trying to hide the surprise in her voice.

The silver-haired girl winced. 'I think I liked it better when you called me Darcy.'

Violet smiled. 'Okay, Darcy, what can I do for you? Any more exes to track down?'

Darcy combed a hand through her hair. Her patched jacket looked extra bright today, like it had recently been washed. The ruby pendant shone at her neck. 'No, just thought I'd come personally to drop something off.' She pointed to the living room.

A young man had appeared on the couch. He seemed a little lost, taking in the apartment with a blank stare. He had on a fraying denim jacket and jeans. He reminded Violet of Eddie, and she smiled.

'Don't worry, I've already briefed him on leaving empty milk cartons in the fridge,' Darcy informed her, reading her thoughts.

'If he steals my cornflakes, you'll be receiving a very disappointed letter from me.'

Darcy's eyes sparkled. 'Can't wait.'

Violet lowered her voice. 'Are Layla and Penny … are they okay?'

'You know I can't tell you, right?'

'Right, I know. But if you do see them, just … tell them … tell them—'

Darcy's fingers slipped into hers. The initial ice-cold still shocked her, but Violet took comfort in the touch. 'I will,' said Darcy.

'Thanks,' Violet breathed, closing her eyes for a brief moment. Her phone pinged again. 'I'm late.'

'Get out of here,' Darcy urged, pulling her out of the apartment and closing the door.

'I'll see you around?'

Darcy hesitated, unable to meet her eye. She shoved both hands into her pockets. It was an unfamiliar look on her, one that Violet found oddly endearing. 'Yeah. I mean, if you'd like that?'

Violet grinned, cheeks growing hot. 'Yes,' she said, 'I'd like that.'

THICKER THAN WATER

A.R. Henderson

Evie stared at the ocean, and the ocean stared back.

Waves rocked back and forth, white caps crunching and crashing against the sand bar. They unfurled into smaller flurries of water, brushing forward in lacy layers over the shallows. Froth and bubbles nipped at Evie's bare feet, cool and sharp.

Evie swallowed hard and tried to keep their breathing even. There was no danger in simply dipping their toes in. The real danger was out in the deep, past those gnashing, breaking waves, where unseen riptides swirled and slithered.

A memory — of cool water moving over Evie's skin, blurring their vision, defying gravity — made them shudder.

Just keep your toes in, Evie reasoned. *Just for a bit.* They tried to focus on other sensations that weren't freaking them out as much. The wet sand under their feet, firm but squishy. The sound of seagulls squawking and squabbling further down the tide line.

In the summer, the beach would have been a rainbow: butter-yellow sand dotted with bright towels, candy-striped umbrellas and sunburn-pink skin. In winter, Driftwood Bay was a sepia photo of itself. The sand was so washed out it was nearly white, empty except for a black raincoat walking a brown dog. The water and sky were a bruised and surly granite grey. The stony waves were churning, roiling, thrashing.

A rogue wave rushed over Evie's feet, the white frothy fingers of the sea clawing all the way over their ankles. They forced themself to stand still for a moment, rigid, ignoring the pounding in their chest. Then they ran, stumbling up the sand.

'Are you okay?' called Griffin. He was waiting for Evie further up the beach. In his berry-purple parka he was the most colourful thing there. It was the kind of outfit that Evie's mother would have called *tacky*, and something about that made Evie love it.

'I'm okay.' They breathed in, trying to keep their voice even. They probably looked like an idiot, fleeing from an ankle-high wave.

Evie glanced down at their feet. They were wet and gritty with sand, and they had turned transparent.

Evie could see the outline of their toes, an indent on the sand, but they were crystal clear. Like they were made of clean glass — or like they were made of water.

Evie offered Griffin the brightest and most well-adjusted smile they could manage and willed their stupid feet to become corporeal again. It usually started in the feet. Or the fingertips. Usually people didn't notice, especially if Evie managed to keep attention on their face. They tried to make a casual gesture, but their hands fluttered around their face like mosquitos.

Griffin let out a gusty breath. 'You don't need to put yourself through exposure therapy, y'know. At least, you don't need to throw yourself into it when you've just arrived. Maybe have some dinner first.'

He offered Evie a wonky smile. He had the same eyes as Evie's mother, his sister. A different smile though. Their mother's smile was always symmetrical and shiny as if it had been painted on.

'What d'you say?' asked Griffin, carefully watching Evie's face, and, mercifully, not noticing their ghostly feet. 'Fish and chips, to commemorate your new life as a salty sea-dog?'

Guilt lodged itself in Evie's chest like a piece of rock. They had made a silent promise not to do anything to worry Uncle Griffin while they were staying with him. He'd had no obligation to take Evie in while his sister was away. Evie was already going to be taking up space in his home, his life, his schedule. The less room Evie's issues took up, the less of a burden it would be.

So Evie nodded and followed him up the beach on their ghostly, watery feet.

Tendrils of tide pushed themselves through Evie's memory. Bubbles raced over their skin. The cold current pinched and grabbed at their arms and legs. It pushed their hair into their face, blinding them. Evie's hair had been longer back then. Twirling in the riptide with no sense of which way was up, in the deep water of a beach not unlike this one.

They remembered a feeling not quite like falling, more like a sudden upset of gravity. As if the laws of physics were different under the sea. As if Evie weighed nothing; mattered not at all.

They remembered opening their salt-stung eyes and seeing a sky so impossibly blue. They remembered someone yelling, sounding very far away. They remembered the smell of sand and the lingering burn of seawater in their throat.

They remembered a doctor saying that Evie had technically

been dead for forty-nine seconds before the surf lifesavers had resuscitated them. The number was so specific that it seemed silly. Had someone been standing there counting? But, all the same, it had lodged itself in their ten-year-old brain forever alongside all the other fun facts they knew about rocks and plants and dinosaurs.

Since the near-drowning — or the temporary drowning, Evie supposed — their parents had diligently kept them away from large bodies of water. That meant no beach holidays, no more pool visits, and nervously changing the channel every time *Blue Planet* was being rerun on TV. Five landlocked years. It also meant some fretting and frowning when Griffin offered to have Evie stay with him while their parents were on their overseas posting. Evie had assured everyone that it would be alright. It wasn't like there were many other options.

Besides, Evie had wanted to know what would happen if they saw the sea again. It was why they'd asked Griffin if they could stop there on the way, between the bus stop and his house. Maybe it was a sign of self-development. Maybe it was some stupid, stubborn idea of unfinished business that had been stewing in Evie since they were ten.

Maybe, Evie had wondered, the waves would surge up and wrap around them, trying to finish the job. Maybe the shallows would gently brush Evie's hands, trying to apologise. Maybe Evie would turn to foam.

Maybe Evie would turn back to normal.

But no. None of those things had happened. So Evie just hugged their hoodie around themself and hid their semi-transparent feet under a spare towel.

They wondered if part of them had stayed under the sea. Or if part of the sea had stayed under their skin.

Griffin drove them to the cliff overlooking the ocean. He pulled to a stop under a corrugated iron carport, dented and drooping in one corner ('From a hailstorm last autumn') and tucked up next to a tall house made of dark brick ('It looks a bit ugly, I know, but in the '70s someone really thought this was the height of architecture!'). Gum trees and ferns cluttered around the house. In the not-so-distant distance was the sound of waves.

'So,' said Griffin, with the chipper gravitas of an adult who doesn't want a child to freak out, 'it's just a short walk from the back garden to the headland. Only a couple of minutes and you can sit on the clifftop looking out at a spectacular view of the sea. Sometimes you can see whales!' He drummed his fingers on the steering wheel. 'I hope that …'

'It's fine,' said Evie, doing their best to sound confident. 'Thanks for letting me stay.'

'Hey, no worries!' Griffin patted them on the shoulder. 'It'll be a pleasure to have you. And it'll be good for me. I've been living a bit like a bachelor, rattling around in this big old house, so having a guest has forced me to get my act together again.'

Evie's mother had said something similar. She worried about her little brother: he travelled too much, he collected too many weird old objects, he didn't go on dates or try to *make meaningful connections*. When Griffin came up for Christmas, he always spent half the day batting her off while she sighed about how he'd never settled down with a nice girl.

'Oh, not that you're a guest.' Griffin added, quickly. 'You

should make yourself at home.'

Evie checked that their toes were solid again, then walked into the old brick building feeling like a trespasser.

Unpacking all their clothes into the wardrobe felt like too much of an imposition. Evie dug pyjamas and toiletries out of their suitcase and left it open and full as they tiptoed towards the bathroom.

There was something about showering in strange bathrooms that felt like visiting an alien planet. Evie felt more exposed than usual as they undressed and left their clothes in a tight pile — not taking up too much space — on the bench. Jeans with hems still damp from the sea, a too-big hoodie, plain nude-tone underwear.

Occasional back pain and complicated gender feels aside, Evie was sort of thankful for being a so-called early bloomer. Once you hit a D cup or so, bras tended to turn beige and white and black. It took the pressure off shopping for them, especially with their mother. She couldn't fuss and flit and hold up the frilly pastel-toned ones and say, 'Oh, don't you think this is cute?'

Evie did think they were cute, but that wasn't the point. It was a good thing Evie had trauma associated with water, they thought. It meant that no one expected them to go swimming, and it meant that their mother had never taken them bikini shopping. Their drowned-as-a-child weirdness created an effective moat around their gender weirdness, meaning they didn't have to talk about it.

They climbed into the shower.

If Evie really thought about it, they didn't hate their body.

Not really. Their body wasn't their enemy, it was more like the neighbour's odd kid that their parents insisted they should be friends with because they had some superficial things in common. At best, Evie and their body were acquaintances, sitting awkwardly together at backyard barbecues, begrudgingly sharing the same space with a sense of mild solidarity.

But when people saw Evie and their body together they always made assumptions. *Oh, look what good friends you are! Oh, aren't you growing into a fine young woman?*

As their mother's voice echoed through their mind, water sluiced down over Evie's scalp and into their eyes.

It happened suddenly, a tectonic shift under the skin. It wasn't right. The water was hot, it shouldn't have happened. Maybe something about the sound of the sea, the feeling of water blinding them. Evie felt gravity shift, their stomach drop.

They managed to crack open a stinging, waterlogged eye and looked down. They let out a yelp.

Evie had turned completely transparent.

'Crap.' They tried to focus. Anchor themself. Become aware of their fingertips, then their palms, then their wrists. They tried the breathing exercises their old therapist had suggested. They stood there swearing and trying not to think about drowning, trying not to think about their mother.

I am okay. I am okay. Lying to yourself could be a pretty effective calm-down technique, apparently. Evie focused on the sensation of slick tiles on the soles of their feet and the droplets of water pinging off their shoulders. They held their hands in front of their face. Their body was still perfectly see-through. Slightly blueish and wavering in the light, like shallow water.

Evie breathed. They stepped carefully out of the shower.

They looked in the mirror and saw half a person looking back, all made of splotchy paint daubs of pale, freckly skin.

'You right?' called Griffin from the hall outside. It gave Evie enough of a shock that, for some reason, their whole right arm reappeared. They wiggled their fingers.

'All good!' Thankfully, they could speak, just. Three-quarters of their face was back. It looked like a scoop had been taken out of the right side of their head. Their reflection had one living brown eye, and one ghostly blue one. It shifted with the light, distorting the tiles on the wall behind it. 'Just slipped!'

Evie wrapped a towel around as much of themself as they could, and curled up on the floor. They told themself they were okay. They tried to believe it.

When they next peeked at their reflection, their whole head was there. They checked themself over, running their hands down the sides of their ribs, twisting around and making sure there were no watery patches on their back. They flexed their fingers, rolled their neck and wiggled their toes on the soggy bath mat.

Un-ghostly enough to handle dinner, they let out a final heavy breath and summoned the courage to get dressed.

They pulled on clean pyjamas and their biggest, lumpiest black hoodie. They vanished into it so thoroughly that Griffin wouldn't notice if Evie went watery again.

Griffin had a nice old cedar table that he said he'd found at a local antique shop, but they ate on the couch. Something about the whole thing felt scandalous — the greasiness of the takeaway, the mismatching décor of Griffin's lounge room, the TV playing on low volume in the background. Evie didn't recognise the film, but it looked and sounded crackly and golden and vintage, showing a blonde woman in men's clothing running around what looked like an old cowboy saloon. Evie wanted to ask who she was, but got too shy, so instead said, 'Mum hates having the TV on while we eat.'

Griffin laughed. 'Well, I hope you don't mind. I can't stand the sound of my own chewing, so I always chuck on an old movie or something.' He bit a chip in half. 'Have you messaged your mum, to tell her you're here safe?'

Evie winced internally. 'I don't want to wake her up. I can't remember what the time difference is between here and Paris.'

'Well, if she's asleep, it'll be a nice gift to wake up to.'

They pulled their phone out of the depths of the hoodie's pockets, took a photo of the living room, and sent it to their mother. First they typed out *Home sweet home!* Then deleted it and wrote, instead, *Arrived safe. Hope you're settling in too.*

If Evie listened carefully, they could hear the waves chomping at the cliffs below. *But they're out there,* they recited. *And I'm safe. I'm okay.*

'You still right to go shopping tomorrow?' Griffin asked.

Evie summoned that false confidence again. 'Yeah, sounds good.' As long as they managed not to turn to liquid if they accidentally stepped in a puddle. They tried not to think about it.

The least Evie could do, they figured, was to make life easy for Griffin. Not be the weird kid who had died and come back to life. Not be the queer kid, dyeing their hair or wearing boy's clothes or doing anything that would make their mother huff with disapproval. Not be the kid made of water.

Just be normal, whatever that was. Just be as normal as was reasonable, as normal as it took for them to blend into the walls until their mum's posting was up and they could unburden Griffin from the weight of their weird, traumatised, drowned body.

As Evie tried to sleep that night, they could hear the sea smashing itself against the cliffs.

Driftwood Bay was one of those little towns where everyone knew each other. Griffin was greeted warmly in every shop they walked into along the main street. In the second-hand bookstore, he gestured enthusiastically to Evie and said, 'This is my sister Christina's kid. Staying with me while she's off at some high-flying new position in France. Typical overachiever move from her, right?'

A bolt of lightning went down Evie's throat. They looked back and forth between Griffin and the bookshop owner, who was laughing and rolling her eyes. The casual way he'd said it — *my sister's kid* — made Evie stare at him.

'So, what book d'you need again?' he smiled at them, scratching his nose. 'It's not *The Outsiders*, is it? They assigned that to me when I was in year nine. They've gotta get some new material.'

'We're doing a Shakespeare unit, actually. *Twelfth Night*.'

'Oh, good, that's way more modern,' Griffin laughed, and Evie laughed with him, the sound surprising them. 'At least that's one of the fun ones. Gender fuckery and sexual confusion and all that.'

He bought Evie a copy of the play, and they watched him the whole time, wondering what that meant. Inside the pockets of their hoodie, they could feel the subtle sickly coldness that told them their hands had turned translucent.

They followed Griffin along the street, taking in the colour and shape of the place: the pastel-pink ice cream parlour, the cracked siding of the fish and chip place, the cinema with its angular art deco façade, the brand-name clothing stores jostling for space next to the local boutiques. The sun was out, wintry and weak, dog-walkers and coffee-drinkers bundled up in decidedly un-beachy coats and hats. Evie wondered if this street would feel familiar in a few months. It was a strange thought.

In the supermarket, Griffin asked what Evie liked to eat. Evie said they normally ate whatever their mum ordered in the weekly meal kit, boxes that came to the door meticulously designed to be healthy and efficient. Griffin screwed up his nose and asked the question again. Evie thought about it for a minute and said, 'I like curry?' So Griffin got a basketful of slow cooker curry sauces, just like that.

'Let's just duck in here,' he said afterwards, nodding to a shop window painted with VINTAGE – ANTIQUES – BRIC A BRAC. The display was cluttered with a chest of drawers, an old baby doll in a frilly nightgown ('That's haunted,' mused Griffin), and a massive stuffed and mounted stag's head. Its antlers fanned out and filled most of the window, necklaces and pocket watches on chains hanging off each point. 'You never know what they'll have.'

It was just as much of a mess inside, and somehow Griffin blended in perfectly. A record was playing on the gramophone at the front desk and it smelled intensely of vanilla-scented candles and mothballs. 'This is pretty cool,' whispered Evie, scanning the room, taking in the furniture and paintings. Griffin grinned and vanished towards a shelf of vases and teacups.

Evie drifted through the dust motes, towards the rack of clothing in the corner of the shop. Making sure no one was looking, they skimmed their see-through fingers over the hanging fabric: a button-down covered in crayfish, an ugly Christmas jumper, a beaten-up tee printed with *Women Want Me, Fish Fear Me*. They realised they were in the men's section and flinched, the transparency washing up to their elbows. But no one, still, was watching.

At the end of the rack were a pair of mannequins showing off what looked like vintage clothes: a shirt and pinstripe waistcoat on one, a cinch-waisted floral dress on the other. Its halter-neck and flared skirt made it look like something a 1950s starlet would flounce around in. Evie ran their glassy, ghostly fingers over the skirt, tracing the rosy patterning, wondering what it would look like on them, how it might feel to swish around in a skirt with that much *whoosh*.

The image quickly flickered out. People would think, *you're wearing that because you're a girl and girls are supposed to wear pretty vintage dresses.*

Evie wondered, instead, how they'd look in the waistcoat. That would make people think, *well, you're dressing masculine because you feel like you have to, right? You know you can be non-binary and feminine?* These thoughts looped and looped until Evie felt like they were caught in the riptide again.

Calm down, they coached themself. They'd never get to have those conversations anyway, since neither the dress nor the waistcoat was tailored for someone as curvy as Evie.

'Evie?'

They whipped around, dropping the hem of the dress, and found Griffin staring at them. His eyes were wide. His lips were parted.

Evie didn't need to look down. They could tell from the look on Griffin's face and from the hazy, cold rush bubbling over their skin. Or rather, where their skin was supposed to be.

Evie was gone. Completely incorporeal, nothing but a silhouette, ill-defined edges swaying back and forth as if seen from underwater. Two glassy hands and a liquid, ghostly head poking out of a hoodie, looking at Griffin with wavering, watery eyes.

Evie stepped backwards, moving sluggishly, as if submerged. They tried to start their *I am okay, I am okay* chant, but all that echoed in their mind was *I've ruined everything.*

They remembered, too well, the feeling of being lost underwater. Of kicking out their feet and touching bubbling emptiness instead of sandbank. Of their heart shooting up into their throat, their lungs squeezing, their stomach tipping as they floundered. That split-second realisation that they needed to take a breath, but they would only gulp down a lungful of ocean if they did.

They remembered, too well, that feeling returning to them even when they should have been safe on dry land. Saltwater rushing up their nose when the girls noticed that Evie always got changed in the toilet before P.E., giggling behind their painted nails as they all got dressed together. The riptide pushing and pulling at Evie's limbs as they scrolled through social media and saw argument after argument about who counted as really genderqueer. Their mother's voice sounding muffled, far away, as if heard from underwater, as she lay out her makeup palettes and toured Evie through them, pinching their chin and dabbing blush on their cheeks.

Deep-sea disorientation when pride parades or trans rights protests marched across the news, and their mother tutted, 'They're not going to get anywhere making a scene like *that*, are they?' Did she want Evie to agree, or argue? Would she have cared if Evie said anything? Evie could never reply. Their mouth was full of water.

It felt like drowning, sometimes. And Evie could say that, because they knew, firsthand.

Griffin's voice pulled them back into the present. 'You right, kiddo?' he asked softly. He extended a hand, unsure where to put it. It landed carefully on the shoulder of Evie's hoodie. 'Is there anything I can do?'

Evie stared at him. Blood was rushing in their ears.

'Let's get you out of here, hey? Have a sit down somewhere?'

Evie numbly, liquidly, nodded.

Behind the antique store was a little park, a square of spongy coastal grass and a couple of benches in the shade of a big old Norfolk pine. Griffin sat quietly, shopping bags clustered around his shoes, as Evie slowly regained colour and substance.

'Sorry,' they said, as soon as their mouth came back. Their words came out with a bubbly, rippled quality.

'Don't be sorry,' Griffin smiled weakly. 'I'm just glad you're okay. Does this happen a lot?'

'Sometimes. Yeah. Ever since the … y'know.'

He nodded, thoughtfully. He was still sitting next to Evie. He didn't look like he'd seen a ghost.

'Everyone deals with stuff like that in different ways,' said Griffin.

Beneath the hoodie, Evie could feel that their torso was back, and their arms were nearly done, too. Their hands still looked like sculpted glass, veined with ribbons of light like sunshine moving through seawater. 'I guess so.'

'It can be a bit claustrophobic in those cluttered old shops, hey?'

'No, it wasn't that.' The last thing Evie wanted was to taint his favourite shop. It made the admission slip out. 'I get … I don't like clothes shopping. I mean, I like *clothes*, but going with my mum always …'

A salty breeze weaved between them in the following quiet. Griffin just nodded. 'Christina's a pain in the ass sometimes, isn't she?'

Evie blinked at him, and he laughed. 'She's my big sister, I'm allowed to say that. It means I know it better than anyone.'

Evie breathed out. 'I just feel like there's a certain way I have to look. I feel like I have no control over it, because …'

Maybe that was too much to blurt out all at once. All that complicated Mum Stuff, all that complicated Gender Stuff, churning like a stormy tide in Evie's chest. They trailed off, but Griffin didn't seem to mind.

'I get that. It's rough.' He sighed, hugging his bright purple coat around him. 'People think you have to fit into a nice little box. Even if they mean well, it can be … well, it still feels like they're shoving you into a crate, even if they're polite about it.' He grinned his wonky grin. 'You just do whatever you feel comfy doing, okay? You're under my roof this year, so I'll look out for you.'

Griffin tentatively rested one hand in the middle of Evie's back, rubbing slow circles between their shoulder-blades. 'There, that's feeling more solid, huh? D'you want to head home?'

Evie nodded.

When they got into the car, Evie asked softly, 'Can we stop by the beach?'

'You sure?'

'Yeah.'

The wind was as bitterly cold as it had been the day before, raking off the waves. But the sky was blue, and the ocean matched. A vibrant fresh-from-the-paint-tube blue, dotted with little sprays of white on top of the waves.

The sea was calmer, the water less hungry, less agitated. Evie sat, very carefully, on the sand and watched the sea ebb in and out.

Griffin sat next to them, plopping down with an exaggerated groan that made Evie giggle. They both pulled off their shoes and buried their bare feet in the cool sand.

'The ocean's always changing,' he pointed. 'Never the same beast twice, no matter what we want it to do.'

Evie smiled, for real this time. The two of them talked, voices flurrying around them on the salty breeze. With the waves so near, Evie was transparent up to their calves. But they were sitting far back enough that the tide couldn't catch them. And Griffin was next to them, a warm buffer against the wind, a listening ear, a wonky grin.

Evie looked at the ocean, and the ocean looked back.

NEGARA

Lian Low

I'm slumped in an empty toilet cubicle, saliva dribbling down my chin. I crawl to a cracked sink and pull myself up while waiting for the vertigo to pass. The door swings open; I hear laughter and voices.

Through my blurry vision I see two identical strangers swaying in crop tops and wearing fluoro pink make-up.

'Need a hand?' they ask.

'Nah, all good, I think. Just a headache,' I say.

'No worries, darl,' they respond as a toilet door slams shut.

I splash cold water on my face and slowly stop seeing everything in pairs. I push the door open to a room packed with sweaty bodies. The fashion is glitter, leather, fluoro, shoulder pads, denim, mullets; it's the queer white community bopping their heads, rolling their hips and swinging their arms to '90s dance music. As I enter the dance floor, the music cuts out and the room darkens until the only light is a mirror ball spinning on its axis. The spotlight shines on a performer on stage who is lean with cappuccino skin and thick, wavy hair. I recognise them: Naager.

A song from a place that I used to call home starts to play.

Ho ho ho balik kampung
Hati girang
Terbayang wajah-wajah yang ku sayang

I see people in the crowd turning to their drinks and talking to each other, ignoring the performance. The crowd is lukewarm as they try to make sense of Naager and the Malay song that my Aunty Ivy loves so much. Naager doesn't seem to care — they're dancing their heart out and miming the lyrics to Malaysia's national icon Sudirman singing about returning home after a long journey and imagining the faces of loved ones. When the performance ends I clap rapturously, forgetting where I am. I'm sad that no one else gets the meaning of the song and why the song is important to Naager. When the ambient lights return the crowd come alive as they start dancing to Kylie Minogue. I try to stealthily move through groups of people to get to the backstage area to find Naager when someone slaps me on the back.

'Fan-fucken-tastic mate!' A giant burly man with a handlebar moustache bellows in my ear, lifting his glass of beer in salute. Some stowaway beer froth on his moustache jiggles when he talks.

'Thanks,' I mumble. He thinks I'm Naager. I decide not to correct him, afraid of sticking out even more.

I feel a damp hand on my shoulder and flinch. I relax when I see it's Naager, their face covered in sweat, glowing happily.

'You okay, my friend?' they ask, drinking thirstily from a bottle of water. 'I looked everywhere for you.'

'Where are we?'

'Melbourne. 1994.'

'199—what?'

The DJ amps up the dance music, so my voice drowns in the beat. Naager puts a consoling arm around my shoulder and walks me towards the entrance.

'Stuck in time, my friend. I need to find Aunty. See, my watch is broken.' Naager points to the broken glass on its face. It's an unusual watch with multiple sets of dials moving at the same time, but I'm too confused to look closer.

'That doesn't explain … *anything*. A few hours ago, I was taking your laksa order in my aunty's restaurant. We talked about Malaysia because 'Balik Kampung' was playing and you said it's your favourite song. I said I'd like to visit Malaysia one day, because my family left when I was small and I don't remember anything. You said if I go, you'll introduce your friends who can show me around, including to that underground queer party Rainbow Rojak. Then you asked for the time, then the cops stormed into the restaurant and now I don't know where I am!' I start to sweat as the words tumble out.

'Relax and stay close, okay? Otherwise, you'll never get back,' Naager says apologetically.

I take a breath and try to relax. Before I've finished the first exhale, whistles pierce the air like grenades and a body of blue uniforms swarm into the nightclub. Naager pushes me through the crowd as everyone scrambles for the exit, bodies on bodies on bodies. Over the top of screams and cries, we hear a commanding voice say repeatedly, 'One hand on the wall, one hand behind your head.'

Police bark orders for people to stand in a line. A mastiff-like cop with huge teeth and angry eyes storms towards us. I don't let go of Naager as the mastiff tries to force us apart. The cop pushes

Naager hard and, as they fall backwards, I feel myself falling into nothingness.

I'm slumped in an empty toilet cubicle, saliva dribbling down my chin. I pull myself up to the nearest sink, slowly standing as the room spins around me. I hear the door swing open and some laughter.

'You okay?' I hear a voice coming from someone wearing a lot of denim.

'Not again,' I groan to myself.

'Sorry, you okay or not?' the person in denim asks with concern.

'Good mate, good. Just a headache,' I say.

'Okay-lah,' the voice says gently and walks away.

I splash cold water on my face as I hear Mariah Carey's 'All I Want For Christmas Is You'. As the vertigo passes, I hear the same song play again with hoots of laughter. I push open the door to what looks like a big house party in a nightclub. An MC in a tuxedo and a top hat jokes with an older woman in a batik sarong at the front of the stage.

'The first time I emceed, Aunty says to me, *if you need to say 'lesbian' just say it once, it'll go over people's heads. But don't say 'lesbian, lesbian, lesbian' too many times.* You remember, Aunty?' The older woman holds her drink up elegantly in a toast to the MC, then turns to the crowd and raises her glass again, laughing loudly. She has a face that reminds me of an eagle. In that one swift turn it feels like she's taken in every face in the room. People in the crowd laugh along to the banter.

'Don't internalise the hate, people. We've been here since

before the colonial empires. Across the seas in South Sulawesi, the Bugis acknowledge five genders: makkunrai or women, oroané or men, calalai or trans women, calabai or trans men, and the transcendent fifth that can be all or none — bissu. Now, let's welcome tonight's main act, Naager!'

Patrons cheer as Naager struts into the light to 'Balik Kampung'. Spurred on by the adulation, Naager grows god-like on stage. They are dressed in an azure *baju melayu*, which is a loose shirt over similarly coloured trousers, with a checked sarong wrapped around their middle and a *songkok* on their head. The crowd sways in time, singing along to every word in the song. Naager feeds on the crowd's energy; their gestures and stance are electric, radiating into the hearts of every single patron in the club.

When the song finishes, Naager bounds off stage with so much joy they look like they are flying. I can see them looking for me. Despite my annoyance at waking up in another toilet stall, I'm happy for Naager. Random people clap them on the back with congratulations, wanting to shake their hand and buy them drinks as they walk towards me.

'We're in Kuala Lumpur in 2018, Sammy! Woo hoo!' Naager grins.

'Naager, is this the Australian?' asks a tall person in denim. Naager nods back with a thumbs-up, still catching their breath. 'Welcome to Rainbow Rojak!' the denim-clad person says to me.

Two other friends of Naager hug me. They wear matching outfits — pink singlets with a black star on the back over silvery white gym shorts, with knee high socks and leg warmers.

'What was that about?' I ask Naager, as the friends talk amongst themselves.

'I asked my friends to look out for someone with an Aussie accent. You-lah! I told you I'd introduce you to my friends at Rainbow Rojak!'

'When will this stop, Naager?'

'I need to find the Aunty who the MC was talking to. She'll know how to fix my watch.'

'Look, I just want to go home. Aunty Ivy will be mad with worry.'

'If we can find the Aunty and she fixes my watch in this timeline, your aunty won't even know you were gone,' Naager says.

I'm angry at Naager: how can they just be so relaxed about all these time skips? But then I'm also elated that I'm in Kuala Lumpur at a Rainbow Rojak party. I've only read about them on the internet, but never dreamed that I would be here in my birthplace surrounded by other queer Malaysians.

I zone back into the conversation.

'You're lucky in Australia because you have laws. You've got politicians, academics, scientists, big shot people who are open about being queer or trans. In Malaysia, we're told that we'll die by god's wrath, we'll die by lightning. You believe or not?' Naager's friend smirks at me.

'Don't scare my friend, otherwise they won't connect with their roots,' Naager says.

'I feel blessed. My Aunty Ivy runs a restaurant called Blue Rice that has a cabaret night every month that is queer,' I say.

'Now my friend is here because this watch is broken. Aunty di mana?' Naager asks their friend.

'Aunty? Don't know. I find for you. Then after, we go to the *mamak* stall and get some noodles, okay?' Naager's friend gives them a kiss on the cheek and winks at me.

'Who is the Aunty?' I ask.

'The Aunty is very, very old and very, very wise. She helped me run away. I was in a bad place. But now, because the watch is broken, I can't stop running,' Naager says.

I glance down at the watch. 'What did you do?' I ask, unable to help myself.

Before Naager can reply, I hear a commotion at the entrance and a few people yelling 'Polis! Polis!'

'Stay close and hold on to me, Sammy. We don't need to get into trouble. Again.'

A police officer who looks like a muscled-up tiger heads our way, then stops in front of a long-haired femme with heavy make-up and a sparkly red dress.

'Mana MyKad? ID?'

The femme cries while the police officer checks her identification card. The officer laughs, then grabs her arm roughly to handcuff her.

Naager yells in anger and pushes the police officer, who raises his baton and whacks Naager hard on the head. As Naager falls backwards, I catch them and then both of us get pulled through the floor into liquid darkness.

I feel a heavy wet mass slumped against me. Groggily, I push with my shoulder to straighten up, slowly opening my eyes to see Naager leaning on me. Saliva and blood dribble from their mouth as their head and torso slump forward.

'Help! Anyone! Help!' I yell as I hold Naager up.

Voices, then footsteps bound down the stairs. The fluoro lights flicker on and I see Aunty Ivy running to us, her flowing pyjama robes are like fairy-wings.

'What happened?' Aunty Ivy asks. 'Oh my god. I'll call the ambulance.'

As Aunty Ivy runs up the stairs, Naager slowly opens their eyes.

'It's okay, Sammy,' Naager says softly and gestures to their watch. 'Take it. Please.'

I gently unbuckle the watch strap and wipe the blood away on my pants. I place the watch in my pocket.

'*Naager baik. Hati girang.* I'm happy, Sammy. Going home. *Balik kampung,*' Naager says gently, before fading into smoke.

For three weeks, my throat burns. Every time I swallow, I feel like shards of glass are crawling down my oesophagus. I can hardly keep my eyes open. All I want to do is sleep. When I'm hungry, I heat a tub of rice porridge from the freezer. When Aunty Ivy checks in on me, she updates me on where my parents are in their Tassie caravan trip.

'Your mum says that the wombats in the caravan park they are staying at are too bold searching for food. It seems they smell bad,' Aunty Ivy laughs.

'Thank you for taking care of me, Aunty.'

'You get one hundred percent better, Sammy. I need all the help I can get in the restaurant,' Aunty Ivy smiles.

We don't talk about what happened that night with Naager. Aunty Ivy doesn't ask. It's like they never existed.

When I'm well again, I return to my job at Blue Rice. Aunty

Ivy gets me to do a bit of everything — cash register, waiting on tables, washing dishes, buying groceries from Footscray Market across the road. Working and staying with Aunty Ivy means I get to save up during the holidays, before I head into first year uni. I don't wear Naager's watch, but I carry it with me in my pocket wherever I go. At night, after my shift, I take it out and look at it, the hands all ticking in different directions.

My days are filled with work. Customers come and go but I don't forget Naager. One morning while making a durian smoothie, I see the Aunty that Naager was looking for enter the Blue Rice. When she walks through the door, I feel like something heavy is sitting on my chest, pushing all the air out of my lungs. She sits where Naager sat when I first met them. She is dressed in a batik sarong that features red phoenixes in battle. I've never seen anyone in Blue Rice wear batik. Even my parents and Aunty Ivy don't wear their sarongs in public. Once I saw Mum wear hers for her fiftieth, but that was it. The Aunty holds my gaze calmly. I look away, embarrassed that I've been staring, and quickly grab a notepad and pen and hurry over to her table.

'Hello, Aunty. What can I get for you?' I stutter, not looking at her.

'May I borrow your notepad and pen?' Her voice is low like a cello.

'Okay,' I say, nervously placing the notepad and pen on the table. I feel my palms becoming sweaty as I wait to see what the Aunty writes.

The Aunty scribbles 'N-A-A-G-E-R-?' on it.

I shake my head. The tight feeling in my chest grows. 'I'm sorry I can't help you, Aunty.'

She scrawls lines over Naager's name, then writes 'N-E-G-A-R-A' and points to me.

'Sorry, I don't understand.'

She gestures to her wrist and taps it. She opens her hand, palm facing upwards. Her fingers are long and thin like the claws of a giant bird.

I feel for Naager's watch in my pocket.

'Naager gave it to me.'

'I know. I gave the watch to Naager. The watch has called me here. My queer families are suffering. The authorities call them a deviant cult, a free sex party, a threat to national security, and corruption from the West,' Aunty says. 'Naager was a good messenger. But you've seen how dangerous the work can be. They got caught in the middle of a fight gathering evidence about human rights abuses that the authorities perpetrated against my queer families. The watch broke, and that's why they're gone. The work is dangerous, but I can fix the watch, and I will need a new messenger.'

'Why can't you be the messenger, Aunty?'

'I'm the Watch Keeper, not the messenger. Naager gave the watch to you. When the watch works, it can take you wherever you need to be, at the precise time, date, hour and year. Your family will never know you've gone because you can always return here in this time. But if the watch gets broken, your life will be in danger, like Naager's. There will be a glitch, and you will be stuck repeating an action, and you won't be able to control time. Then you must find me, to fix the watch. And you must find me in time.'

'It was too late for Naager, wasn't it?' I say. The weight on my chest returns. I see storm clouds gathering outside Blue Rice. I place Naager's watch on the table.

'You don't have to say yes. This job is not for everyone,' the Aunty says as she carefully places the watch into her clasp bag.

'Is there good pay?' I say, trying to lighten the conversation.

The Aunty doesn't reply but looks at me seriously in return. 'Truth is like fire that will never go out. It will burn until the end of time, until the truth is told. Will you be the new messenger?'

I nod, on instinct. All my worries about uni, about the future, they all lead here. This is what I'm supposed to do. 'Yes, Aunty. I'll do it.'

She stands up to head to the door. 'I'll be back when the watch is fixed,' she calls over her shoulder.

'Wait!' I say. 'What is NEGARA?'

Aunty turns, her smile radiating like sunshine cutting through the storm clouds.

'Negara means country.'

TASSEOGRAPHY

Emma Di Bernardo

Luna let the white noise of the house party soothe her into a trance. Muffled sounds of a raging house party, of laughter, underage drinking and dangerous spell casting, echoed beyond her consciousness. She drank deeply from a cheap porcelain teacup, until only the drowned dregs of homebrand tea leaves remained. She closed her eyes, holding up the question in her mind like an offering. She felt the thrill of premonition shiver through her. Luna placed the saucer on the rim of the teacup, turned the cup clockwise three times and removed the saucer lid. She looked at the fragrant tea leaves and the intricate patterns they had scattered across the bottom of the cup.

'Well?' Rose asked excitedly. 'What does it say?'

Luna looked up at the row of faces watching her. Rose, her best friend, took a sip from a drink with the taste and the colour of a Life Savers' packet. She hesitated. This wasn't exactly the scenario her oracle ancestors had probably envisioned when they thought of passing their ancient skills and practices on.

Rose had asked for Luna to see whether she'd get a boyfriend this year. The tea leaves hadn't spelled out the message Luna had predicted for her. A warm flush rose in Luna's cheeks. The watery tea mixed uncomfortably in her stomach with the cheap vodka she'd drunk earlier. She got the sinking feeling that the message was for her, not Rose. She looked at the shape on the right, turning the cup.

'It shows a broken path,' Luna finally told her friend, 'and a new one forged.'

Luna stood up and immediately felt a shock of pain in her abdomen. The pain tugged and ached so fiercely that it winded her. She let the cup and saucer fall to the floor as she hunched over.

'I think I need to lie down.'

Rose glanced at the people who'd watched the tea leaf reading with her. Some of them had moved on to more raucous activities, but a few lingered, concern etched on their faces as they watched Luna stumble. Rose put an arm under Luna and helped her stagger to a nearby room.

'Had too much to drink,' Luna heard Rose explain to someone. Luna, in her haze of pain, was confused. This wasn't drunkenness; this was pain. This was something she knew all too well. Rose closed the door and conjured a light to hang above them. Luna curled up on the bed amongst the party-goers' assortment of bags.

Her vision swam. Pain scratched at her insides. She curled in on herself, trying to shield herself from the pain. 'Can you call an ambulance?' She asked.

Rose was across the room, her back to the door, arms across her chest. Rose's smudged smoky eyes bulged at Luna's question. 'In the middle of my party?'

'I think something's really wrong,' Luna whispered. The last time she'd had this pain, she'd ended up in surgery to remove cysts.

'My parents will kill me if they find out an ambulance was here.'

Luna understood the underlying worry, but her pain compounded, deepened — it was a higher priority than Rose's worry. She tried again, her voice wavering. 'Can you get someone to drive me to the hospital?'

'I–I don't think anyone is sober here right now.'

Luna inwardly despaired. What was she going to do? She couldn't drive in her tipsy and ill state. She was going to have to call her mums. Both of them would be mad at her for drinking, but then maybe she wouldn't be in pain anymore, so maybe it was worth it.

'Just sleep it off,' Rose soothed, trying to push Luna back down on the bed. She handed Luna a couple of pills. 'Take some of my dad's codeine. I'll come back and check on you soon.'

Rose quickly retreated, closing the door behind her. Luna was left alone in a sea of undulating pain and knock-off handbags. She cried out in pain, but no one was there to hear.

After a long while, Luna heard the door open. She heard the frantic voices of other people. She could barely focus as someone's cold hands checked her face. A flash of blue hair, someone repeating her name. Someone else came forward, someone strong. Luna was lifted, taken out the back door, crumpled into the back of a car. Luna thought she saw Rose's worried eyes above her as pain pushed into blackness.

Luna slowly became conscious of the mundane white light of

her local hospital. Her mind churned in a thick soup as the anaesthetic wore off. Her parents buzzed around her bed like flies. The doctor came after half an hour to tell Luna the results of an emergency laparoscopy.

'We couldn't find any cysts,' the doctor said brightly.

Luna's mum, Selene, spoke up. 'Then what caused this pain for my daughter?'

'We're unable to determine that at this stage. Luna has symptoms of pelvic floor dysfunction. There is a high likelihood she has developed neuropathic pain, or nerve pain, so her neuropathic system has learned to be in pain.'

'You're saying I'm pretending to be in pain?' Luna blurted out.

Her other mum, Nova, squeezed her hand tightly. The doctor murmured reassurances, but Luna barely heard them. She felt as though she were observing herself in the hospital bed from the other side of the room. The doctor left them alone. Her mums tried to soothe her as tears fell. Luna withdrew under the starched hospital sheets with a sniff.

'We're going to go look down at the gift shop,' Selene said eventually. 'Do you want anything?'

Luna shook her head. Nova squeezed her shoulder. 'How about a cuppa?'

Luna tearily nodded at this. Nova ducked out and found the hospitality staff. She soon returned with a sad-looking cup of off-brand English Breakfast, tea bag still floating, in a thick plastic teal mug. Selene helped Luna to set up the tray attached to the bed, and Nova set the cup down.

'Be back soon,' Selene said.

Nova paused at the doorway and gestured towards the cup. 'Drink up,' she said with a wink.

Luna sipped at the tea, relishing the too-hot temperature. She checked her phone. She didn't have any messages. She composed a quick message to Rose, keeping her tone chill with a few emojis at the end.

Thanks for getting me to the hospital. They have a few ideas of what is wrong. Hope the party was awesome!

A tiny little tick next to her message showed that Rose had viewed it. A few minutes went by. Seen, but no response, no little floating dots to show a message was being written. Was Rose mad she had to leave her party to drop her at Emergency? That's all the nurses had said, that Luna had been dropped off by friends. Had Luna ruined her party?

It was just past eight in the morning, so maybe Rose was still hungover. Luna didn't want to think about being left on read, so she decided to google nerve pain and pelvic floor dysfunction.

Absolute colossal mistake. Luna read words, but couldn't truly comprehend them: *biofeedback*, *trauma*, *pain cycle*.

The silence from Rose was torture. This unknown, potential diagnosis of nerve pain hung over Luna like a shadow. She checked the time — she estimated she had at least fifteen more minutes of alone time, the way Selene would flit around a hospital gift shop in appreciation of useless kitschy knick-knacks. Luna remembered Nova's hint. She drank down the scalding tea and held the drowned tea bag above the mug. She removed the staple, opened up the bag and dumped the leaves into the bottom of the mug. She ignored the dull ache in her pelvis. With her eyes closed, Luna took a deep breath in and out, focusing on the answers she sought from the leaves. *What condition do I have? Will I be in pain forever? Is there a cure?* Luna turned the cup clockwise three times, and then looked down into the dregs to read the message divined there, as women in her family had done for generations.

And it was just a clump of wet tea leaves.

Luna closed her eyes and immersed herself in the soundscape of the tea house. The loud chatter of Celestial patrons, the sharp tinkling and scrapes of cutlery against plates, the industrial whirs and clunks of the outdated coffee machine. Luna breathed in deeply, smelling the pot of peach and cinnamon tea she was brewing. The pain around her pelvis kicked into another gear as she reached high for a spoon. It had been a month since her surgery, and the semi-diagnosis of pelvic floor dysfunction still hadn't brought any insight.

A gruff, wet cough spat through the pleasant white noise. Luna looked up to see a man in his mid-thirties with a sour look on his face. He shook a takeaway cup of coffee at her.

'I ordered a soy latte, made real,' he said.

Luna felt her customer service smile knit itself into place. She tried to push the pain to the back of her mind, shifting her legs slightly. She pretended to check the scrap of paper the man's order had been scrawled across. 'One large soy latte made real. No magic.'

The customer frowned. 'It tastes burnt. It's clearly been transmuted.'

Luna's smile slipped a stitch. She'd made the order with no magic, she was certain. The man had ordered a coffee in a tea house — his order stuck out like a thorn on a rose. Luna reluctantly reached for the coffee. 'My apologies, sir. Let me make you a new one, on the house.'

The man ignored her outstretched hand and threw his coffee into a nearby garbage bin, which hadn't been lined with a new bag yet. The disposable lid fell off and hot liquid sloshed up the sides of the bin. He muttered something about hexing the place before stalking off.

Luna stared at the bin. As a Seer, her magic was restricted to small transfigurations. She could turn the coffee into tea, or soup, if she wanted. But she couldn't get rid of it. Her mum should really hire a proper witch.

A tall figure in combat boots and black denim jumpsuit suddenly appeared. Luna briefly wondered if she had untapped summoning powers.

'Let me help you,' the tall figure said with a smile. A click of their fingers and the mess disappeared from the bin.

'Thank you,' Luna replied absently. She looked at her smart watch, counting the hours until her shift ended. She looked back at the figure, who hadn't moved. Blue hair, freckles, a bored look on their face.

'You're Luna, right? You're in Year 11.'

Luna paused. 'Yeah, that's me.'

'I'm Talia. We go to the same school. I'm in Year 12.'

Luna followed Talia's gaze as Talia raked over Luna's messy bun, her standard black t-shirt and pants combo, her discoloured 'she/her' pronoun pin, for signs of recognition.

'Are you the girl who went to hospital at Rose's party last month?'

Times like these Luna wished her claim to fame was still Luna the Lezbo who had a crush on her best friend (which she protested in vain, as she was firstly, queer, and secondly, not in love with her best friend. No one cared. They liked the insulting alliteration).

'Yeah, that was me,' Luna confirmed, clearing her throat.

Talia looked impressed. 'Wicked.'

'I had to have surgery.'

Talia at least looked sympathetic. 'It was a shit party anyway.'

Luna didn't know how to respond. She busied herself restocking the fridge, willing the hot flush of sadness and anxiety that had welled up inside of her to dissipate.

'Can I order?' Talia asked.

Luna nodded. 'Right. Sorry.'

Talia looked at the list of teas on the board overhead, slightly obscured with an overzealous monstera vine. 'What do you recommend?'

Every barista's most beloved question. Luna peeked around to look at the special of the day. 'The lemon, lavender and rose tea is quite nice this early in the morning.'

Talia's brown-painted lips turned up in a smile. 'That sounds perfect. I'll have a pot of that, thank you.'

Talia paid for the tea and took a seat. Luna took a brief moment out back near the industrial bins to eat a few painkillers before coming back to brew the tea. She looked at her watch again, scrolling through her chat messages with Rose. She re-read the dozen apologetic messages she had sent to Rose. The little tick next to each message signalled that Rose had seen them, but Luna had still not received a reply. Rose had been icing her out at school for weeks. The coldness made Luna's insides ache almost as bad as her ovaries. She flicked her screen off, not wanting to face the loneliness anymore. She started to make Talia's order as the light fog of painkillers stirred and rose in her body. She poured hot water from the coffee machine into a cup, and then reached for the rows of jars that lined the back wall of the tea house. Celestial was a cosy tea house in an overgrown suburban alley. Her mums, who owned the place, refused to allow staff to refer to it as a café. The only food was a small selection of pastries in the front display window that were imported from a local bakery every morning. To Luna, Celestial was a fragrant second home.

Luna brought the tea over to the far back table Talia had chosen. From the ornate silver carrying tray, she gently placed the tea set and hourglass timer down. Talia turned the timer over, the lavender grains of sand falling in a steady stream.

'Give it three minutes to steep,' Luna directed.

Talia was transfixed by the timer for a moment. Then, confusingly, they turned the timer over again. 'When is your break?'

'Oh, any time, as long as it's twenty minutes.'

Talia looked around the room, and Luna followed their gaze. The morning rush had finished and had settled into a slow drip of few customers. Talia gestured for Luna to take a seat. 'Take your break now with me?' Talia asked, but to Luna it didn't feel like a question.

Luna waved to her mum in the back, signalling she was taking her lunch break. Luna grimaced through the blooming dense pain coming from her bones as she took a seat. Talia hovered their fingers over the steaming porcelain teapot. They retracted their fingers, and the teapot rose, as though it was a puppet on strings. Talia magically poured them both a cup of tea in the technicolour, rose gold-rimmed cups. With a wave of their index finger, they not so gently led the pot back on the table. The cups rattled in their saucers with the force of the action.

Talia looked sheepish. 'Sorry, I'm still working on my levitation skills.'

Luna tried to act cool about it. She shrugged. Her eye caught the stack of books peeking out of Talia's book bag. 'Are you revising for exams?'

Talia groaned. 'Unfortunately. I'm going to study politics, with a minor in magical law. My dad's a lawyer so it's pretty much a given.'

Luna picked up her teacup and blew the steam away. The steam curled tangerine in the air. She began to ask Talia more about their career, but was stopped short with a loud sigh.

'So, what's your story?' Talia asked, a dreamy expression upon their freckled face. 'I heard you were a Seer.'

Luna froze. *Here we go.* 'And you want intel on whether you'll get into your stupid uni degree?' Luna asked dryly. 'Your source must not have told you I only see bad things. I don't see positives. A big hiccup in the Seer line, I'm told. That's what I get for my mums picking a non-magical donor.'

Talia shook their head. 'I was just making conversation?'

Luna wished she could melt into a puddle or spontaneously burst into flames. 'Oh.' She tried to back track. 'Sorry. Do you want me to try and see something for you?'

Talia shrugged. 'Not if it's a drama. I'd love to see tasseography in action though.'

Luna was surprised Talia knew the technical term for her kind of magic.

Luna directed Talia to drink the last of the tea, until they felt the tea leaves kiss their lips. They placed the cup down on the saucer. Talia pushed their empty cup and saucer across the table. The sound scraped at Luna's nerves. She peered into the teacup.

'Do you want to know something about your career?' she asked, slowly looking up from the leaves.

Talia, for once, seemed flustered. 'I mean, yeah, I do, but why do you ask?'

'The leaves show there's a fork in the road, and a road less travelled. You seem to have options.' Luna met Talia's confused gaze. 'Does that make any sense?'

Talia shook their head. 'Can you make the message any clearer? Should we brew another pot of tea?'

Luna checked her watch. She only had five minutes left of her break.

'Hey, don't worry about it,' Talia shrugged off-handedly. 'I can make my own future.'

Luna gaped. Was it that easy?

'I wish I could shake off worry like that,' Luna said.

'Seems kind of ironic that someone who sees so many futures gets so caught up in getting an answer.'

'Or the past,' Luna mumbled.

Talia sighed. 'You don't remember me, do you?'

'Yeah, I do. We know each other from school.'

'No, we don't,' Talia said, biting their lip. 'I mean - yes, we do. But I know you from somewhere else.'

Luna's face flushed in embarrassment. She apparently was as bad at remembering the past as she was seeing the future. 'Oh, I'm so sorry. I … uh … when did we first meet?'

'At Rose's party,' Talia explained. 'I drove you to the hospital.'

Luna shook her head. 'No, Rose drove me.'

Talia snorted. 'No, I definitely did. Nice to hear she's claiming credit for it though. She asked me and some of the guys to sneak you out the back so it wouldn't interrupt the party.'

Memories of cold hands and blue hair rose like steam in Luna's mind. 'I can't believe she lied to me,' Luna whispered.

Talia rolled their eyes. 'I can. She seems horrible.'

Strangely, Luna didn't feel angry. She felt a little deflated, but also relieved. The anxiety that had haunted her for weeks slowly melted away. She was over wasting time on someone who wasn't a friend.

She remembered the vision she had scried that night at the party. A broken path, a new one forged.

Luna's mum signalled her to finish her break. She got up from the table. 'I have to go back to work. See you around sometime?'

Talia nodded, distracted as they packed up their book bag. 'Definitely,' they replied before rushing off with a smile and a wave. Luna wondered when, and how, and why.

An influx of customers threw Luna back into mind-numbing work, where she had too little free brain space to worry about the future.

'Dear godddddd,' a voice came from above.

It was early morning at Celestial. Luna looked up from making her latest order to see Talia standing at the counter in bat-wing shaped sunglasses, a hand over their face.

'Do you have a tea that cures hangovers?' Talia groaned.

Luna hadn't expected to see Talia properly again - and not so soon. 'No …' she said feebly, '… but we have coffee.'

'One black coffee, three sugars.' Talia ordered and paid with a practiced swipe of their bank card. They dragged their feet to the same table as the other day at the back of the tea house. Luna nervously made the coffee in a large mug and delivered it to Talia. It was a good pain day, so she moved with an ease she wished to relish on days when her body was trying to destroy her from the inside.

Talia waved Luna down to sit opposite them. Luna obliged as Talia took a long sip of coffee. Their mouth twisted in a grimace. 'This coffee is shit.'

'It's made real, no magic.'

Talia's dark expression grew. 'Oh, that's why. Nothing beats magic coffee, mate.'

Luna froze. 'Oh. Sorry.'

Talia waved the apology away. 'Stop apologising. It makes my hangover worse.'

'Did you have a party last night?' Luna ventured to ask. The loneliness at not even knowing a party was on sat thick and gluggy in her stomach.

Talia sipped at their coffee again. 'Nah, a spell hangover.'

Luna sat straighter. 'The future spell worked?'

'Nope. I transfigured your terrible friend Rose into a cane toad.'

Luna barked in laughter, and then slowly realised Talia was serious. Horror crept over her body, making her arm hair stand on end. 'You didn't.'

'I did. Don't make that face. It's temporary, she'll be back to normal tomorrow. She may never recover from the social humiliation, though.'

'I didn't ask you to do that.'

'You didn't have to. That's what friends do.'

Luna settled herself into the seat more comfortably, the ghost of scratchy chronic pain not haunting her for the moment. *Friends.* While she didn't completely agree with using magic for revenge purposes, she had to admit it did feel nice to have a friend. A real friend. She tuned out the bustle of the tea house. She focused in on Talia, and the kindness they had shown her. The greedy way Talia slurped coffee, the melodramatic angst as they recounted the night before's events. The way the sun glittered off Talia's many rings, the way Talia's face glowed in the daylight. A small warmth grew within her. For once, she stopped worrying about her future.

The present, Luna decided, was nice enough for now.

FIGMENT

Elizabeth Bourke

I rearrange my legs on the stone park bench — our stone bench — and press a button on the side of my Augmented Reality headset. A digital clock illuminates mid-air. My girlfriend Halley is 31 minutes and 29 seconds late. Not that I'm counting. Her last message hovers in the corner of my Aug headset's display.

I just need more space, Petra.

I scan the glade of hologram trees around me. These are paperbark trees, *melaleuca quinquenervia*. I picked their species from the list on the Aug headset's online store, before uploading them to the app, Figment. I lean close to a white trunk and count the pixels. They roll up its flank like fish-scales. When I scuff my unlaced school shoes under the park bench, they ricochet off concrete concealed under glowing augmented leaves. Water slops somewhere close by and car motors growl, so I turn up my audio input so loud that the augmented track of cicada-song vibrates in my chest.

Halley appears in the glade, materialising out of nothingness as my Aug headset picks up her shape and feeds her into my display. I tell myself that she's emerged from the forest beyond, or maybe the pale flaking tree trunks, or maybe the imaginary oxygen exhaled from paperbark leaves. She's wearing an Aug headset, too. She picks her way over synthetic tree roots. Ladybugs loop in front of her eyes, tracing paths that Halley mapped for them ages ago.

One lands on her forearm. Translucent wings wink with augmented light. She slams the heel of her hand onto exoskeleton. *Splat.*

The silence between us makes my toes curl. Halley stands over me and I consider assuming the brace-position, but it might be a bad look. We stare at each other. I glance away to check there's no beetle juice or pixel smeared in her palm.

I hate you, Halley finally says, but it comes out as, 'Hey, Petra.'

I'm sorry, I say, but it sounds like, 'Hi.'

Her face is a folded piece of paper. Heat flares in my cheeks.

'How was Mrs Nguyen?' I offer. I add for good measure, 'Did she give your test back yet?' That's right. Give her something to talk about. Anything.

'Nah.'

There's warm wetness around my fingernails as the scab that I've been scratching on my knee flakes off.

'Well, I had her last year, and she's so weird about homework you know, she just gives so much, but did you know that she—'

A plane zooms over our heads and it's probably for the best because more dribbly words are bubbling up in the back of my throat and I need a sec to swallow them back, like when I smell watermelon and nearly puke. The plane concealed behind the Aug display is so close that there's a magnitude 10 earthquake inside me and there's an earthquake under the paperbark trees and there's an earthquake under the entire city, probably. I wonder if there's an earthquake under Halley. I wonder if she feels it. She's always levitating a few feet off the ground these days, head tilted back to watch something far-off, never quite hearing what I say to her. She's looking for the plane now, searching for its vapour-trails as they unfurl like pieces of an exploded star. But the fake sky peering between paperbark branches stays empty.

I try again. 'Want to go for a walk?'

'Sure.'

I stand from the park bench. We take a few faltering steps together side-by-side — as if we're two toddlers learning to walk — and then we're moving in-sync again, my shoulder bobbing beside hers, our steps matched and mirrored like a dance. Augmented sunlight collects softly in her palm as she takes my hand. She smiles at me and I go all floaty and weightless like we're in our own little anti-gravity chamber. I smile back.

We wind in and out of the ring of paperbark trunks. Boughs are heavy with skirts of pale yellow flowers, pregnant with dew and sap. I pass through a low-hanging branch that should scrape over my cheek, but I don't feel anything. It's a branch that I sculpted myself, ages ago, code moving through air, pale whorls of bark springing up like tributary rivers or the lines in my palms. I point to the branch.

'Do you remember how we made that together?'

Halley presses her mouth into a narrow line. 'I wanted it to be higher,' she says.

I liked it lower. I liked being able to squeeze between the branches as if climbing between the glade's fingers. I liked feeling enfolded by them, green all around, my own little verdant cathedral with its own paperbark disciples.

'We can make it higher, if you want,' I say.

'No point.'

Something twists in the back of my throat.

'What do you mean?'

Halley shrugs. 'It's okay, but look at it. It's so pixelated. All of this is.'

There's always a *but*. She rounds on me and I take a step backwards.

'You should see the Figments that you can make these days,' she says. 'Better specs. Better resolution. Better definition.' She jerks her hand from mine and for a silly, stupid, hopeful moment I think she's reaching to touch my cheek. Instead, she pushes her hand through a robed paperbark trunk over my shoulder. Pale pixels part and reform like the surface of a lake as she wiggles her fingers in and out. 'You can actually interact with the new Figments.'

I turn my face into the synthetic sunlight so the glare blocks her out. I wait for my forehead to warm and the oily tip of my nose to burn, but there's no heat in the augmented sun. My voice is strained and wire-thin, 'We can make a new Figment together. It'll be fun!'

She shakes her head. 'I don't have time.'

I don't have time. My smile weakens like too-milky tea. *I need more space.*

I linger in the trees as Halley walks ahead of me. She's right. The paperbark trunks are fuzzy and out-of-focus. They lurch wildly at drunken, manufactured angles. I kick a gnarled root and wish that the scuffed toe of my school shoe would ricochet against damp wood. But my foot just sails through the air.

Halley's shoulders slip behind a veil of green leaves, and then I'm alone and lost in this glade. This museum.

It's all so far away.

Halley doesn't see me open a new window on my Aug display. I flick through the Figment app, directing the cursor with my gaze.

Generating new Figment. This could take a few minutes …

If there's a world's-slowest-Aug-headset competition, mine's winning it. The Figment app is still loading. It was loading all afternoon after Halley left to do *urgent* homework. It was still loading as I sat on the park bench listing all the things wrong with our glade. It was still loading during dinner as I pushed defrosted peas around my plate with a fork. I ran upstairs when Mum asked me about Halley ('Stomach ache,' I told her.). It was dark when I finally pulled off my Aug headset, but the Figment app was STILL LOADING.

There's nothing else to do while I wait so I spin around on my desk chair again, again, again, and then my room is whizzing past and it's like I'm launching into outer space. My bed, desk, bookshelf are far-out exoplanets behind the loading bar on my Aug display and the plastic glow-in-the-dark stars on my ceiling are the entire galaxy. I'm still spinning when my headset chirps.

Please select what Figment you would like to create:
>Person
>Object
>Animal
>Landscape

Finally! I snap my gaze over the Landscape option, but

pause. There's too much wrong with our glade. It's unmendable, unfixable. I have every error, every kinked branch and out-of-tune cicada, saved on my Aug headset in HD, 1080p, 60fps footage. I open a new window on my Aug headset to take stock of it all and replay the afternoon at 3x speed. I slow down at the pauses between Halley and I, the hesitations, the sentences started but clogged somewhere in our throats. The silences feel as though they stretch forever, past the exoplanets and galaxy, past even the most distant stars. Those silences stretch all the way to the very end of the universe, where there is nothing but entropy and awkwardness and lost frequencies.

Earth to Halley, do you read me?

I replay the footage of my words to her. *We can make a new Figment together.* Good one, Petra. Stupid, stupid, stupid. I tug off my headset and my desk chair groans as I lean back in it. Blu-tack shows through the glow-in-the-dark stars on my ceiling, but they're no longer a galaxy, just hunks of cheap plastic. I watch myself up there amongst the stars, an imagined version, a new-and-improved-Petra who says all the right things and smiles at the right times and crafts paperbark branches at exactly the right heights. And when I put the Aug headset back on I select Person.

I'll make a new Petra. One that belongs up there in the plastic stars constellations. The Aug display flickers over my eyes and then there's a grey person standing in my room. I slide off the desk chair. No, it's not a person, not yet. The Figment is more like one of the mannequins at the abandoned clothes shop in the Westfield near my house — all cool white plastic with a blank face and motionless limbs held at unnatural angles as if its plastic bones are broken. The Figment stands on a crumpled school shirt so snippets of white fabric appear between its grey toes, but the shirt doesn't buckle or crease with weight.

When I blink again, there's a small starburst from my Aug display as it throws holographic buttons around my bedroom. *PRESS TO SELECT. HEIGHT, WEIGHT, EYE COLOUR, MOUTH WIDTH, FINGERNAIL SHAPE.* My head whips round my bedroom as buttons come to rest on my desk, on my pillow, on the duvet with the dancing-giraffe pattern. One balances on a pencil I left standing in a paper cup. It wobbles for a moment before settling there on the rubber eraser. The buttons orbit us like asteroids, caught up in our gravity, a miniature Kuiper belt right here in my bedroom.

I step into the Figment. I wriggle my shoulders into theirs. I shimmy my hips so they're phased over with the Figment's. I match my stance to theirs and the school shirt crumples beneath the arched soles of my feet. The Aug headset catches on to what I'm trying to do, or maybe the Figment itself does, because I swear it moves slightly, ever so slightly, a trembling in the grey forearm muscles and the ribs like the flank of a nervous animal as it finds the planes and gullies of my posture and copies it.

I lift my arms and turn my palms to face me. The Figment does the same a fraction later: its movement an insubstantial blur like the tail of a comet, just spacedust and pixel chasing after flesh and bone. My fingers shiver as I hold them under my nose and they're pink in parts and grey in others. I wonder how I must look, wearing this Figment like a bad-fitting coat. It's a little taller than me so the grey triangle of its shoulder appears from the muscle of my neck like a growth, a grafted limb on a paperbark tree. If someone saw us now they wouldn't be able to tell us apart — Figment from Petra, Petra from Figment — but they could tell which parts of us belonged to me, which parts belonged to it.

I whisper to the Figment, as if whispering to my reflection in a mirror, 'Can you hear me?' But of course it can't. It's still in Generation Mode.

I need it to hear me. I need to be able to tell it what to do, what to say to Halley, what heights to place paperbark branches at and what tune the cicadas should sing (insect song #845). And the need is so great and sweeping it's as if I, *we*, grow hands and hands and hands because I'm then scratching at myself, at the Figment, and its hands chase mine as I pinch grey pixel between thumb and forefinger to tear it away and I smooth grey synthetic muscle down thighs and squeeze my, *our*, waists like the spinning neck of a vase on a pottery wheel. And then I'm thinking of Halley in the glade and I'm taking fistfuls of pixels and ripping them from the Figment and I'm taking fistfuls of myself and ripping it too. It's a violent, vicious tethering of unreal to real. I stare at the grey matter in my hands as the pixels dissolve through our grey-pink fingers like seafoam, then we're the same. My outline matches theirs, theirs matches mine.

The Figment and I paddle through virtual buttons as if wading through a ball pit. There's a brass hook drilled into the back of my bedroom door that strains under the weight of my unzipped school backpack. A button has settled there in the back of my bag's throat, amongst textbooks lolling like tongues. The button is labelled *HAIR COLOUR*.

Halley and I are in the same grade at school, but we never hung out before we dated. On the first night I met her, really met her, we were at a house party. I can't remember whose house. Long halls like airport runways had been close and dim and hazy from kids puffing on grape-scented vapes. My hair was sprayed bubble-gum pink that night. It crackled and snapped like chicken bones as I leaned my head against the stair banister and pulled Halley's lips to mine.

The Figment and I now extend a grey-pink finger and poke the *HAIR COLOUR* button, then wave our hands mid-air to flick through the available options. When I glance down again, the Figment's ropes of hair that hang down my shoulders are bubble-gum pink.

After the house party, Halley and I waited at a bus stop together. The others had left for kick-ons. It was just us, congealed together in the fluorescent lights of the bus shelter like week-old sausages at the bottom of the fridge. When Halley switched on her Aug headset to check the bus timetable, my cheek tried to find the jagged knob of her shoulder, but I was too tall. I stared at the blisters on my pinky toes instead and snuck little looks at her to check she hadn't noticed. Halley gazed into the night, eyes unseeing and glassy and shifting with light behind her Aug headset. I stab the virtual button on my desk. *HEIGHT*. The Figment shrinks like a strip of gum between teeth.

Halley and I were at the beach when she told me, 'If only your eyes were blue.' I smash a button. *EYE COLOUR*.

'Have you tried the gym on Second Street?' *WEIGHT*.

'That pastel blue dress you wore at the party was cute.' *CLOTHING*. But I leave the Figment barefooted.

The bus never came after the house party. I think Halley read the timetable wrong, but I didn't tell her that. So I slid my heels off and carried them in one hand with my Aug headset as we stumbled home together. We took wrong turns and doubled back on ourselves and giggled when we passed the same postbox three times. We took a shortcut along the river with the waves sloshing in our ears. We cut through a glade of paperbark trees with spongy soil between our toes and ferns crawling up our bare ankles and rain-smell clogging in our nostrils and the cicada song making the night itself grow wings and tremble with dark. My feet ached and ached and ached so when we found a stone park bench I collapsed there and demanded that Halley do the same or else she'd simply *have* to carry me home (secretly, I was hoping for the latter).

She didn't carry me home, but we talked as the nearby river's tide came in and then we made out again and then talked some more, until even our Aug headsets ran out of battery. Dawn light warmed our cheeks and made the river shine when we finally left the glade's cupped palm.

Then, all-at-once, the Figment is complete. Blue binary-stars in her head stare unblinkingly at me. She's still frozen in Generation Mode, still poised on my school shirt, a nebula of freckles over her nose, pointy-eared and snub-nosed. I look up, a little giddy from the soaring feeling in my chest. The plastic stars on my ceiling are real and glowing again. I motion on my Aug display and yank the Figment out of Generation Mode.

And when she inhales, I take a breath, too.

They don't allow Aug headsets at school so I sleepwalk through class instead. I bump into Mrs Foster on my way out of English, my fingers slacken around the ballpoint pen in Science and the numbers grow branches — paperbark branches — in Maths. My headset weighs a million tonnes inside my backpack.

During lunch I march into the middle of the deserted school oval, where the teachers won't bother coming to tell me off for using my headset. I can't find Halley so I message her instead.

Where r u?

She doesn't reply. I lie on my back and dead dandelions crackle. The sky is fierce blue behind my Aug headset. The Figment appears there, leaning over me, ghostly see-through. I reach up and touch her cheek and her augmented skin dimples and for a moment I can nearly feel her, nearly. Tiny hairs raise on my forearms with goosebumps. *You should see the Figments that you can make these days.*

I want to show her to Halley. I murmur to the Figment, about the house party and our first night in our glade and the imperfect branches and all the out-of-focus paperbark trees. A plane passes overhead and slices the Figment in half as she listens.

After school's done, the Figment and I walk to the paperbark glade. We follow the railway and trains pass us with their windows greasy from handprints. I shrug on the Figment's shape as we step between the augmented paperbark trees. I upload her to the glade file on my Figment app.

I can barely hear the car horns now, barely notice the acrid stink of exhaust fumes from behind the Aug headset, barely make out the sound of gnawing waves over cicada trills. The Figment girl's chest rises and falls under my nose with simulated breath. She can interact with this glade, she speaks the same language as these hologram-trees, and by wearing her skin I can too. Her hologram shifts over the backs of my hands like a haunting as I reach for the low-slung paperbark boughs. We lift the branches up, up, up. Robes of white bark bubble and melt away and pale pixels drip to the synthetic ferns between our feet. The branches re-form. We make them perfect.

We drift like a cloud in a gully, amorphous and whimsical. We grow large as we reach upwards and cradle the pale yellow flowers. Pollen falls as sleep dust. We make more flowers. Make the trees groan with the weight of them. We make them pink, like our hair. We grow small as we fold over our bellies and stoop to watch Halley's ladybugs. We make them butterflies instead. Make them beat wings like eyelashes in the fluorescent lights of a bus shelter in the early hours of the morning. Remove the sun. Make it night. Lower stars into the slices of sky between branches, like diamonds lowered into the metal cages of necklaces.

'Petra!'

Halley's here. I didn't notice her load into the glade. There's jetfuel in her, a livid, stinking blackness in her voice.

'What have you done?'

I turn to face her. She staggers backwards as she looks me up and down. She's holding her school backpack in one hand but it slides out of her grip and slumps by her ankle. She points to me, no, she points to the Figment. 'What is that thing?'

'I thought you'd like her.'

'God, Petra. Take it off.'

I do. Halley's lips are pale as she takes in the Figment: a silent, sparkling reimagining of myself as I first appeared to her two years ago at that house party. But then she looks past the Figment and her head's whipping round like a spinning top to look at my new-and-improved glade.

'Where's the glade gone? Is this a new version? You saved the original, didn't you?'

I look down. A butterfly crawls over my school shoe.

'You saved it, didn't you?' She leans forward and hugs herself with elbows jutting out like broken ribs. 'Right, Petra?'

'You said you didn't like the original.'

And just like that, Halley comes crashing back down to Earth. She's sobbing as she glares at the augmented ground. She smacks the power button on her Aug headset with the heel of her hand, as if squashing a ladybug.

'I can't do this,' she mutters.

Halley vanishes from the glade.

'Come back—'

The last thing I see in the glade is the Figment girl. There are solar flares in her eyes as she gawks at me. I suck air between my bared teeth as I grip the Aug headset and wrench it off. All at once, the paperbark glade and the Figment girl and the sweet augmented night are all clenched there in my fist. Reality slams the air from my lungs. The waves sound too close, because behind me is a sea wall. Murky water lurches below and car exhaust reeks and the planes over us scream and the nearby trains chatter over rails and the concrete wedged under my shoes is a blank and uncaring face. The entire afternoon gathers me up in a fist and hurls me out of orbit.

Halley hunches beside me. She squints in the glare of light off water.

'I miss how it was,' she croaks.

We've been here before. Last year, Halley and I looped fingers between the wires of a chain-link fence and pressed our noses through its holes so hard it left angry red marks on our skin. We watched as the real paperbark trees of our glade were sliced up like sashimi. Sweet sap dribbled and stank and ghostly white boughs clawed against the clouds as if trying to cling to their homes in the sky. As they fell, Halley had squeezed her eyes shut and mumbled the same words, *I miss how it was, Petra.*

The construction workers prised paperbark roots like fingers from the dark earth. When the concrete slab was laid down and the river's rising water levels were wrestled back, we stood on the newborn sea wall with our Aug headsets on. We re-grew the paperbark glade together, grew it out of pixels and code rather than cells and genes.

I can't look at this place anymore. I haven't been able to for a long time.

'I miss it, too.'

There's salt on my upper lip. The river spits on my sneakers and grey waves are driven by a bitter wind. I've sat here with my legs dangling off the sickle-shaped sea wall for three hours and 29 minutes. Not that I'm counting. Every time I've tried to load into the paperbark glade, tears make the Aug headset slippery on the bridge of my nose and I have to watch 'Top Ten Funniest Cat Videos' on repeat until I can look at the water again.

I'll do it this time, before the tears come. I fumble with the Aug headset's power button, fingers numb and unwilling with cold. I boot up the Figment app when the Aug display flickers on.

Welcome back!

The paperbark glade lurches onto the display. It's been months since I was here last, months since Halley broke up with me, but a keening still peels from my lips so I clamp them shut and grip the headset to hold it steady over my eyes.

The glade is exactly as I remember it. Waxy eucalypt leaves shimmer and the augmented night cranes its neck to watch me stumble between trees. The wind over the sea wall still lashes hair against my skin, but it can't touch this glade. Halley and I never programmed a breeze. The trees are motionless as if cast in resin, and the drifting butterflies turn slowly in the air.

I blow warm breath over my chilled fingers. I can't decide if I'm cold from the wind beyond, or from passing through this glade; I'm passing through a ghost.

The lump in my throat is a knot that unravels. It tugs me through the glade. As I walk, I dip my hands into bark and moss and stone. I don't mind how the pixels shift and reform like water, but I miss the ladybugs and the golden-hour sunlight and the glade's sweeping skirts of low branches. I miss how it was between the real paperbark trees. I miss the night that Halley and I met, really met, at that house party. This place is only an echo of the original glade. It's as if a portion of its spirit still remains here, barely, both real and imagined at once, but all ghosts must pass on.

A butterfly lands on my shoulder. It trembles as if nervous, and its antennae twitch in my direction. I wonder if it has grown fat on augmented nectar sucked through an imitation proboscis. Maybe I should squash it, like Halley squashed our ladybugs. Movement in my periphery makes me turn. The Figment girl emerges from the trees, or maybe the pale flaking tree trunks or maybe the imaginary oxygen exhaled from paperbark leaves. She treads towards me. I let the butterfly flit away as I reach out for her. There's only cold air between my fingers when our hands interlink. My hair looks very, very brown beside her pink pigtails. These days, I like my hair brown. I scry her face for signs of Halley and signs of us both from that first night. It's written everywhere: pressed like flowers into her cheeks, in the smattering of freckles, in the blue eyes. I redirect my gaze into the corner of the Aug display and open the Figment app menu.

Are you sure you want to delete this Figment?

>Yes

>No

I choose fast. But for a moment, the cicadas trill louder and the paperbark boughs creak as if calling out to me and I swear even the butterfly wings thrum in my ears.

The Figment girl smiles. 'Goodbye, Petra.'

I know it's just automated dialogue. But it's as if I'm watching a comet on the horizon, blazing green for a triumphant, fleeting moment.

I raise my hand to wave goodbye, and then they're gone.

THE GRAVEYARD SHIFT

Jes Layton

12AM

The servo is a blurred glow. Its lights cut through the rain like someone bat-signalling 'SCREW YOU' into the sky. With the night pressing in all around him, Theo steps under the sensor of the door and slips inside.

The graveyard shift isn't anyone's idea of a good time, let alone Theo's. It's not normal for the junior staff to start this late, but Theo figures Nate's decided they can get away with rostering him on because it's school holidays. It means more money anyway, he reminds himself.

Nate stands behind the counter, pressed up against the locked cigarette display the way melted cheese sits on top of a Parma. They only speak when Theo comes back from dropping his bag in the office and placing his phone under the counter, carefully stepping over the line of salt in the doorway.

'Nice shirt, very formal,' they say, like Theo doesn't know when he's being mocked.

Theo shoots them a look.

'Aww c'mon,' says Nate.

'What?'

'You look like a puppy that just got told off,' says Nate. 'I hate puppies.'

Theo stares at them. 'You hate puppies?'

Nate winks. They clap their hands together, kicking off from the display. Theo notes the way their eyes linger, just for a moment, on the little badge pinned to his collar, a small homemade thing reading in glittery purple pen *he/she*.

'Alright baby-gay, I'm off. Left side till's been closed and counted. There's some stock out the back that needs shelving. Should be quiet tonight.'

Their face is lit up by a set of headlights from outside, but when Theo glances out the pumps are empty. The only other car in the car park apart from his nan's is Nate's.

'Just me on?' Theo asks.

'Friday's still about,' Nate answers dismissively. 'Haven't seen him or nothing, but he'll pop up, sooner or later.'

Theo swallows and picks at a flap of loose skin by the nail of his thumb. He doesn't know exactly where his worry is coming from. He has a feeling — like thunder in the sky, only the thunder is in his stomach.

'So, really I'm just on my own tonight. Sure, sounds safe.'

Nate picks up their bag and does the zip. 'Boss's cutting hours. Whattayagonnado.'

'Yeah,' Theo says, 'I know.' He ignores the expression on Nate's face. Ignores the furrow in their brow, the lines by their mouth. Ignores the way both start to smooth out as they begin: 'Look, Theo—'

Theo clears his throat and avoids their eye. Hard to do — Nate, with their face full of piercings and spiked hair, is hard to look away from.

Some of Nate's piercings clink together when they sigh. 'Just chill out, mate, okay? Grab a Coke or something. I already salted the office.'

'Yeah. I'm sure Friday's all for that,' says Theo.

'You'll be fine,' Nate says again. They bump Theo's side, slide across the still un-mopped floor and offer a salute as they rush out the door. 'Stay out of trouble, yeah?'

Right. Theo thinks, suddenly alone. *Stay out of trouble.*

1AM

The servo is quiet after Nate goes. There's the rain outside, and there's Theo inside shelving Doritos. He places them in neat, layered rows. Someone will only mess them up again, but he does it all the same.

Sometimes, when he's on the night shift, after he's mopped and cleaned and all the aisles are tidied and straight, when everything is totally ready for whoever is on in the morning, he stands by the door, the sky inky black outside, and thinks, *okay*. For a moment, everything is okay.

Loneliness, Theo decides, is the third most cool emotion after leucocholy and nothing.

It's while he's staring into the frosty glass of the freezer that the back door bangs open — kicked in by a bright red heel. It's Friday.

He's close to seven-foot with the heels. His face is done up with glass-sharp eyeliner and bright pink lips to match. *A man with decoration* Friday had described himself on Theo's first shift. His hair had been blonde then, platinum. Right now it's chocolate brown and bounces against his shoulders.

'Why are you looking at the freezer like that?' Friday says with a deep, raspy voice.

Theo frowns. 'It needs cleaning regularly.' It only comes out a little defensive.

'I cleaned it Thursday.'

'Oh,' Theo says. There's no one outside, no one about to come in. He means to say, *okay*, and leave it at that. Instead, he says, 'Okay … Saw the movie you're always talking about.'

He clenches her jaw. But when Friday stops and looks at him, he doesn't look confused, like he's forgotten what Theo means. He looks pleased.

'Yeah?' he asks.

'It was on TV. *Ghostbusters*,' Theo adds, in case he has forgotten, and is trying to be polite.

Friday blinks, once, and then smiles. He has this nice expression, sometimes. His eyes go kind of curious, kind of soft. Like something personal. Almost like … well, it's enough to forget—

Theo glances down, feeling very weary with himself.

He can sense Friday grinning. 'So, did you like it?'

Theo considers. 'Yeah,' she decides. 'I liked it.'

'And, you know, it's about time, too,' Friday adds. His tone has shifted seamlessly to something lofty. He can do that. This had been Friday's original point, the last time that they'd talked. Where Friday could go on and on about old things, Theo only knew of them through the osmosis that was popular culture. A point of fact that Friday had taken as some sort of challenge.

'Seriously Theo, everyone has seen that movie.'

Maybe forty years ago, Theo thinks. 'Everyone?' she says,

while giving Friday a look.

Friday laughs. 'Yeah, everyone. Even my—' he stops, but he recovers quickly, the wrinkles around his eyes lessening. 'Nate says you've finished school? What, Year 11 now?'

'Twelve,' Theo amends. 'You've been talking with Nate?'

'We often have special moments where I come into a room and they immediately leave,' Friday says, pink lips kicking up into a smirk. 'I treasure those times.'

Theo's binder pulls in tight across her chest as she snorts half a laugh. She's always looked at Friday and seen something, a flicker of the kid he probably once was, maybe not even eighteen, but, god, so feral. She tries to imagine herself Friday's age, forty or fifty-something. It's hard to know, and Theo reckons it's rude to ask. But she can see it, kinda, going about life comfortably wearing dresses and binders and make up and facial hair all in equal measure. Rocking gender like an outfit. Pronouns as accessories.

The goddamn dream: just not giving a single fuck.

'*Ghostbusters* is a classic,' Friday tells her. 'Proper ghost hunting, none of this unfinished business healing with the power of love sappy shit that ain't even scary.'

'There's—' Theo stops. Starts. Tries to arrange her thoughts. 'There's a friggen marshmallow man—'

'—terrifying.'

'And the graphics—'

'—seriously kept me up at night, for real.'

Theo shakes her head, disbelieving. The graphics were so bad. 'Gonna have to show you *The Haunting of H—*' she stops. Her mouth snaps shut.

Friday frowns. 'The haunting of what?'

'Uh,' Theo says. She feels a flush ruddy her cheeks, her ears. 'Nothing. Just,' she glances at the window, 'still raining.'

'Yeah,' Friday says slowly, still looking at her, 'it is.'

Theo averts his gaze. 'Right. I'll, uh, just recount the till.' She scoots down the furthest aisle, a sudden chill running through her as she passes Friday who just stands there, trying to catch her eye.

Theo's servo is a small one, right on the turn as you head out onto the Princess Highway. A red-brick-painted-white building surrounded by leagues of paddock and a snake-back highway. There's something grey and quiet being the only stop for kilometres out here. A muteness like fog, that lays low over the Great Ocean Road, making the sharp twists in the road bracketed by plummeting cliffs all the more dangerous. But even here at the servo there's a vague almost-darkness that Theo's sensed but never seen. He doesn't think it's a problem. It's been here for a while, and it isn't causing anyone harm. It's just quiet. Thick and slow and in-between. And sometimes, Theo thinks, when she lets herself think about it at all, that if she could really see herself, she'd see something grey and in-between and quiet too.

She straightens up the lollies by the till. The Skittles packets and Milky Ways. It's something to focus on. Something that Nate should have done during the day, but he spends all his hours responding to YouTube comments on his phone, and none doing any actual work. So Theo gets to do it instead.

In the meantime, she drinks a lot of coffee. She's tired tonight. She's tired most nights, the kind of tired where you can't sleep.

Friday's disappeared wherever it was he disappears off to.

While alone, Theo stands behind the counter and watches the shadows shift on the wall in front of her. At this point it has become a near nightly routine. Some people counted sheep. Theo counted shadows. One by one.

The sky is dark. The rain and wind are loud outside. The servo's been empty for the last two hours, which is of course when it suddenly isn't.

Theo's first customer — a hairy, thick-necked man — comes in and decides that his struggle to find a particular brand of smokes must be due to the servo's goddamn incompetence. Theo watches the man's pale face for a while, the angry movements of his mouth. She waits for him to stop talking.

He does not stop talking.

'You here on your own then?' he says.

The man stares at Theo with an unsettling intensity. Eyes so brown they're black. He raps his knuckles on the counter between them, leaning on it heavily, leaning in.

'Bit young for that, don't you think?' the man asks.

Theo's grin does not fade; he has perfected customer service to an art. 'That all for tonight, sir?'

The man doesn't blink. 'Sign says help wanted,' he points out unhelpfully.

Theo glances at the sign out front. It's been up for weeks. The servo's always hiring. Nobody wants to work the graveyard shift.

'Any interest?' the man asks across a ciggy-yellow grin.

Theo takes a deep breath.

The lights flicker. There's the sound of the bell ringing as the servo door slides open. Theo sees the man jump and draw back at the same moment a woman enters, dripping water onto the whitened tile, her jacket sitting weirdly about her shoulders, as if she had been trying to use it for cover.

'Bloody pouring out there,' she tells Theo without really looking at him. She ducks into a far aisle. The whirl of the coffee machine kicks on.

Theo returns his attention to the counter. 'Is that all, sir—'

The man is gone. The pack of Marlboro Reds sits on the counter in front of Theo. His chest relaxes a bit. *Oh*, he thinks. The man was one of them. There isn't long to dwell on it. The woman approaches the counter. She buys two sludgy coffees and a pack of chewy, then leaves, jacket drawn awkwardly up over her head.

Theo watches her drop one of the coffees in the car park outside. He goes to bring the woman a new one, but she's already gone, the lost coffee abandoned to the rain. Theo stands in the open doorway and watches the rivulets of dark brown run slowly towards the drain.

Her car had been parked next to Theo's nan's: a tired old Holden with Theo's shiny red P plate slapped onto the back windshield. The man, of course, wouldn't have a car.

'Theo?' Friday is now standing behind the counter. Theo blinks before turning back inside.

2AM

It's right before the witching hour that Theo gets a call.

'You still alive then?' Nate asks sleepily.

'Shut up.' Theo's hunched up behind the counter. 'Friday's here.'

Nate hums down the line, a tired sound. 'Told you he would be,' they say, like they don't take day shifts just to avoid Friday at every available opportunity.

'You should be asleep,' Theo counters. Friday is wherever Friday goes, while Theo's curled over his phone as though it is the only spot of light in a dark night. 'Nate …'

'Oh, god that sounds serious,' says Nate. 'Far too serious for this time of night.'

'Morning,' Theo corrects, soldiering on. 'Just wondering if it's … cruel, y'know? I mean, y'know what Friday's like.' It occurs to him that maybe Nate doesn't know what Friday's like.

'I do,' Nate says surprisingly. 'If the conversation isn't his idea he gets that weird look and, and—' and then the line goes silent.

Theo sighs. 'Nate? Are you still there?'

'I'm still here,' says Nate.

'I don't think this is good for him,' says Theo. Carefully, he pulls the left till open, flipping through the sorted arrangement of notes and coins. He silently counts a fistful of silver fives, almost able to see the lines around Nate's mouth as they audibly frown. 'I mean how long has he been here? Longer than me, longer than you.'

'Theo, you can't.'

Theo clears his throat and snaps the till closed. 300 to float, yep, everything is fine.

'Yeah,' he says. 'I know.'

Theo buys and eats a Kit Kat on his break because chocolate is a natural antidepressant. It's not really any sort of dinner or breakfast, but labels like that don't really fit when you start at midnight.

There's a crash from the back room, the sound of something breaking.

The servo's back room is next to the toilets and behind the chips. Facing the used-to-be-mens-bathroom which now is appointed as FOR ALL, there's a sliding door that leads into it. Theo ducks his head inside, one arm reaching to find the light switch. The room lights up in a dull orange haze and from the doorway Theo sees cases of energy drinks ripped from their pallets, cans scattered all over the ground, leaving a sticky puddle on the floor.

Theo stares at the mess. 'Friggen,' he starts, annoyance flickering like a flame up his spine, 'seriously!' He turns—

There's a pale carroty-haired girl standing in the chip aisle. Theo closes the door behind him. The girl fizzles. Another one he hasn't seen before.

'Uh, hey,' says Theo.

The girl doesn't blink or look away as Theo edges past her, heading for the mop bucket. Her eyes follow Theo's feet out of the aisle, stopping when he stops. She stares at the floor under Theo's boots as though there's something there. Theo pauses just off from the counter, glancing down. There's only white tile beneath and his own shadow.

The girl turns and bolts. Feet pounding the tiles as though something's after her.

3AM

Theo can't always spot them, the people — ghosts or spirits or whatever — that come to the servo, but mostly he can. They tend to pop up more and more as night fades, getting weirder and weirder, less conspicuous he supposes. Flocking to the servo like little bugs to a phone screen. Attracted to that small glimpse of life in the dark empty void of the Great Ocean Road. Mostly, Theo just tries to roll with it.

Time crawls. One man, stepping out from the freezer in the back, asks Theo what it smells like here now. The servo, the highway, the land, Theo isn't sure which he's asking about. She listens as the man says he can still remember walking through the gums with his eyes turned up to the canopy, the dense wilderness of unspoilt coves and caves, the salt and tea-tree scent on the wind. Can Theo smell it now over the steel trap machines that hurtle down the flattened land at impossible speeds? Theo, while cleaning windows and rotating stock, tells him his land smells like armpits now, sweating in the sun, like dust in an aircon, like warm Coke and petrol.

The man asks what Coke is.

Another one appears in the corner of the store, half in the wall and half out and starts shrieking. Ragged, wet hair, sallow cheeks, she is never not screaming while she's here. Perma-frightened, constantly lit under oncoming headlights.

It's a good thing she never hangs around long. Theo fetches the mop and bucket to soak up the rainwater she's left behind, then has to sit down for half an hour out back, pressed against the wall, knees pulled up to his chest.

4AM

As three turns to four then begins nearing five, Theo thinks the worst of the night is behind him. That is until all the lights go out, and the entire servo is swallowed by darkness.

He has to remind himself that loneliness, being alone, is a super cool emotion and not at all terrifying.

'Friday?' Theo calls out, unsure if Friday can hear him. 'Friday!'

'Theo?'

By the till. Theo moves blindly through the aisles, trying not to hit anything. It's so dark in the store, no headlights, no hint of rising sun outside, that Theo can barely see his own hands. He goes forward, step by step, until he reaches a familiar nook behind the till, fumbles under the counter and pulls out his phone.

Theo thumbs on the torch and sees Friday, leaning against the counter. Friday smoothes one hand over his dress, the other hand taps long painted nails on the completely black screen of the till.

'So,' Friday says, 'lights are out.'

'Yeah,' Theo croaks. 'Got that, thanks.'

Friday looks away from the screen and directly at Theo, winged eyeliner looking like stark shadows in the phone light. He shrugs one bare shoulder, a jerky movement. 'Not creepy at all.'

'There's a power box in the office,' Theo says. A switch might have tripped, if she can flick it, the lights will return. 'Gimme a sec.'

'Oh right, sure, splitting up, that makes sense.'

Even though he says it, Friday stays planted on the spot as Theo, phone in hand, heads back through the main floor to the office. The rain outside is loud, pelting against the windows, a steady background drumming that Theo wishes wasn't so damn fitting to the ambiance.

Careful of Nate's salt line, she works her way into the office. The door clicks shut behind her. Her phone is a spotlight on the wall and it only takes a second to spot the metal box behind the dead desktop. Some fiddling to get it open, some more fiddling to actually flick any of the switches inside.

There's no shock, no sudden jolt. The lights are off and then they are on. Theo breathes out, relaxes a little, thumb sliding across on his phone to shut off the light.

It's then that the door swings open. Theo whirls around and looks up, fast.

It's the man from before.

Theo blinks. Customers aren't allowed back there. He tries to stay rational: this man, this spirit, is just like the others, just passing through.

The spirit takes a step forward, and Theo remembers its cigarettes left on the counter — Marlboro Red.

'I'll be with you in a minute,' he says, hating the pitching of his own voice as the ghost steps closer, booted feet coming right up to the salted boundary of the doorway.

Its eyes stay on him, staring him down, looking dark and pupiless.

'I won't be long. Just wait by the counter, okay?' he tells it.

'Don't think I'm gonna do that, no,' the spirit replies simply.

Theo feels his gut swoop.

'You can't come in. I'm sorry.'

The spirit leers, and with a painful wet squelch against the tile floor, steps *over* the salt line.

5AM

The compression of Theo's binder is nothing compared to the stranglehold of his lungs as the man — not spirit — steps over the salt line and into the office.

175

I'll die today, Theo thinks.

'You keep quiet,' the man says, his voice like the roll of a wave, threatening to dunk Theo under. 'And nothing funny. Nobody has to get hurt.'

Theo's phone is in his hand. He slides his thumb across the screen, holds it down until the emergency—

Whipcord fast, two hands reach out and shove hard at Theo's chest, sending him toppling backwards. Theo hits the ground with a painful *crack*, able to keep his head from bouncing off the floor by landing hard on his arm. Pain ricochets like a crescendo, rattling up his wrist. Theo gasps, fingers clasping around his wrist as he tries to sit up. The man is now towering above him.

'Theo!' Friday shouts.

The man turns. Theo looks up.

Friday stands just outside the doorway, looking furious. Friday can't move forwards, though, barred from entry. Seeing this, Theo turns quickly back to the man who snarls, 'Don't you fucken—'

'Let me in!' Friday bellows, fist slamming so hard on the door frame it splinters. The servo rattles. The lights flicker.

The man jerks forward, eyes wide on Friday. At the same time, Theo slides the phone across the floor, between the man's legs, to and *through* the salt line.

Friday bursts into the room, like he's been pushing against a wall and now the wall is gone. The man yells, an expression of pure fear on his face. Theo would feel sorry for him, but instead he thinks of the man's goblin-grin and feels nothing. Friday roars.

The man grunts in pain when Friday rushes him. His eyes wide in shock as he is grappled and begins to slump, just as

Friday's knee comes up. His jaw cracks like the sound of a gun. With a growl, Friday — heavy and physical and real, so real — crashes his fists down onto the back of the man's head. Down and *through*. Into and *in*. The man jerks, stiffening. A gurgling noise rises, not from his throat but from his chest, from deep down, as if he is fighting for something. Struggling.

'Fr-Friday,' Theo chokes out, blinking through tears, 'stop, you'll kill him.'

Friday jerks his arms back out and the gurgling stops, one prolonged exhalation of breath. Free of Friday, the man falls face first into the floor.

A moment. Theo holds his breath until the man's chest slowly, stuttering, rises and falls. Once. Twice.

Theo rises to his knees and after one painful breath, two, stretches his good hand out to make absolutely sure that the man is … because if Friday hadn't … if Friday wasn't *trapped* here … then maybe tonight Theo might've—

'Hold still,' Friday orders, and Theo draws his hand back to take up his throbbing wrist. He looks up at Friday, even though it feels impossible, even though his head is filled with the very worst things. Friday's hand, large, cold, so cold, friggin *burning*, encircles his injury. Pulling it out from his chest to look it over. The pain, once sharp, is immersed by just how cold Friday is. The perfect kind of ice pack, that wraps right around him, numbing everything.

Friday's frowning, worrying one painted lip in his teeth. 'Theo, I don't—'

'There's a first-aid kit,' Theo manages, gritting his teeth. 'Under the counter.'

The relief leaves with Friday but returns when he brings back a bandage, and wraps it up and around Theo's neck in a sling. Then Friday drags her out from the office and kicks shut the door between them both and the man.

Back on the main floor, Theo drops to her butt on the tile, head tipped back against the counter. Her vision blurs.

'Jesus,' Friday says, 'shitting … Christ.' He kicks the counter once, and Theo startles at the sound. Then Friday is crouching in front of him, one hand hovering over his shoulder, the other near his arm. 'Sorry, sorry. You okay?'

Theo looks at him. His own eyes feel too wide, but he can't seem to help that, head ringing. He can't help the ragged breathing, either, much as he might like it to stop. He can't seem to control the shivering. He feels as though something has unearthed itself. Something is crushing down on his lungs.

'Friday?' he asks, at last. Because it doesn't make sense. He tries to focus. To concentrate. Friday, he realises, looks scared, too. Bright and sharp with fear. It makes him seem younger than he usually is. It makes him seem like somebody unsure. Theo knows how that feels, at least. He reaches out his good hand, gripping the edge of Friday's dress, but it falls right through like smoke. He wants to reassure Friday, but he can't even do that.

'Sorry,' Friday coos, soft but raspy, 'used a bit too much energy. Let's get you outside, yeah?'

Theo manages a nod, and shakily gets to his feet. He staggers a little, still feeling stunned. His shoulders curl in with the cold emanating from Friday, or maybe not the cold coming out, but rather all of his own heat getting sucked in.

'Button under the register,' he manages to say. Friday leaves his side for a moment to slam the button down. A silent alarm, somewhere, rings in some nearby station. It doesn't exactly make Theo feel any better.

'Okay,' Friday says, 'let's go.'

6AM

Doused in the beginnings of early morning light, Theo locks up the servo one handed, fumbling as the rain falls hard, soaking his hair and clothes. Friday stays like a shadow behind him. The servo with all its lights off looks half-dead itself. With shaking fingers, Theo unlocks his nan's car and then they're immediately rushing to get in. The doors click shut, one after the other.

It's quiet in the car. Friday reaches across Theo to turn the key, starting up the engine and then turning on the heater. Rain pelts against the glass. It's heavy all around, the car headlights illuminating patches of the downpour, strange waves of water, blown by the wind. Inside the car, it's sheltered and growing warmer. A small bubble, separate from the world outside.

Friday pulls off his wig, and places it in his lap.

'Are you all right?' Theo asks him. It's probably a ridiculous question, but he asks anyway.

'Yeah,' Friday says. 'Yeah, m'good.' He looks away, out the windshield. He taps a hand against his leg. One. Two. Three. One. Two.

The edges of Friday, the lines of his body, waver a bit, like looking at the surface of a pool after someone has just dropped a stone in. He ripples.

'Y'know, I didn't die here,' he says, after a while. 'Was out. Karaoke, friend's birthday, just another night of, shit, doing so much of what I wasn't supposed to be doing. Just acting young and reckless and like nothing in the world mattered but that moment, then, next thing I knew a valve in my heart just went *pop*. Dropped down dead. Fifty-five years old. That's no age. That's no age at all.' Painted nails tapping. One. Two.

Theo replies quietly. 'If you didn't die here, why are you …' *here*. He lets the silence finish his question and sees the way Friday tenses beside him, suddenly less human. More spectral under the hazy glow of early morning and servo light.

'Never was good at staying in one place,' Friday says low, like a hum. 'They tell you to follow the light, y'know. When you pass. What they don't tell you is sometimes that light is a goddamn servo in buttfuck no-where. Run by some kids who barely know what to do with themselves.' He sighs. 'It's funny, you remind me …' his fingers pause between one tap and the next.

'Yeah?'

'Of him,' Friday answers. A faint smile appears on his lips. 'My son.'

It is the nicest thing he could have said. Theo sucks in a tight breath, his heart all at once swelling up in his chest. It makes him want to do some wild alloromantic shit like have Friday's babies or give him both of his kidneys. She'd still probably offer his kidney, but she's definitely not into the baby thing.

'He'd probably be more Nate's age now, older maybe. Hard to know. Time is … weird.' Friday frowns out at the foggy windshield. He swallows hard enough that even with his shimmering form, Theo *sees* it. His Adam's apple bobbing. 'Reckon I was probably an alright dad, before the end.'

It's too quiet, and Theo wishes, again, that Friday made those tiny noises that alive people make. He's always so damn quiet.

'You should call Nate,' Friday says. 'Your parents, your mum. Won't be able to drive yourself home like this.'

'My nan,' Theo corrects, looking up at Friday from the corner of his eye.

'Yeah, alright. Call your nan.'

Somewhere out on the highway, Theo hears a siren wail.

All at once, the words claw their way out of his throat. 'Y'know that you can go, if you want to. You don't have to stick around here.' It hurts Theo's chest — hell he hurts all over — but he sucks warm stale air in through his teeth, and continues. 'Probably have more important things to do.'

Friday allows himself the space of three heartbeats to look Theo over. Theo can count them, because of the way his own heart pounds in his chest.

'There are other things,' Friday admits, looking out at the blurred blue and red glow slowly approaching them through the rain. He gives Theo a sideways smile, painted lips highlighting his face. 'But nothing more important.'

THE BOY AND THE WITCH

Ash Taylor

The steep hillside was dark and wet, lashed by pouring rain. Far below shone the lights of a small town, twinkling invitingly in the night. I forced my way up the hill, yanking my legs through heavy muck and grime. Despite gathering my now-drenched skirts around my knees, I still struggled. The strong wind whipped my hair cruelly against my face and the cold dug its fingers deep into my bones. The incline grew steeper and steeper. What was once slick waterlogged dirt gave way to barren rock and rubble as hillside turned to mountain and rose higher out of the fog. Small muddy rivulets ran down the mountainside, carving deep pathways towards the valley below.

Up ahead a small gate swung wildly in the howling gale, its creaking moans carried off by the wind. I steeled myself and pushed it open. The wind died down as I crossed the threshold. Even the rain ceased, waiting in expectant silence as I approached the door.

Thunder cracked loudly overhead, drowning my knock. The door slowly opened. I tensed, my instincts screaming at me to run.

'Well?' a harsh voice demanded after a few moments. 'Are you coming in?'

I froze. 'I—'

'Well get a bloody move on then, or you'll catch your death. We haven't got all night lad. Your parents will be looking for you soon.'

The door opened wider, revealing an elderly woman. Her skin was lined heavily with age. Though dressed for bed, she appeared wide awake. Her eyes were sharp and bright in the gloom of the cottage. She was shorter than I was, with a hunched back and wild grey hair like a stormcloud. I paused, glancing warily at the eaves of the house where charms made of bones and twigs hung. The charms danced wildly in the storm as the wind tugged on their strings like an invisible puppeteer. In the darkness they seemed to grin.

I entered. There was no going back now.

'How did you know?' I demanded, keeping the witch at arm's length. 'How did you know I'm not …?'

'You think you're the first to come here, seeking my help?'

She waved me through, closing the door with a gentleness I did not expect. The latch clicked home of its own accord, momentarily glowing with a brilliant white-blue light.

The hallway was long, lined with old charms and decorations that hummed with power. A shiver that had nothing to do with the cold ran down my spine. Strange paintings hung on the dark walls, with eyes that followed my movement. They seemed to whisper. We walked in silence, the hall extending much farther than the size of the cottage would allow. There was no end in sight. The witch paused, grunting as she tapped on an empty portion of the wall. 'Behave,' she warned under her breath. The walls shuddered briefly. The floor rumbled and the hall shook in response to her words.

'What was that?' I asked, gripped by the sudden urge to flee.

'Just the thunder lad, don't worry,' the witch assured me cheerfully. 'Have a seat.'

I glanced around at the empty hall.

'A seat? Where am I meant to—'

She walked past me, taking a seat in the cosy looking kitchen that had appeared at the end of the hallway. A fire crackled merrily in the hearth — warm and inviting — and a kettle sat already boiling on an old woodfire stove. The room smelled of smoke and herbs. Two mugs waited on the hardwood table. It seemed normal. The only sign of strangeness was the way the shadows twisted and leapt, writhing in ways too unnatural to have been cast by firelight. I took a seat opposite the witch. Awe and fear warred within me as she leant forward, her hungry eyes gleaming with an inhuman glow.

'You have come to make a deal,' she said.

'Yes.'

'And what will you give in return?'

'Anything.'

She threw her head back, laughter echoing until the room was filled with it. The flames leapt, growing brighter.

'Anything he says! What a thing to promise to a witch! What happens when 'anything' is your first love? Your still-beating heart? Your soul?'

My eyes widened as I stared back at her. Taking a deep breath, I steadied myself and focused on calming my wild heart. It took me a moment before I could hold the witch's powerful gaze. When I finally spoke, my voice was sure and steady.

'Grandmother,' I began, 'I will give you whatever you see fit as payment for what I want.'

'And what is it that you want? You'll have to be very specific, my boy.'

'I want to shed this skin — this identity. I am not my parents' daughter, and they will not accept me as their son. I want — I *need* — my body to match my true self. If you can do that, I will give you anything you want from me.'

The witch leant back in her seat, the shadows behind her growing until they nearly engulfed the room. Behind her the flames died down as thousands of disembodied voices whispered and moaned from every direction, pleading, crying, gasping. They rose to a breathy crescendo and then — silence. A heavy feeling hung in the air. I waited.

'It can be done,' she assured me. 'But there is a price to pay for all things, you understand? You must play an equal part in your own creation. Your payment is service, but first you must prove your worth. Prove your use to me, prove to me that you have the necessary skills and wit. I give you three tasks that you must complete — before the sun rises in the morning.'

I stared across at her, clenching my fists in determination.

'I will do anything,' I repeated. 'But I want to know what they are first.'

The witch grinned, baring too many teeth that were far too sharp.

'Very astute of you, lad. I have here within my kitchen a pile of clay dust, but I am old, and my hands aren't as steady as they once were. I dropped some poppy seeds and they're all mixed together. Separate them.'

Shifting in her seat, the witch revealed the pile of red earth and seeds hidden behind her — a pile I was certain had not been there before.

'Then, you must collect the rain — using this.' She waved her hand across the table, and a battered sieve appeared upon it.

My heart felt heavy in my chest as I stared at the sieve, and the burden of my current reality began to set in.

'And finally, you must bring me blood drawn from a stone.'

'Why?' I asked, embarrassed by how petulant I sounded. 'Why make me do all this?'

Shadows gathered at the corners of the room as the witch stared across the now much longer table. Her eyes flared with power. When she spoke, her voice was low and simmered with authority.

'You have come to me, in the middle of the night. You have roused me from my sleep and asked for something that, although within my power, involves a great deal of magical working and energy. And now, you have the gall to ask me why?'

I swallowed; my throat was tight. I met her gaze unflinching, fists clenched until my knuckles turned white. 'Yes.'

Her eyes narrowed. I did not dare look away.

'I live every day feeling that I am wrong,' I continued, my voice thick with emotion. 'I have no future like this. So I came to you, to ask for your help because I know you have the power to change things. So yes. If you want me to serve you in payment, I will do that. You want me to do these tasks, then I will do that. It's a small price to pay. But I want to know why.'

The witch smiled too large. 'Because if you are to serve me, you must first prove your value to me.'

The flames flickered and crackled in the hearth, waiting patiently as silence hung between us. I stared into the flames.

'And if I fail?' I asked.

'Then you return home wiser than before. Or, I eat you.' Her eyes sparkled with good humour, but the way her jagged teeth glistened suggested it was not entirely a joke. She held her hand out, bony knuckles sturdy and strong.

'Do we have a deal?'

I reached across the table and gripped her offered hand. Her sinewy fingers were stronger than I had expected, and when she squeezed my hand it tingled.

'Deal.'

'Good!' The witch released me, clapping thrice and sending the shadows scurrying back to the corners of the room where they lingered hungrily. 'Then your three tasks begin.'

Lightning flashed outside with a deafening crack, filling the room with blinding white light. When it cleared, I was alone.

An hourglass sat on the table, sand trickling away my time. The kitchen was quiet and still, save for the faint flickering of flames and the way the shadows still danced eerily in the dark recesses of the room. I stared across at the pile of dusty clay soil and seeds, my thoughts flinging themselves wildly in my mind. This was impossible - one task I could finish by morning, but all three? And how was I to draw blood from a stone? Slowly, resignedly, I sank to the floor and began to separate seed from dirt. One by one by one I went, creating a second smaller pile which grew with agonising slowness. If I kept going at this rate, I wouldn't be done with the first task come daybreak. I began to work faster, my fingers and heartbeat trembling. The seeds were small and hard to grip. They slipped through my fingers, tumbling back into the mixed up pile. I had to pause to inspect each one, to ensure they were seeds and not dirt. I had to succeed - home was a living hell, and I could no longer bear it.

Hours dragged by, until the hourglass was half empty and the storm had begun to ease. Rain still fell, beating a heavy tattoo against the window panes and roof, but the wind had died down. I stared at the pile of seeds. It looked no different to when I had started. Tears of determination welled in my eyes, dripping into the rich, red dust where they mixed together, creating a meagre amount of slurry. It trickled into cracks in the stonework, turning the grout a light red. I stuck my fingers in it, tracing sweeping trails on the stone floor, and watched in quiet contemplation as it began to dry. I had an idea. A sieve would not hold water, but clay — clay would. I only needed to separate it; of course I needed the sieve. I laughed nervously. It was all so simple now - the tasks, which had seemed so impossible, now made sense.

Hurriedly — so hurriedly I tripped and stumbled over my own feet — I dashed to the solid wooden table and snagged the witch's sieve. Only a few hours remained in the trickling sand. In the firelight I could just make out the fineness of the mesh; it was just tight enough that the dry clay soil would pass through, collecting the delicate seeds within.

Feverishly I shovelled handfuls of the mixture into the sieve, shaking it with trembling hands. Slowly the pile of seeds began to grow, hundreds of tiny black dots pooling together as the fine clay dust piled higher. Outside, the rain continued to slow. The storm no longer raged, the rain instead pattering encouragingly on the roof. A gentle breeze whispered through the leaves of nearby trees. It was almost peaceful. Almost.

As the hourglass continued to solemnly drain away, I paused to survey my work. I now had three piles, one noticeably smaller than the rest. My confidence grew, and I returned to my task with renewed vigour. Eventually only two separated piles remained. One clay, one seed.

I wiped sweat from my brow and got to my feet. Now for the clay. There was enough there to make a small amount, if I could mix it with water. I glanced around, a frantic feeling rising in my chest and sitting heavy in my throat. There was a deep basin, fitted with a heavy cast iron hand-pump at the back of the kitchen. It protested loudly as I began to pump. I didn't need much — just enough to wet the dust. Water splashed into the basin with a metallic echo. I grunted, arms straining with the effort as I continued to pump until there was enough water in the sink to grab a handful. The walls closed in, as if the house was fighting me. I kept an eye on the hourglass and the sky through the window, mindful of the time. The sun was yet to rise, but with heavy clouds obscuring the light of the moon and stars it was difficult to gauge the hour.

Slowly, carefully, I gathered water in my cupped hands, and began to trickle it into the clay dust until there was enough to mix. I needed only enough to coat the inside of the sieve and plug the fine holes through which water would otherwise drain. The fire had died down in the hearth, leaving red-hot coals and small, weak flames. The slurry squelched between my fingers, but soon I had a workable paste, thick enough to spread inside the sieve. The poppy seeds were left to one side; they served no purpose to me now.

With the clay spread and the holes plugged, I stared at the remains of the fire. Its heat would bake the clay (I hoped) without melting the metal. Praying to whoever would listen, I cast the sieve into the fire and looked around for a poker to spread the coals. I couldn't find one. There was very little sand left now — and my time was running out. The walls of the house vibrated, the sensation almost like sinister laughter. The coals were red hot, but I plunged my hands into them, hissing as my skin blistered and burnt. I hurriedly spread the coals, then sat back and waited.

Nearly half an hour passed before I dug the sieve out from beneath the coals. I grabbed the sieve, using my skirt to shield my blistered hands from the heat. My hands ached, their skin angry, red, and raw, as I pulled it from the fire. Its wire was losing its shape, but the clay was baked enough. The rain was no longer as heavy as it had been, but it was still sprinkling, and that was all I needed - after all, she never said how much rain I needed to collect. Desperately, I searched for a door. The room had been closed off, but now as I watched the wall began to shift and change. Its stone brickwork gave way to a wooden door with iron bolts and a heavy wooden latch. I flung it open and was met with the cool night air, the rich earthy scent of rain — and the first rays of light beginning to break free from the horizon.

My time was almost up.

I ran, the cool rain hitting my face and soothing my burnt hands.

The ground was slick and uneven, roots and stones littering the path, but still I ran. Rain sizzled as it hit the still-hot clay, steam rising from the bowl. I was so focused on the sieve-turned-bowl that I wasn't watching where I was going. A root snagged my foot, catching and twisting.

I fell.

The bowl went flying.

It skidded and came to a stop, spinning in place. Pain seared across my palm, blood mingling with rainwater that had pooled on the ground. I grimaced, inspecting the cut. It was deep and bled profusely as rain washed over it, throbbing intensely. A sharp stone jutted from the ground, covered in blood.

I scrambled across the ground, and heaved a sigh of relief when I reached the bowl. The clay was still intact, and at the bottom of it, a small pool of water slowly gathered. I fell backwards, lying in the slowly growing puddle and just breathed. Rain plastered my hair to my face and my clothes to my body. I was wet, muddy, and cold. I didn't care. I had rainwater, and I had the seeds. Through the faint mist and slowly dispersing clouds, I saw light on the horizon.

The sun had started to rise.

The fall had damaged the fabric of my skirts, creating a small tear that I grabbed at and ripped. It was wet and slightly muddy, but it would do. Wrapping it around my palm, I took the makeshift bowl with both hands, cradling it like a newborn. I headed back to the witch's house, taking careful steps. It was difficult to open the heavy door with my hands full, but I managed with a thrust of my shoulder and a slight stumble. Drenched and exhausted, I returned triumphantly just as the sun broke free of the horizon.

In the faint half-light, the room seemed smaller. I breathed heavily, my heart roaring in my ears as I waited. Nothing.

'I'm done!' I cried. 'I've completed your tasks!'

'Have you now, lad?' The witch's voice came from behind me. I turned and lifted my chin triumphantly.

'Yes.'

I placed the bowl on the table carefully, and motioned to the pile of seeds on the kitchen floor.

'Your seeds are separated, and this,' I pointed at the bowl, 'is filled with rainwater. The tasks are complete. I held up my end of the deal.'

The witch raised an eyebrow. 'And the blood drawn from a stone?'

My heart sank like a ship. The blood. I had forgotten about the blood — how had I forgotten about the blood? I sagged, my shoulders slumping forward as my head fell in defeat. All of this was for nothing. I was tired, wet, and bleeding, and it had been for nothing.

I was bleeding.

The witch waited patiently, leaning on her staff.

I thrust my hand in front of her, unravelling the cloth bandage to reveal the ragged gash along my palm. 'I tripped when collecting rainwater,' I gasped, 'and cut myself on a rock.'

'Very good,' she chuckled, moving around me to survey the table. 'You have proven your resourcefulness, and quick wit. Yes, you'll do nicely. Give me your hand.'

I placed my injured one in hers and watched as she made a fist out of it, squeezing until blood dripped from the wound and into the collected water.

'There's no point to a test if you learn nothing,' the witch grinned. 'You are to serve me, remember? My eyes, my hands, my legs when necessary. You swore to do as I say.'

'I— yes.' I nodded. 'I did. I will.'

She clapped her hands together. 'Get yourself out of those wet clothes lad, you shan't be needing them much longer. Now, the real work begins.'

The morning had scarcely begun, but birds were already awake, their gentle songs soothing in the early light of day. The witch's garden was sprawling and overgrown, bushes, trees, and vines all vying for space. The rain had stopped completely. A vaguely humanoid lump of clay sat in the middle of the garden. I stared at it in trepidation. Occasionally I glanced over at the hunched figure of the witch as she worked, using the mixture of my blood and the water to paint sigils on its 'flesh.' I stood naked as the day I was born, arms crossed protectively across myself.

'Grandmother … do I have to be naked?' I glanced down at my body, scuffing one bare foot in the dirt.

'You weren't born with clothes on boy, and you shan't be reborn in them either. Now, grasp it,' she ordered, straightening her back with a series of painful sounding pops. 'Let it know you. Your family will find this empty shell and presume you dead, while you live on in this body. Over time, it will become yours.'

'It's clay.'

'For now.'

Hesitantly, I reached out and took the clay figure's hands. The thing shuddered, red earth running like water over my hands until it engulfed me all the way to the elbow. I yelped, trying to pull away.

Slowly, features began to take shape, wobbly and uncertain.

'Picture your ideal self, your ideal form,' Grandmother

instructed. 'Let the clay learn that shape so that it may take it on itself. It might help if you close your eyes.'

I closed my eyes, focusing on myself, my body, on details I had never thought about in depth, but often seen in my dreams. Features which were previously uncertain began to morph into something real. Eyes, a nose, hair — shorter than before, but still reaching wide, strong shoulders. The clay learned them all.

'Think about the shape of your body, injuries from childhood.' The witch continued to guide me as she began to paint mirrored symbols on my skin. 'Birthmarks or scars that you wish to keep, give that to the clay. Your age will not change, but this body will now grow with you.'

With a final, decisive brush stroke she stood back, observing her work. A naked young man now stood before me, our hands slowly separating as the clay retreated. As the last of our fingers parted, colour rose in the clay figure's skin, matching that of mine. Grandmother nodded, pleased with her work.

'I cannot promise that this will not hurt, nor can I warn you of what you might see. Your soul is going on a journey, shifting from one body to another. Where it wanders — what it finds — before I call it back to its new home, I cannot say. You will have to be prepared, and on your guard. Do you understand lad?'

I didn't understand, but I nodded anyway.

Closing her eyes, the witch spoke a single word that reverberated deep in her chest. It sounded like the warm earth and the cool wind, the clammy damp soil and the wind whistling through the trees.

My once living body dropped, now little more than a lifeless shell.

His vision flashed, then — nothing. He was nowhere and everywhere, floating on a turbulent current, tugged to and fro by the forces of the Otherworld.

Seasons came and went, the sun rising and setting and rising again a thousand times. For a brief moment, he experienced infinity. Then everything stopped.

'You shouldn't be here. She's calling for you — listen.' The voice was unknown, yet familiar, and spoke gently into his being. Wispy, ethereal hands pushed against his shoulder, and he was tugged back by a thin tether, slowly at first and then gaining speed until he was slammed back to earth and into his body.

'W—what?' The voice that came from my mouth was both mine, and yet not mine at the same time.

'Easy now, lad. Open your eyes slowly.'

There was only darkness, but the witch's voice was close to my ear, and the birds continued to warble gently nearby. I slowly opened my fresh eyes, blinking in the harsh morning light as I adjusted to my new body. My old body, now empty and still, lay beneath a simple shroud.

A laugh escaped me, bubbling forth and then erupting into great heaving sobs of relief as I drew my knees into my flat chest and held my body close. The witch placed a hand on my shoulder. It was reassuring and gentle, but ironlike strength lingered beneath the surface, reminding me that I was hers.

'Remember your promise, boy,' she warned. 'If you try to leave this place, if you try to circumvent our deal, this body will return to clay, and your soul will forever be unbound.'

I nodded solemnly.

'Thank you, Grandmother,' I murmured, my voice thick with emotion. 'Truly.'

She smiled, and this time it wasn't too large. 'Well, best get up. We've got work to do my boy. But first — what do I call you?'

I glanced around the garden, looking at the overhanging trees and greenery. I recognised some of them, their bright red berries, and knew their purpose. I knew my purpose — and my name.

'Rowan,' I said. 'My name is Rowan.'

THE PARADE OF THE WEEDS

Clover Lake

Under dream-heavy blankets, it started with a soft cough in a young boy's sleep. Elias was an aspiring man of ten; he went to a local public school, lived in a homely cul-de-sac, had a family. Until this point he was destined for ordinary-hood, for his name only to go down in the memories of family, friends, a potential lover or lovers, yearbooks, and that was it. To say that he lived, somewhere, sometime, was all that was necessary. But that night, this all changed. Awoken by his cough, Elias had found that a dandelion had sprouted within his mouth. It had taken root at the back of his throat, its stem curling and weaving its way up between his teeth, and its soft yellow flower just barely escaping his lips.

He felt faint. Flowers draw part of their life from the dirt below them. But the flower now growing inside Elias did not draw life from that earth. Indeed, as Elias grew fainter, he could almost feel his blood being intercepted and robbed by the weed inside his throat.

His first thought was to rip the thing out. But its roots were nestled deep — Elias wondered if pulling it out would take some of him with it. Elias took his chances, grasped his small hands around the stem, began to pull, and screamed. Small boys aren't meant to feel such pain, their hearts not yet big enough. The weed remained. Its roots had burrowed in deep. Only blood fell out of his mouth.

Weeks went by as weeks do, and Elias found himself atop an operating table within the Saint Augustine Hospital. The dandelion, its leaves now suffocating Elias's airways, its stem growing thick and long, its flower now ready to disperse its seeds, was to be surgically removed. The doctors found with their machines that the dandelion's roots, ravenous and greedy, had entangled Elias's brain stem and penetrated every bloodway they could reach. The surgery was arduous but successful. The dandelion was extracted and burnt. Its roots were left inside Elias to rot. The room was silent and cold. And that was the last Elias thought he would hear of the weeds.

Not one second after Elias's dandelion had been plucked, an elderly lady, who tended to her garden most days and picked fruits on the others, felt an itch upon her back. It was a nagging thing, buzzing around the confines of her brain like a fly stuck in a jar. She continued with her day; ignoring the itch was quite easy for her as in her old age she had learnt to ignore a great many things. She thought back to her ex-husband, who had been a nagging itch upon too much of her life — though she did like her and Paul's grandchildren. She missed those little rascals.

Two days later, Agnes felt something much more peculiar on her back: a sprout. She imagined it stuck up its two leaves with resilience. Agnes had never heard of a plant growing from someone's back, but she admired the hardy thing. She didn't consider what it could lead to, or perhaps that was exactly what she wanted to see. She spent the rest of her afternoon picking strawberries from a local farm she had often trespassed upon before. And at dusk, she baked these strawberries into a pie. She would not share any with the farmer whose farm she had taken from. He was a wicked man with deceitful eyes. This idea made her feel more just in her trespass and theft.

Agnes awoke that night in a coughing fit. The sprout had tripled in size, and she could feel it now, feel it properly. She could feel its roots burrowing into her skin, coiling around her veins and strangling them for all they had. She figured enough was enough and tried to yank the sprout out but upon her first pull she realised that it would take half her back out with it. She hated it. She had never so quickly gone from admiring something to despising it. She could have pulled it out in her youth. She knew it. Her back would have been too muscular and firm for it to take anything with it. This thing was capitalising on her ageing body and she hated it for that. She would book a doctor's appointment as soon as she could.

Two weeks passed, and a doctor from her local practice found themselves at her door. Given Agnes's advanced age, her missed appointment was cause for concern. The doctor tried the door, found it was open, and stepped inside. The house smelt like absence. It smelt like nothing had ever lived here. The doctor found old Agnes lying in her bed. An invasive plant commonly referred to as Bridal Creeper spilled from her body, its long ropes grabbing onto shelves and the ceiling fan above. The weed's bulb was outgrowing Agnes, its fleshy organs extruding out of her body, contorting, stretching, and breaking her skin. It was unsightly. The thing had left her head untouched, which felt like a grace the weed had granted her.

Agnes's untouched head was preserved, and her valuables were taken from her house and given to her grandchild whose chosen name was Elly. The house, the weed within, and the remains of Agnes were burnt to a cinder. Agnes would be remembered.

Elias had returned home safe and sound after his hospital stint. Many doctors and his family assumed it was a freak occurrence, brought on by Elias perhaps being too fond of the dirt and frolicking in the grass and eating bugs. However, this notion was destroyed when a second patient with a plant growth arrived at the Saint Augustine Hospital. Paul had checked into the hospital three days after attending the funeral of his ex-wife, Agnes. Paul was not told how she died, only that it was peaceful. Whispers started to pick up around the hospital: nurses and doctors would gossip about the new disease, pathogen, and the weed. They would wonder about how it transmitted itself. You could eat it; you could go up to it and kiss one of its delicate leaves. It did not spread that way. The doctors weren't concerned. They didn't see Agnes's mangled body after all.

A week passed and young Elly came to see her grandfather. Paul had been distant; Paul had been cruel to her. Paul called her by a name that was not her own. Paul's condition had degraded. The roots of the thing had entangled every inch of his body. Despite what Paul was to her, just another man she knew who didn't respect her, Elly felt sorry for him. Seeing him like this, with every wheeze and pained movement of the lungs met by a prick of the plant's thorns, was distressing for her. He had spent all his life stepping over others, but now, in the end, all he amounted to was living soil. Paul's weed had been far more resilient than Elias's. And it was here that the gossip of the Saint Augustine Hospital began to sour. They worried about how they would ever get the next weed out. And as time went on, and as Paul's time flickered out, they were all now certain there would be a next patient. It was not this belief that brought about the next patient. The weeds had determined humanity's downfall long ago, and they had already selected their path.

Elly was there that moment. That moment when Paul let out his last strained breath: his lungs churning with blood, an entirely separate aquatic plant living in that sea of blood. When Paul let out his final breath, every single person in that room was taken by the weed's cradle. They grew faint, their heads spun, and in just a few moments, they felt that itching under their skin. Many of the family, doctors, and nurses grew terrible weeds. Weeds that robbed them of life and dined on their soul. The only person to survive that day was Elly. She instead saw a single red flower petal had sprung out from her fingernail.

There was nothing the hospital nor the saint it was named after could do. These new patients waited for death in hospital beds, alone. It was now far too dangerous for anyone to visit, after all. Reporters would come and go, all in face masks, hazmat suits, or anything they thought would protect them. Nothing did. Their reports would be echoed in bingo clubs, derelict disco halls, offices, and schools. And then this was not an incident isolated to the Saint Augustine Hospital. Throughout county houses, small towns, and extravagant cities, every child born was born with a weed. And as this newborn decayed and gave way to new life, their family too would be joined in death through the parade of weeds.

Elly watched from her hospital bed as each patient hosting the weeds was entombed in the hospital's walls. The theory was concrete could trap the weeds, but Elly knew that was wrong. She just felt it. She felt it in the tip of her fingernail where a delicate flower had now blossomed. Before it was her turn, she hid. She hid inside herself as she had learnt to do her entire life by pretending to be someone she was not. And it worked. She was spared.

As the weeks went by, more and more patients were brought into the confines of Saint Augustine Hospital. Elly watched them walk in, and then when their recovery had failed, she would see them be taken. Doctors who could still walk would run tests on Elly. They were trying to discover why her weed spread so slowly and lived with her in coexistence. Her weed latched onto non-vital veins, took what it needed, and left the rest for her. It was spreading, there was no doubt about that, but it seemed to be harmless in its spread. Eventually, another patient like Elly arrived at the hospital. She looked at them, and she didn't think they were happy. From the look in their eyes, Elly knew they had learnt to hide within themselves like she had.

She thought on this for some time. Perhaps this was why the weed had spared her. It could not find her soul because she had hidden it. She had hidden it as she had been forced and taught to do her entire life. So there was nothing of her true self it could take. This flesh she found herself in was not her, not truly. So the weed was indifferent to it. That's why she thought the weed spared the other patient. They too had hid within themselves.

The TV was left on in her room some days. When she was lucky, there was anything else on but the news. But today, news is what it brought her. The entire population of some city somewhere had been dragged under the earth by some great writhing plant thing. She didn't care that much. It was odd to her, to be indifferent to so much death. The truth was, if she had been dragged under by the coiling tendrils of the weeds she would think she deserved it. The why eluded her. But when she saw on the news that the situation had been changed from 'pandemic' to 'cataclysm', it felt deserved.

Tendril-like stems were popping out from the back of Elly's television. The staff must have noticed it too. Their idea that the concrete would entomb the weeds was wrong. They had only given them another host to live within. The stem living inside the television had a tiny flower poking out. Elly knew how much death the plants had caused, but this seemed so very fragile. The beauty of flowers has often been written of by poets struck with either the natural world or unoriginality, but even now, after it had taken and devoured and subsumed so much life, it was still beautiful to behold. What neither Elly nor the hospital staff knew was that this tiny flower was adjoined to a weed unfathomably titanic. The thing festering within the walls of the hospital and under the earth was monolithic. And soon, in just a single month, it would end the world as humans had known it.

The vinyl flooring of the hospital gave way to the weed's wooden tentacles. The hospital itself became lethargic. It had never been noticed by humans, but buildings too have their own soul. And when that soul is subsumed and robbed of them, the building changes, it becomes sick. Dark spots appeared deeper than the wall itself, plumbing pipes began to coil in on themselves, the air within the hospital became decrepit. A hospital robbed of its soul and devoid of the life that once pulsed through its wall becomes warped. Halls circled in on themselves so that it would take years to reach the end. Doors became so rotted that upon stepping through one, you would lose something of yourself. Hospital beds began to clump together and congeal into something more modern. New floors, basements, and alcoves began to bring themselves forth. Parts of the hospital began to plunge deeper than the weed itself. They were taken under the earth, and they were never to be heard from again.

But once more, Elly was spared. The room she stayed in remained intact and untouched. The other patient like her had begun to roam: unsure of why, but certain that the maligned walls would not harm them. They had stumbled into her room, and she found out his name was Gregory. He said there was another patient like them, someone who had been spared by the carnivorous weed. And they no longer hid within themselves. They had said that they had lived their entire life hiding themself, so if they were going to die, they were going to do it as their truest self. But they had left.

'Why are you still here?' asked Elly.

'There isn't anything left out there,' replied Gregory.

'There isn't anything left here either.'

'Well, there's you I guess,' Gregory said in a soft voice.

Gregory left the room soon after. *Maybe I don't need to hide anymore*, Elly thought to herself.

Elly and Gregory both knew that the weeds had escaped the city's confines, but they were unaware of just how far the weed had spread. By now, it had crossed countries, continents, and the world over. A new epoch was about to begin. A kinder epoch. Gregory chose to leave in the end. Elly left the hospital shortly after. Outside, her city was barren. The weed had dragged many buildings under. Those that still stood appeared gaunt and sickly as if their skin had been pulled taut around them. But, the dirt was the same as she remembered. The sky was the same as she remembered. Taken by a wistful emotion, Elly laid down in the soil of her former life. She was going to get up eventually. She just needed to lie down for a bit. Under the cloudy sky.

She lay there for forty minutes before it happened at last. The hospital, now devoid of any inhabitants, was pulled under the earth. In an instant, the weed removed that intangible thing that kept the sky in the air. It removed the difference between a second and a minute and it remoulded the earth into a softer portrait. Cities and lives alike were rent in an instant. And then they were pulled under. Their blood, spilled at last, gave back what the earth had given so many eons ago.

The sky fell. It lay with the dirt and flowers and there it stayed. Its immeasurable corpse was a mercy to the flowers and the animals and the insects it blinded, for now they did not have to see what was to come. There were few humans spared. These few were spared because they had the capacity to change, to be different from those before them. Elly and Gregory were among them. They had already proved to the weed that they could transcend what they were told to be and what was forced upon them. These people who would survive, but be changed nonetheless after it was done, reconciled themselves with the earth. Elly and Gregory found themselves sound asleep at this moment; the weight of the sky's slumbering body providing them with comfort enough to rest through humanity's final hour. The ground ruptured all around them; the titanic mass of the weeds was impossible to understand now.

Much of the world was pulled beneath itself. It was changed and morphed into something new. And yet Elly still slept, but she was changing too. The weed inside her grew. It never harmed her. Elly's head began to ripple and her flesh was changed to petal. Her bone was changed to stem and her brain was made into something more intangible. She could still think and feel to the same capacity she could before. Gregory was changed as well. Just as the others were that had been spared and would soon reconcile themselves with the earth. They knew they were no better than the dirt under them nor the sky above them. That they were a part of it, and thus harming any of it would only harm themselves.

The weeds hoped that these new changed survivors would be different.

The weed had done it. It had ended it all. Those that were left, such as Elly, could no longer be called human. They were a hybrid of the best of what was and all of what was yet to come. The wind blew over dirt and never again would it touch concrete. The weeds set themselves to lifting the sky back into place and restored that intangible thing that kept it up there. They let the seconds be different from minutes and they patted the dirt back into place where they had broken through. The clouds returned to the sky and the wind blew all the same. The waves danced upon the ocean and the rain drizzled just as it should. And then, with their job done, the weeds let themselves die. They let themselves be consumed just as they had done. The animals, the insects, the fungi, and the bacteria all fed upon the weed's body until all the nutrients it had taken into itself were returned. The weed breathed life back into the earth and with that those once-humans who had been spared awoke once more.

And so as everything must, the parade of the weeds had ended. Elly awoke to a world that was quieter than before, but she was still a part of it. She and Gregory found the others after some time. And they lived. They lived in a way that was impossible before the weeds. They came to harmony not just with the earth and its dirt, insects, and animals, but also with themselves. No longer did they hide within themselves. They were as much themself as they all could be. Elly, to her surprise, had never been happier. She would spend her days tending to vegetation and animals, laying in the dirt where it was warm, and walking along coastlines. Sometimes, she would walk hand in hand with others like her, but even when she was alone she was still happy. She never felt alone. She knew that the dirt had given her form and she would return to it in the end. This comforted her, knowing she would never truly die either. The memory of who she was would persist within the earth for eons to come. She was finally herself. She was finally happy. And she was happy to be herself.

THE SWAN KING

Alexander Te Pohe

The whole room seems to sparkle around Eros Avian — the chandeliers above, the faeries swirling just overhead, the shimmering jewels adorning those attending. He relishes in it, his white skirts brushing against the floor as he dances. He clasps the waists of a procession of beautiful gentlefolk — delighting in their smiles, their laughs, the soft touch of fine fabric, and the delicious tidbits of gossip. It is the same as every night here in the palace except for the tall figures of The Eagle Queen and Diana, The Queen Consort. Even when the music sweeps his gaze away from theirs, he can feel their judging eyes on him. Tomorrow they will tell him he danced too little with Olive, Consort Olive as they so often corrected him. She was to be his queen — this he would debate them on, with a smile and a laugh to stay in their favour. But that is tomorrow. Tonight is not for tedious duties, but for frivolity.

The crowd of dancers part, side-stepping servers carrying plates of tiny desserts and small glass cups filled with amber liquid. A stern looking knight strides towards Eros, dressed in a black robe imprinted with Eros' swan sigil. *His* knight, Bradley Freesia.

'Consort Olive wishes to see you privately,' says Bradley, his tone stilted.

It was their pre-arranged signal. Instead of going to Olive, they'd sneak out. All the appropriate arrangements had been made and the servants paid for their silence. This way, they could spend uninterrupted time together.

Eros smiles mischievously. 'Dance with me first?'

Bradley frowns, his hazel eyes darkening. 'That would not be proper.'

The man had always been a touch too bound to duty. Eros had once found it endearing — their strained public conversations a fun game. But now that marriage is in his sight all he wants is the kind, soft spoken man to drop his mask.

Eros is tempted to hook his arm around Bradley, but he holds back. 'You always spoil my fun.'

'Come along your highness.' He drops his voice, 'They are watching.'

Eros makes a show of looking straight at his mothers. His mothers are both tall and their matching black feather cloaks make them appear like two imposing eagles. They watch him leave without intervening. Eros can always count on the Queen not wanting to draw further attention to his misbehaviour.

Eros' white heeled boots clack against the black marble floors as they make their way through the castle. Bradley stays a few steps behind, moving silently through the halls. It has been like this from the time they could both walk. Always Eros in front and Bradley behind — a reminder of their stations and the Great Shame that originally locked their families together.

As usual, the guards and knights do little to conceal their

whispered insults. Eros ignores them but only because that is what Bradley has asked him to do.

They descend the creaky stairs into the old servants' passages and join hands. The buried tunnels are dark and damp, the limestone walls partially covered in moss. Here they can be two anonymous young lovers. Still, Bradley walks stiffly beside him. He'd often told Eros of his dislike for this place. It made sense. It holds the history of Bradley's cursed ancestors — the Freesians. The tunnels were just one part of their sprawling stronghold. Bradley's royal bloodline culled their own citizens and turned the once fertile land to dust. It is a past that Eros wants to erase. Scrub away the blood, the uprisings and slaughters led by Avians desiring to snatch the crown back. But it is that very tangle that brought him Bradley.

They exit the passage into a barely used back alley beyond the palace walls and jump into the waiting carriage. It is plain and small, but in it they'll make their way through the city undetected. Their driver takes them through the heart of the city. The inner city is beautiful — the buildings made from black stone, the streets lit by green faerie lights, and the eagle sigil is carved above every doorway. Stores are open, street vendors are serving food, people sing in public houses and perform on the streets. Eros drinks in the scents, the sound of rumbling applause and twittering laughter. The commoners enjoy these freedoms in a way Eros is envious of. He's tasted that life but always in disguise and only for an all too short period. He peeks out the window, towards the gothic palace perched in the middle of the city. His life — his duties — at the palace always close around him eventually.

The driver turns and they enter the western part of the city. It's much older than the rest of the city and still has the original red limestone buildings. Here there is less light, the buildings smaller and crumbling in parts. White freesia flowers are painted on walls, signs, and above doorways.

Bradley frowns, worry pinching his brows. 'There's more than usual. We should take an alternative route next time.'

Eros wraps his hand around Bradley's. 'It's just a symbol. It means nothing.'

'People are behind that symbol — that means something.'

'If you're that worried about it, I'll alert the Queen.'

Bradley squeezes his hand. 'Thank you.'

There is truly nothing to be concerned about, but Eros can't stand to see Bradley flustered. He'll tell the Queen and she'll have those flowers painted over. Crisis averted.

They hit the road leading to the ocean. The buildings dwindle to wooden shacks and the gravel becomes dirt. Pinpricks of light flicker on the sand and as they get closer, Eros can see Princess Phoebe and her servant, Bradley's sister Rosamund. They have at least a dozen guards with them all dressed in black.

Eros crosses his arms in frustration. 'What a waste of a night.' He turns to Bradley, flicking his long white hair over his shoulder. 'Did you tell them?'

'Of course not,' Bradley says. 'But–'

Eros groans, anticipating another one of Bradley's grand speeches.

His partner ignores him and continues, 'It's for the best. Your safety is paramount.'

'What's there to be afraid of?' asks Eros.

'The Six,' Bradley replies.

'Those dried up petals? They're nothing to worry about.'

The carriage stops. Bradley opens his mouth to speak, but Eros steps out of the carriage before he can say anything. The old supporters of the Freesian's may have been strong in number many centuries ago, and sure, their members had risen from a decade ago and yes, the Freesian symbol is sometimes painted here and there, but flowers are nothing to be afraid of.

Phoebe approaches them, smiling weakly, with Rosamund following behind her. Phoebe's hands are dirty and the hem of her patchwork skirt is stained. Eros's sister has come straight from the palace gardens dressed like a servant. If not for the golden duck pendant in her short brown hair, she might have been mistaken for one.

She dusts her hands on her skirts. 'I'm sorry about this Eros. Rosamund let slip about your secret outing and I had to tell Mother. She has allowed it so long as the guards remain here.'

Rosamund doesn't meet his glare, but in the dim light he can see her trying to fight back a smile. She always *accidentally* spills their secret. And she always seems to enjoy it. Rosamund shares Bradley's black hair, hazel eyes, and brown skin, but that is where their similarities end.

Bradley steps forward, a picnic basket in his arms. Eros raises a brow at his boldness. 'I apologise for speaking out of turn, but I would like to accept the Eagle Queen's kind proposal.'

Eros had been prepared to offer a quick no and turn his heel on this shamble of a night, but he will stay — for Bradley.

'Then we shall accept,' says Eros.

'Very good. I'm departing for the gardens. There's a particularly interesting carnivorous flower that requires my attention. Don't have too much fun,' says Phoebe, poking his arm on *fun* for emphasis.

The Princess bows to Eros and heads for the waiting carriage with Rosamund. Bradley squeezes his sister's arm as she passes and her expression softens somewhat.

The guards scatter across the sand, some staying close and others patrolling further away. A few of the Eagle Queen's faeries sit on their shoulders, providing Eros and Bradley with a little light. The faeries nibble pieces of bread and watch the scene curiously. Bradley acknowledges the guard closest to him and the guard curses under his breath. The faerie on his shoulder giggles — their green light shining a little brighter. The creatures hold great power but their light has become a novelty over the centuries; the price of their power is too great for anyone to desire it.

'I can punish him, if you wish,' says Eros. The guard deserves at least a little time in solitude.

'It's really nothing. I'm used to it,' says Bradley.

'But you shouldn't have to be.'

Bradley strolls away, his shoulder length hair ruffled by the breeze. He sets up a blanket and their basket close to the water. Eros reclines next to Bradley and watches the man eat pieces of fish and bread. He feels himself relax for the first time all day. Finally, he can just be.

One of the faeries lands on his shoulder. Up close the faerie has the same features as a human, save for the pointed ears. The creature points at the basket so Eros hands them a slice of cheese. They snatch it from him and fly away. The faeries all love human food. It is one of the reasons they allow their light to be used. That and their desire for destruction. Eros had watched them delight in it and even encourage it. Without it, they would leave this place.

'You should eat,' says Bradley. 'When was the last time you had a proper meal?'

'I've had bubbles and tiny treats all night long,' says Eros. 'You should eat. It'll make me happy.'

'Wine and desserts are not food.'

Eros quickly devours some fish and bread. 'There.'

The faeries giggle to themselves. They think the same thing as his mothers and every person in the kingdom: that this union is doomed.

'How was your day?' asks Eros.

'Bow practice, sword fighting, hand-to-hand combat. The usual things we do when we're not on a mission,' says Bradley.

'What about your poetry?'

Bradley's hand immediately goes to the dagger sheathed at his hip. 'There's no time for that.'

'Tell me one of your old ones then?'

Bradley peers cautiously at the guards nearby. Their disgust has been replaced by distant stares of boredom and apathy. He clears his throat, 'bury me beside you / where flowers grow / birds shall sing / as our hearts become dust // be with me always / from sweet sunrise / to bitter sunset / keep me always // whether love blooms / or dies / never leave me / i shall always be at your side.'

Eros kisses the blush rising on Bradley's cheeks and that only makes it deepen. 'You would do quite well at my poetry evenings.'

'My poetry, maybe. My person, absolutely not.'

'I'll get you there one day.'

After their meal Eros and Bradley strip off their clothes and wade into the ocean. Their skin-deep differences become clear under the moonlight. Eros has always been different in body to Bradley, the scars on his chest were enough of a reminder, but they share the same heart. Eros dives beneath the still water and emerges as a beautiful white swan. The faeries fly above them, dancing and laughing to themselves. Eros and Bradley float atop the ocean long into the night. Even under the watchful eyes of the palace guards it is peaceful. Eros wishes they could stay like this forever.

Rain pinpricks the water in the early hours of dawn. As the sun rises, the Eagle Queen arrives to fetch them. She stands on the shore under the cover of many umbrellas. Half of her flock traverse the sands to call Eros out of the water. He emerges from the waves — his wings became arms, the webbed feet skin once more as he changes back into his human form.

Under the cover of umbrellas he's dried and helped back into his clothes; Bradley hurriedly dresses beside him, damp from the drizzle. Only when they're dressed does the Queen speak with them.

'Someone will be here soon to bring you back to the palace,' the Queen tells Bradley. She turns to Eros. 'Come, my son. You'll be in the carriage with me.'

The Queen's black eyes are expressionless as she leads Eros to the carriage. His mother had given him her brown skin and prominent nose, but he'd gotten his green eyes from Diana.

'We expected you to return to the palace much earlier,' says the Queen, dabbing at her damp face with a black handkerchief.

'We were—'

'I don't need the details. It's time this foolishness ceases. From tomorrow more of your time will be devoted to Consort Olive. Do you understand?'

Eros feels his throat tighten, but forces a half-smile. 'Yes, of course your Majesty.'

'Very good.'

The rain picks up, pelting all sides of the carriage. Eros peers out the window and through the grey he just makes out Bradley's blurred figure on the shore.

The next morning at breakfast Eros finds himself seated across from Olive, his bride-to-be. Her strawberry blonde tresses seem to glow in the dawn light. At this early hour she's dressed in an elegant white gown with long sheer sleeves, perfectly matching Eros. Crowned with a pearl encrusted golden circlet, she certainly looks the part of a princess.

'How are you this morning?' asks Olive.

'Well,' replies Eros, without looking up from his seafood soup.

'I missed you at the ball last night.'

'I was busy.'

The conversation continues in this stilted way. It has been like this for their entire courtship. Olive exudes the quiet and wholesome beauty the Eagle Queen loves. But no matter how handsome, she could not tempt him.

The Queen and Diana do not appear for breakfast. Instead,

Eros is given a letter and a pile of books. The letter specifies that the Queen has a cold and that Eros is to study with Olive. Two of the Queen's ladies make sure Eros and Olive depart for his rooms after breakfast.

Eros is kept in his rooms with Olive for three days. His time with Olive is dull and although she is kind, he cannot suppress the inkling that something is not quite right. He petitions the Queen to leave, but each letter is returned with an official order to stay. The guards go so far as to forcefully push him back in whenever he steps even a toe outside.

On the third day, Phoebe arrives. Her face is damp with tears and she's barely able to speak before she bursts into tears. An accompanying guard coolly tells Eros that he is to go directly to the Queen's chambers.

Eros bolts out of his room; this time no-one stops him. Wings rip out of his back, tearing holes into his gown, and he flies through the castle, gliding down hallways and soaring up staircases. He doesn't stop until he lands at the Eagle Queen's bedside. His mother lies with her head in Diana's lap. Her breathing is shallow, laboured. With each cough, black feathers ripple across her skin; an attempt from her body to break away from the sickness. Eros's heart drops. This is all wrong. She is only supposed to have a cold. She'd been fine.

Diana gestures for him and he sits at her side. She tells him that the Queen has been unwell for years. He can't understand. Was her face always this thin? Her skin always so pale? He'd shadowed her for years and she'd never had one day off. It doesn't make sense. None of this made any sense.

The Queen slips away in the early morning. Eros, Phoebe,

Diana and Olive spend the next twenty-four hours with the Queen's body. Diana and Phoebe clean and dress her, scattering black feathers over her form. They tell stories about her, cry, sleep beside her, and at dawn, her body is burned and her ashes scattered in the gardens. Bells ring throughout the city to mark her passing and there is the unexpected sound of cheering from the palace gates.

Although pale and unkempt, Eros rushes to Bradley's private rooms. He needs him to make sense of all this. But his room is empty and covered in a fresh layer of dust. Eros stumbles out, asking a passing servant where his knight is.

'The knights' quarters, your Royal Highness,' replies the servant.

His heart thumps erratically in his chest. These have been Bradley's rooms since he was a child. He belongs in the palace, not in the shared rooms of the knights. He races to the knights' quarters, but once there he is told that Bradley was sent on an important mission days ago. He left no note and even his poems, scribbled on scraps of parchment, are gone.

The Swan King returns to his rooms. As soon as he's through the doors he collapses in a fit of tears — grief compounded by isolation and the growing fear of being not a prince, but a king: a king with the responsibilities of the entire kingdom and all its subjects.

In his first act as king, Eros signs orders allowing Phoebe and Diana to temporarily rule in his place — Phoebe will take care of the palace and Diana the affairs of the kingdom.

He stays in his room for days on end. The silence is broken

only by Eros's crying and the screams of the rebels at the palace gates. He sees them every morning (just before he shuts the curtains that Phoebe opens on her morning visits), dressed in their well-worn and patched-up clothes, waving signs painted with the white freesia flower. They call for Bradley, their king, every day and well into the night.

be with me always / from sweet sunrise / to bitter sunset / keep me always. That's what Bradley had said to him. But he hadn't come back. Hadn't visited. All that exists of Bradley is the drumming of his name beyond the gate and in Eros's heart.

Three months pass in this melancholy state. His wedding to Olive is planned, Phoebe sits with him every morning and evening, but Bradley does not return. One early morning, hours before sunrise, Phoebe arrives with three of her ladies and Rosamund. Eros, caught in a tangle of grief, does not know how to feel upon seeing her. Rosamund wears a gleeful expression. She is likely enjoying his despair.

'Brother, it is time,' says Phoebe.

He is fed, bathed, and dressed. Phoebe links her arm in his and leads him to the gardens. For once she is in her formal wear: a long brown shirt with golden buttons, a brown skirt flecked with black, and a brown feathered cloak.

'Have you heard from Bradley?' he asks.

Phoebe pats his arm. 'No, not yet. I'll send him to you when he returns.'

He'd lost count of the times she'd told him this. He still wants to believe it, believe the lie, even after all this time.

It is still dark in the palace gardens. Faeries dance between the still-closed flowers like fireflies. The guests stand amongst a grove of trees with heart-shaped leaves. They bow to their king as he passes. He searches their faces and doesn't find Bradley anywhere.

Eros waits for Olive in the middle of the grove. The crowd of gentlefolk murmur amongst themselves as the shouts by the gates grow in volume. Faeries watch from above, their faces split with wide grins.

Olive arrives wearing a matching outfit to his: a thin white gown with a thin golden belt. Olive's ladies slip thick white gowns over their heads and place feathered cloaks over their shoulders. They add accessories: golden circlets, necklaces, bracelets, and dangling pearl earrings.

Phoebe hands them each a white feather. Olive extends her arm and holds hers out to Eros. No matter how hard he tries, he can't move his arm. He does not want this.

There is a loud crash as the garden walls are breached, and half a dozen of his own knights surround Eros, dragging him away from his wedding. They carry him to the palace gates, to the rebels with fire burning in their blood and there, at the front of the pack, is Bradley — his Bradley, his knight — sword in hand and hundreds of people at his back. Eros is pushed forward. Instead of welcoming him into his arms, Bradley spins him around, pins his arms to his back, and puts the sword to his neck.

'What are you doing?' hisses Eros.

'Be quiet!' says Bradley.

Eros's entire body goes numb. He floats somewhere above himself, watching as he is shoved into the palace by Bradley, the Freesian King, followed by the masses. They break and tear down everything they can, some stopping to hastily paint white flowers over the portraits. They arrive at the throne room. Sitting in his mother's marble throne — his throne — is Rosamund. She is dressed in a delicate white gown with a long white cloak. Adorned with strings of white pearls around her neck and wrists, she almost appears to be a princess.

Bradley takes him towards the throne and forces him to his knees.

'Do it — kill him,' commands Rosamund.

'Not yet. We agreed you'd tell him why. Humiliate him, in front of everyone.' Bradley's voice, once so soft, has become cold.

Rosamund crouches in front of Eros and slaps him across the face. His head swims and Bradley holds his shoulders to keep him from falling. Rosamund tells him that he is selfish, his mothers cruel, and that the royal family has abandoned the people most in need of their help. She lists all his failures in excruciating detail.

Now,' says Rosamund to Bradley, 'kill him.'

Eros's body trembles as Bradley forces his head down and places the blade upon his neck. He doesn't want to die, not like this, not at the hands of his love.

'I still have the poison,' says Bradley. 'It would be the humane option.'

Rosamund laughs, high pitched and without mirth. 'Humane? There is nothing humane about this kingdom. Our bloodline, these poor people, will only be free once he is dead and you are king.'

Sweat drips from Eros's forehead. He wants his mothers and his sister with him instead of the cheering and jeering crowds.

Even the faeries watch, their laughter like high-pitched bells.

Bradley raises his sword, and swings. There are screams from all around as palace guards flood the throne room. Eros blinks — his hands are free. He's jerked to his feet and suddenly he's running with Bradley beside him. Arrows, rocks and bits of broken furniture rain all around. A faerie clings to Eros's gown. Bradley takes Eros' hand and leads him through the castle. They turn this way and that, racing through the halls until they arrive at the old Freesian tunnels.

Bradley pushes Eros in front of him and they run for their lives. In the dimness of the tunnels, Eros fails to see the thin tripwire. He stumbles over it, the metal cutting into his ankle. There is a loud *BOOM* behind them. Eros and Bradley are flung forward as the tunnel rumbles and stones fall around them. Bradley hauls Eros out of the tunnels, using the light of the faerie. Eros's ankle bleeds, but Bradley pushes him along from behind. Finally, the exit appears. They stumble into a back alley, where a carriage waits. Bradley stops. His face is much paler than normal and when he coughs, blood splutters out.

'What's wrong?' asks Eros. 'Are you hurt?'

Bradley touches his hand to Eros' face. That's when Eros sees them: the arrows piercing Bradley's back which is slick with blood. Bradley's eyes roll back into his head and he collapses. Eros tries to find Bradley's pulse but there is none. He's dead.

Eros grabs the faerie hovering joyfully beside him. 'Give him his life back!' He hadn't waited all this time just to see Bradley die.

The faerie opens their mouth and what comes out is not words, but a three-dimensional picture of the scene. In it, Eros vanishes and Bradley rises in his place.

Without thinking Eros says, 'Make it so.'

The faerie slips from his grasp and waves their hand. Eros's heart seizes and he falls backwards onto the black cobblestones.

Bradley gasps and rises from his death, the arrows in his back dropping to the floor.

He scrambles over to Eros and searches for any sign of life. He finds none.

'Please,' he begs, 'open your eyes.'

All he wants is to see those green eyes once again.

The faerie lands on the Swan King's chest. They pretend to wring their neck and close their eyes in a mock death.

'What did you do? Bring him back!' yells Bradley. He hadn't wanted any of this. After he was stolen away by the rebels, he'd played the king they'd wanted, only so he could save his Eros. In the end, he'd suffered for nothing.

The faerie opens their mouth. The image they project shows Bradley dying and Eros coming back to life. This must have been what Eros had done. If this continues they'll be trapped in an eternal cycle of death and revival. 'There has to be another way. We both have to live.' Bradley holds out his hand. The faeries flutters into his open palm. 'Please.'

The faerie sighs and holds out their hand. They want something. Bradley gives them all the jewellery on Eros's person, the gold in his pockets, but still, it's not enough. The faerie throws the trinkets aside and waits. So, Bradley gives them the only thing he has: his poems. This intrigues the creature. They handle each one gently, stopping at the one that begins with *bury me beside you*. They point one hand at Eros, the other at Bradley

223

and clasp them together. Bradley's heart skips a beat and on the next, Eros inhales.

Eros and Bradley grasp onto each other. Their hearts beat in sync and they realise, at the same time, that they now share a heart. Their lives belong to each other — they both live or they both die.

Eros and Bradley take the carriage out of the city and vow to return to the kingdom, united. As they travel they discuss everything: the riots, why it happened, the poverty, how Rosamund was right. Eros has the heart to listen now and Bradley the strength to speak the truth.

They discuss the future, the changes they could make, how they would both be kings — Avian and Freesian bloodlines combined. They will unite the kingdom under both their banners and rule more fairly than their ancestors.

When the rioting is over they return to the city, they hug Phoebe and Diana, apologise to Olive, and visit Rosamund in her private suite. Eros takes every verbal sting of hers and in the end, he learns a great deal. They promise to take action on it all with her, but not tonight. First, they need rest.

At last, they retire to their rooms and embrace each other. Finally, they are home.

TRANSMISSION SCARS

Lukah Roser

The lock twice refuses him. It's a game they've been collectively playing for as long as he's had possession of a key. He tries a third and then fourth time before the steel door eventually gives way, shifting with it a collection of dust that has accumulated in the absence of human occupation.

The workshop — the type dedicated to cars and bikes and masculine dick-measuring — sits in a relatively stagnant state. To the untrained eye there is nothing to indicate occupancy. Everything is quiet, in the purposeful sort of way. A mourner's silence. Calvin Cross matches this at first, small and unobtrusive, though no one who knew him would ever think to describe him as either of these things.

He takes this silence, drinks it in. It's almost unknown for such silence to exist here, in a place that thrives predominantly on one's ability to make as much metal-on-metal noise as possible, where the sound of engine and exhaust is a love language shared amongst all those within.

His phone vibrates against his thigh from the prison that is his pocket — also on silent, both because it is on theme and because he is purposefully ignoring it. It is likely his mother:

world's best mother, but also the world's leading nag. She knows where he is if she truly wants him. He continues to ignore her for now. He has other priorities.

Outside, afternoon is shifting to evening as the sun drops low against the horizon, drawing Calvin's long day to a slow conclusion. Inside, the workshop reflects this. Drowsy orange light breaches the space through high rows of elongated windows at the building's front and far side. Shadows eat shadows where this light can't reach, stretching thin and dark to match his mood.

Above him, vehicles sit aloft. High upon mechanical platforms, their bellies spilled of exhaust systems, axles, and engines. Cables keep these entrails out of arms reach — or more accurately, out from under the feet of those too dazed by each vehicle's mechanical splendour to pay awareness to trip hazards and debris.

Before him, the floor is a series of makeshift bays, divided by workbenches and oil drums, misused car parts and faulty circuits of extension cables. Each of these bays homes a car. Some of them stock-standard, some of them functioning more on willpower than mechanism. Others are constructed from parts hotter than a '90s hit single. Tuners and junkers and old Australian muscle, crowded close.

Calvin takes stock of them as he passes. The names of their driver's come and go, because although passion is limitless, money is not. In comparison, the names of the cars are forever imprinted within his mind, permanent in ways so few other things can be: Henry the sore-headed old Morris, the winsome smile of Penelope the Fairmont, the wily and unpredictable Luna the Skyline, Hugh the HT Monaro, Ringo the GT-HO, Macca the Vermilion Fire ZD Fairlane. On and on, he knew them all by make and model, by engine code and all their oddities. He knows them better than he knows himself.

'Gareth?'

The disembodied voice should shock him. Words from a workshop that should be otherwise empty. Calvin knows better, though.

'Not Gareth,' he replies.

He doesn't immediately expect a response. He knows this voice and he knows its barer doesn't like him much. He knows it's somewhat pointless, but he wants to say the words anyway, wants to cement them in as fact, maybe more for himself than anyone else.

The voice elicits a deep, guttural grumble.

Calvin turns around and is faced with a sloped brow and metallic frown. Henry. The Series II Morris Major.

This was the secret of Cross men: they could speak to cars.

A genetic trick of magic and mechanics passed from father to son for as long as the Crosses have had fathers and sons and the cars to go with them. It became their trademark, though no one knew so but themselves.

They made it into a business. Collecting and refurbishing cars and keeping them as lifelong companions. It was any enthusiast's dream. It was any race competitor's nightmare. The Cross family did not simply understand cars on a mechanical level, they knew them closely as friends. Any secrets and benefits lay simply with their ability to effectively communicate, a trait that seemed to come so easily between the cars and themselves and not so much so between each other.

Henry pipes up again. 'Where's Gareth?'

Gareth was the workshop's owner, making him by default the car's owner. Gareth was also Calvin's father, and as such he was the only other living person to have ever shared in Calvin's power. *Was* being a keyword in all these situations as all Gareth was now was—

'Dead.' Calvin tells Henry. 'He's dead.'

Silence. It is expected. Cars can't comprehend death. To them, death generally proposed little more than a pause in thought or a shift in form. When a car died, it only took the arrival of someone with the right amount of stubbornness and passion to resurrect it again. In the cases where this was not an option, then at the very least it could be stripped of parts, each piece holding a sliver of consciousness that would then transfer to another vehicle entirely, shared souls intertwined.

When humans die — depending on what you believe — it is a permanent removal. The ceasing of life means the end of all else.

To a car, death is but a short-term interlude; to a human it is everything.

To Gareth, death meant he wouldn't return to this workshop again. It would take the cars a long while to realise that. Calvin reminds them anyway.

'He's not coming back.'

Henry sputters and backs further into his bay. His park-brake makes a pained crunch upon engagement. Despite himself, Calvin makes a note to check on it when he can.

Equally annoyed, Calvin pulls his necktie loose, social graces replaced with a sufficient oxygen intake. He could never stand social gatherings. Gareth had despised them as well. If one could boycott their own funeral, Calvin was sure his father would have done so.

Calvin couldn't, so instead he had been forced into pants that told him peace with his body would never be an option. Forced to talk with people that either believed he was odd because he preferred his company with four wheels and a V8 engine, or people who thought he was odd because he wore his Anglican high school's male uniform.

He wants to change. He wants to wear his coveralls. They are his usual choice and he'd wear nothing else if school and his mother's insistence never forced otherwise. With an unwashed quality, the overalls made him feel he was nothing and everything all at once. A formless figure of grit and grime, grease and gender nonconformity.

He considers changing but decides against it, if only because his current plans required an unsoiled seat. He'll have to suffer for just a while longer.

The heartbeats of engines rise and fall as he listens for the sounds amongst the silence that only Cross men can hear. The warm lifeforce of the otherwise lifeless radiates through grazed fingers on fenders, of palms on bonnets. Coolant cools their running gear, but not their distress. They don't understand death, but they understand absence just fine.

'You old bastard,' Calvin growls into the workshop.

The workshop growls back.

Calvin looks up. Two orbs of bright white snap at him through the black of the workshop's furthest reach. Beast's eyes, unblinking in their approach. He isn't afraid. He had been the first time, many years ago, back when he was a boy smaller than the already small near-man he is today.

Calvin was eight when the cars began to speak to him. Not in the metaphorical sense of the word. Not in the privy-to-the-point-of-near-genius kind of way often associated with motor vehicles and machinery. In the linguistics kind. In the mouth-to-ear way in which animals often communicate. Or in this case, the grille-to-(according to information found during a late-night internet search on the inner workings of telepathy) right-parahippocampal-gyrus way in which cars and humans apparently do.

It was his dad who found him. Tucked between a herd of clunkers, YuGiOh cards fanned haphazardly against the ground, explanations spilling freely, the implausibility of their voices lost to the wild reach of Calvin's eight-year-old imagination.

To Gareth however, the strangest part about this had not been the power itself, but more Calvin's privy to it. This was a power of sons after all and at the time this wasn't something Gareth had known Calvin to be.

The creature in the workshop approaches, clawing its way through the lengths of bays to meet him where he stands, stopping before him with a startling squeal.

Calvin registers the sleek angles and sharp details of a Ford XC Cobra, blue-on-white detailing more signature than the scribble Calvin had provided to call her his own.

'Calvin.'

Cal-vin. Not Cal. His father called him Cal. Genderless. This was not quite love, but it was certainly a step to the left of it.

'Moe.' He calls her by her name. *For moe-power than your average machine* his father had once said. She must have liked it because she'd never asked to be called anything else. How easy it must be, to care so little about those kinds of things.

When younger Calvin had found older Calvin beneath a layer of social dissonance and genital hatred, it had been because of Moe. He was eleven, gangly, awkward. He spent more time amongst the cars than he did other children. If not the cars, then his father, who generally accompanied the cars regardless.

That day Moe was his project of choice, his fingers lovingly running along her cobalt pin-stripe, foot shifting a stray oil rag this way and that.

'Are you a girl car or a boy car?' he'd asked.

'I am just a car, but your father calls me her, so you may call me her as well if you like.'

'Okay.'

'And yourself?'

'Myself, what?'

'Are you a girl human or a boy human?'

He'd stopped, contemplating the question.

'I asked mum once and she said I was a girl.'

'And what do you think?'

Another pause.

'I'm a boy.'

'Okay.'

And that had been that. As clean as Moe's freshly polished paint. No complications needed.

Moe had been Calvin's favourite from that point, though he'd never let the others know. After all, she was also Gareth's favourite, so the shared bias had always seemed a betrayal.

This was love. The touch of his hand upon paint and the rumble that radiated along his arm to his chest. 'Hi Moe.'

'Did you say goodbye for me?'

Cars may not understand death, but Moe had never been any typical car. She understood at least the significance of Gareth's passing, both to Calvin and the workshop at large.

'Yeah.'

There is an audible *click*. The automatic unlocking of Moe's driver side door. 'Come on then,' she says. For all his love and adoration, Calvin had never been allowed to even breathe the air of Moe's interior, let alone delve within. But who could stop him now?

Calvin slips from his shoes and toes off his socks, kicking them aside, wanting nothing more than to feel the unfiltered sensation of pedal upon pad. Gareth had been a barefoot driver, and despite the cautionary words of many, many driving instructors and an equal number of complaints from the cars themselves, Calvin was as well.

Slipping inside, Moe is a time capsule of an era Calvin's father had never abandoned. A crisp twenty-one at the time of her release, Gareth had held her in the state of 1978 all the way up until his death over four decades later, solidifying both her resale value and her sentimental one. Gareth had always claimed that he had only ever been in love thrice. Once when he met Calvin's mum, Olivia Huong, at a car-meet in his early thirties. Once when Olivia had given him Calvin. And once, before either of those loves, when he met Moe.

Calvin feels something tug within him, a sensation he chooses to ignore. Instead he begins his intended nosing: slipping open drawers, and drawing slips from between crevices that would otherwise be ignored. Buttons are buttoned. Switches are switched. All these things are then returned to their default state before he continues.

He finds it by accident, the photograph tucked neatly behind Moe's driver's side visor.

It's a childhood photo of Calvin. One he'd thought to have been disposed of years ago in a barrel bonfire on his fourteenth birthday. His father had saved this one from the sacrificial bounty it seemed, hiding it in Moe.

It doesn't feel real to look at. It also feels too real to ignore. It stings like Calvin hadn't thought such a tiny thing could. It is the split second of pain from a coolant cap opened too early, but not quite early enough to be disastrous. Such a small pain, but a pain nonetheless.

Calvin forces the picture inelegantly back behind the sun visor. Another habit he had picked up from Gareth — out of sight, out of mind, like so many other things.

The centre console is next. Unlike that of his mother's poor Hyundai Accent — Bob, if you can believe it — that is filled to the brim with receipts and rubbish and what remains of her limited daily fucks, Moe's console contains only a single pack of Winnie Blue's and the lighter that accompanies them. A vice that to Gareth had been long-lived, but ultimately deadly.

'I told him smoking would kill him,' says Calvin.

Moe, who has maintained a complacent silence throughout

Calvin's photo discovery, finally opens her traitor's grille, 'And he always said—'

'—if not the darts, then something else.'

Calvin grabs the pack in a crushing grip, flipping it open to survey what remains. Just under half. He tugs a stick free, placing it between his lips, worlds away from ever lighting it.

Had it been worth it? Calvin wonders.

Calvin falls back against the headrest, hands fisted nine-and-three upon the steering wheel. The lighter lingers in the console, an enticing mistress. He leaves it be, allowing the cigarette to lay limp upon his bottom lip.

He feels like a kid again, playing pretend. A youth-sized enigma in the driver's seat of one of his father's project cars. Legs too small to reach the pedals. Ego too large for the keys to be left in the ignition. The keys are missing now, though Moe had never really needed them. Once you know the language of cars, keys are redundant when compared to the word *please* and its runner up phrase *thank you*.

He needs neither today as Moe's engine once again thunders to life, the sound of her reverberating off the open ceiling, knocking against the far-flung walls. Calvin's bones shake with the force of it, a rumble in his veins that feels like coming home.

The stereo switches on, its signal lost to the workshop's steel frame. It is a familiar sound. Gareth loved the radio, having never adjusted to the streaming services that now rule the world. Cassette tapes litter Moe's glovebox, a system as analogue as the workshop's key or Gareth's nicotine habit. It is so unapologetically his father that it's almost as if Calvin can see him now, perched broad and boxy in Moe's passenger seat, doling out stern and impatient instructions.

Calvin switches from the radio to the tape deck. Another mistake. The infamous sound of The Angels greets him, asking questions he will never have the answers to, guitar chords sounding like heartstrings pulled tight and finessed painfully but masterfully.

Am I ever going to see your face again?

His chest feels tight in ways years of binding had never achieved.

He turns the stereo off entirely.

'Let's go for a drive,' Calvin suggests, rationale already forfeit to the waiting road.

'You haven't got a licence.'

'It's dark out.'

'Barely.'

He is also barely shy of having a licence. Two months out of the provisional glory that will be his freedom. It also hardly matters. An adept driver despite his years, Moe knows she has nothing to fear from him, except possibly the instability of his grief.

Still, she wouldn't take this away from him. She wouldn't know how. Love is funny that way. It is both blind and all-knowing. Fractured and functioning. Questions and answers and questions again. Even for a car that's seen Calvin's lifespan twice over and then some, she does not know how to deprive him of this, consequences be damned.

The garage door opens with a hiss of the remote-operated roller system. Calvin and Moe inch towards it, hesitancy the result of Calvin's conditioning over Moe's reluctance.

There is no turning back now.

As they drive, they bisect the workshops and warehouses that make up the industrial area of his timeless Goldfields hometown. An everyman's maze of machinery and passion and Steel Blue splendour. They leave behind a varicoloured mirage of signs painted over in their wake. Business atop business atop business again; years of profit, turned bankruptcy, turned ruin to refurbishment. They'd seen places and people come and go, all the while the Cross's business flourished under the TLC of their family's unique vehicular insight.

Moe breathes in and her engine roars. Calvin breathes in and his heart follows suit, kindred pistons pushing and pulling blood through his system as Moe's own do for her. Blood, because Calvin Cross bled red like everybody else. Not a lick of oil in sight, despite what they say.

If he were something closer to a car then maybe things would have been easier. Cars have no concept of society, no connection to any sort of binary other than the ones programmed into their coding. Cars have it easy. Run and run and run until you can run no more. Beloved by most. Even the shit boxes are loved by somebody, seen and cherished either for their ability to get someone from point A to B, or simply for the beauty of their improbable existence.

If he was a car, maybe he wouldn't care at all.

They exit onto the highway, an unbounded stretch of blacktop and bushland that spreads from one town to the next, with three digits marking this distance as insurmountable in his brain. They'd never reach the end from here. They'd never have to. The road was enough, boundless and dark and marked with intention.

Calvin shifts through gears, easily, flawlessly, a natural in every sense of the word. He hits the throttle. Moe is heavy, but she's made for speed. The XC's were Bathurst cars. Racing was built into her from axle to angle. She'd give him her all if he asked for it. Lo and behold, he doesn't have to utter a word. The world outside blurs, moving so fast that there's nothing at all.

That's the beauty of being a Cross. The cardinal rules of cars still applied: clutches and gears and brakes and skill. However, after years of close association with cars of many kinds, Calvin knows that these rules are not the only ones. A car has a limited but otherwise significant amount of freewill. A car, if it so wishes, can come and go as it pleases so long as no one is around to question said motion. Calvin's input is unneeded. He puts his foot down anyway, feels his feelings spill over, supercharged. He is speed and control. He is grief and love. He is resentment and anguish and mourning. He hates his father and misses his father in the same breath of exhaust.

Gareth is dead.

He'd never accepted Calvin. He'd never have the chance. The cars had always gotten more of Gareth Cross than Calvin ever had and now that's how it would stay.

He thinks he hears Moe trying to speak to him, but her words are lost in the speed. His mind feels lost to the fuel-injected rush of this race. This race with no competitor outside of himself. His mind is gone, racing faster than even Moe is capable. Lost to the road.

'Calvin,' Moe warns with no response.

Fuck you, dad. Calvin thinks but does not say.

'Calvin.'

Fuck you fuck you fuck you fuck you

'Calvin!'

FUCK YOU

'Jesus take the wheel,' Calvin finally says aloud, tacko touching red, speedo touching infinity, the rev limiter squealing for liberation.

'That is not my name,' Moe replies.

Calvin laughs. The sweet, searing irony of a phrase well-worn but not much beloved.

That is not my name.

He lets go of the wheel.

There is a momentary lapse of control as Moe veers ominously to her right-side, toeing the ceaseless blur of white that divides safety from destruction, before wrangling control of herself and setting them straight once more — another irony from which Calvin is not lost.

His laughter rises, overwhelming all else.

They come to a stop roadside, albeit not as gracefully as Moe would have preferred. There is a crunch of gravel and a clunk of indeterminate origin preceding Moe's sigh of relief.

The sudden stop shakes Calvin as well, throwing him as far forward in his seat as his seatbelt allows. The shock dislodges both his ego and the contents of Moe's sun visor, where the earlier photograph greets him again, this time flipped over, revealing the time-stamped back that had been previously ignored.

A black mark is all that remains of a name since slashed from the register. In its place the name 'CALVAN' is written in messy block letters.

There is a moment then, post the hysteria, but only just, where Calvin lets the last of his laughter fizzle out. Where anger and resentment make way for something else, something more convoluted than even that. There is no emotional flash card for this feeling. No easy way to put it into words. This is what it is to be human and not a car. This is what it is to grieve.

'He spelt it wrong,' he says.

Calvin turns the photo once again, inspecting the face of the child who has always known something was off, but hadn't known the words until a car had given them to him. A child with hair past their shoulders and a skirt their mother had loved until it had been painted in grease on a workshop floor.

Calvin had buried them long ago, this child, and despite the slow progression, it seemed his father had too.

He returns the photo once more to the sun visor, a burial in and of itself.

Moe sighs. 'He tried.'

'That old bastard.'

'He loved you.'

Calvin sighs. 'He tried.'

And wasn't that the hardest part? That his father had not loved him fully. For how can you truly love something if you do not truly know it?

But he had *tried*.

OUR TIME, OUR HOME

Alistair Ott

Sleep flung themself between the soggy wooden fence slats, almost slipping on the mud below. With a relieved sigh, they collected themself and glanced back at the old farmhouse, its porch light flickering in the storm. *I'll only be away till morning; she won't even notice I'm gone.* If Aunty caught them running off again, Sleep would be in for yet another lecture about the dangers of the whitefullas night.

Aunty remembered her time in the Northern city, where people never slept, and she and her wife had kept close when walking alone in the dark. That was what night meant for her. For Sleep, night meant they could freely explore the desolate streets and the bush surrounding them without any suspicious glares or whispers. This land was their family's country, where their aunty and mother were born, but Sleep was nothing but a bored stranger to the locals. When Sleep first moved here, to the town called Otherwhere, Aunty ran around all day working for others. She never had time for herself, let alone them, even if she was always quick to tell them what they were doing wrong. *Too lonely, too quiet.* Sleep just didn't know how to speak to her.

Sleep jogged down the gravel road and into town, water

sloshing around in their rain boots. When Sleep could no longer see the porch light behind them they stopped, resting on a tree trunk and trying to calm their hammering heart. *Not too long now.* The lights of town glowed just past the bend in the road. The rain and wind called for them to push on through the storm to *their* place, the tall grass beneath them pulling them onwards.

Rain pattered onto the pavement, falling from the rooftops and slinking into the gutter. This time in the evening was Sleep's favourite — these moments when the streets were empty of people and alive with everything else. The night took over, and it felt closer to their time. Just like the stories Aunty would sing as she baked, watching them from across the kitchen counter, never daring to close the distance and hold them like their mother once did.

Trudging down the pavement, Sleep finally made it to the other side of town. To the end of Otherwhere before the bush took over. They lifted their hands towards the falling sky — raindrops sizzled and sparked as they bounced off them. A deep *caw* rang out from the trees behind them, crawling up their spine and tussling their hair. They spun around, trying to catch what bird could be about this late in the evening, but only rain filled their ears. The moon impatiently rose over the horizon. Sleep picked up the pace, running off the mud-slick highway and into the retreating scrub below with a newfound fever.

Time sped past as Sleep made their way further into the bush and finally found what they sought. An old mossy sign, which once must have stood as tall as them, now leaned onto a fallen gum tree. They could just make out the carved words

'Recollection Falls'. Sleep always wondered what this place's true name was. His mother would tell stories of the rivers being shaped and carved by a great being, but never of this place. Although the tingling that spread from Sleep's fingertips and deep into their belly told them it was special, sacred.

A short walk from the sign ran an impossibly deep river etching through the bush before disappearing seemingly without a trace. Well hidden by blue gums and brush sat a sinkhole, where the water fell from the river into a magnificent waterfall. Sleep was careful not to fall over the ridge as they slipped between branches and down the cliffside.

To get to its floor, Sleep carefully climbed down carved stairs, permanently slick with water sprayed from the falls. Forgotten by others, this was their special place, where roots twisted and told forgotten stories and moss-covered sandstone surrounded a pool of deep, chilled water. Slivers of quartz and mounds of opal shone amongst cracks in the walls. Despite the overcast sky the rock walls gleamed with their own light, their colours reflected off the pool in an iridescent rainbow.

The storm above raged on, full of fury and frustration, but it died before it could meet the water below. The towering gum trees above and the undisturbed sanctity of the falls protected Sleep. They moved around the pond's edges and sat in a dry spot next to it. They took off their gloves and tried to massage warmth into their hands; their raincoat could only do so much. Sleep had waited impatiently for weeks for this storm to pass before returning here, but it just raged on. And during those weeks they had found themself unable to rest: nothing was as calming and safe as these falls, where the air around them sang stories lost to time and the water called out to them from deep below its surface.

Leaning over and dipping their hand into the pond, Sleep found it just as icy as the air around it. The deep blue seemed to go on forever, no bottom to be seen despite it being as clear as glass. But just as they truly relaxed, a flutter on the other side of the pond caught their attention. Eyes met eyes. Sleep scrambled back as the crow on the other side cawed with delight. The crow danced around in the falls before skimming the surface of the water and landing in front of them. Sleep clenched their hands as it cooed and rattled, pecking at their rain boots.

'You were the *caw* from before?' Sleep leaned in. They laughed as the crow fluffed up, cocking its head at them, before strutting around them and returning to the water to play. Sleep knelt up, crawling closer to the water's edge. Trembling, they dared to reach out, brushing against its tail feathers.

'Whatcha following me for?' Sleep asked as the crow cawed softly, snuggling into the palm of their hand.

The crow ducked down and settled at the water's edge, cawing in what they assumed was approval as Sleep joined it. It peered down into the pond, lowering its head and drinking. The water sparked and hummed as it did. Smoke filled Sleep's vision and they remembered their mother's stories: she'd told them tales of their family's moiety, *Crow*, a crafty and wise mischief maker. Although they may find themselves far away from each other, Sleep would see *Crow* and feel her spirit through it.

Crow fluffed up and peered over at Sleep, before shooting up and flying straight down into the pond, disappearing into its depths. The water around it crashed and swelled, rainbow light glittering around the sinkhole.

Sleep watched as the water calmed back down into soft waves. They shuddered, their whole body electrified, and stepped forward. Deep below the surface, warm orange and purple light shone through the water, calling out to them. They gazed back up, where the stretching leafy branches hid the storming sky, and grinned. They took a deep breath and stepped into the water.

And fell.

And fell …

And fell …

They finally emerged back onto land. Coughing up water, they pulled themself out and touched not cold sandstone but warm sweetgrass. Their lungs burned, but as they stood and patted themselves down, they found their clothes and skin were dry. Rather than a sinkhole cocooned in moss and quartz, they found themself next to a lagoon covered in nardoo and bulrush at the top of a flowering hill. Opalescent scrub and white gums that glowed like moonlight covered the valley below. The sky was deep dark indigo and covered with more swirling stars than Sleep thought possible. Even though it was still night, everything was clear and bright; the stars' collective light shone as bright as a single sun.

A deep honeyed voice cawed out from above them. Sleep whipped their head around and up. Looking down at them was *Crow*, its body spread out immeasurably on the eucalypt above. Black wings dripped down to the ground from where it sat. Its feathers were black as night, splattered with swirling stars akin to the sky. Its beak curled up in a smile, peering at Sleep in amused consideration.

'*Crow*? You … ah … you brou—'

It interrupted, preening its feathers. 'Brought you here? No. You jumped in all by yourself.'

'I—I guess. Why?'

'Oh, because you were doing so much where you were, huh? What a busy human.' Sarcasm dripped from its beak.

'I'll just go back then, huh!' Sleep turned, face hot. The water below was still in anticipation. *Crow* swooped down, landing on the other side of the lagoon. At full height it towered over Sleep.

'Well, you could go back. Just jump in. Or …' *Crow* spread its night-sky wings, gesturing to the land before them. 'Do you *really* have anywhere you need to be?' It sang out, a cawing laugh.

Sleep mulled their choices. Their heart hammered in their chest. Excitement and fear spread from the ground and filled them from toes upwards.

'Go on child. I'll be right behind y—' Before it could even finish, Sleep spun around and ran down the side of the hill. They heard a burst of joyful barking laughter follow them down before they slipped between two enormous trunks and into the bush. *She won't even notice I'm gone.* They made that promise one more time. This was just the adventure they'd been looking for!

Sleep strolled through the glowing white gums and weeping willows, jumping over jingling lilly-pillies and swerving out of the way of dancing waratahs. They kept an eye out for the black feathers in their periphery and followed the silver river that spread across the bush, watching the honeybees and butterflies sway and bop across the still water. They passed a great fen spotted with water lilies and rushes, walking just a little bit faster when they spotted a broad grey croc sitting in the wetland, watching them with keen interest.

Pushing their way through thorny brambles, Sleep found themselves in a vast valley. In front of them stood a mountainous silky gum, its branches spanning the horizon and its bright golden-orange flowers contracted against the night sky. Birds of all colours sang and danced amongst the foliage and cuddled up in the shade. Nectar seeped down from the great flowers and formed streams where they drank. A grand old sulphur-crested cockatoo spun its head around and fluffed up when it spotted the teenager standing at the end of its domain.

'AH! A Spirit? Or a Human?' It bellowed out with curious excitement. 'Who approaches? AH!'

A band of lorikeets, rosellas and galahs rose from their perch and surrounded Sleep before they could step back or explain themself.

'It's not a ghost!'   'Look! It's bruised.'
'I don't trust it!'
'It's real, it's real!'   'Who let it here?'

The birds fluttered around Sleep, softly brushing up and clambering on top of each other for a peek. Sleep tentatively reached out and stroked them in greeting, relieved when one by one they nestled up and chirped in response. A smaller galah sat down close to the crowd, watching them with wide curious eyes.

The great *Cockatoo* rose from the tree and plunged down. The breeze made by its giant wings pushed Sleep back off their feet and scattered the other birds. This one was much bigger than *Crow*. It ducked down to meet Sleep's gaze, cocking its head side to side.

'AH, did you fall here child? This is not your place. Not yet …' *Cockatoo* chuckled, its kin around it joining in and echoing laughter across the valley.

'Yeah, something like that. I'm kind of just, travelling I guess.' Sleep tucked their hands in their raincoat pockets, shrugging, realising its shiny black plastic stood out amongst the colourful birds.

'Travelling? Or seeking something? It can be quite dangerous here. Follow me, child.' It rose and tottered down the valley, following a stream of nectar past coves of bumbling bees.

'Dangerous? Yeah, I guess. I've seen that big croc,' Sleep snorted.

'Oh child. Not *Croc*. You keep running too far and you'll lose your way home.' *Cockatoo* waddled further down the valley, where chirping chicks nestled together in fluffy nests.

'That doesn't sound like the worst thing,' Sleep retorted.

'Wouldn't you miss someone?'

Sleep scrunched up his face, shrugging his shoulders. 'Maybe, but I don't think I would be missed.' Unable to stop the words from tumbling out, their heart fell at their own confession.

'And how could you know that?' A familiar voice bellowed from behind them. *Crow* swooped down and settled next to the now glaring *Cockatoo*.

'AH! So you're how this poor human got here!' *Cockatoo* squawked, flaring its crest.

'Nice to see you again, *Cockatoo*,' *Crow* preened.

'Well, if *Crow*'s your guide you best go on, you have elsewhere to be!' *Cockatoo* cried, puffing up, before rising and sweeping Sleep off their feet with great gusts. The others rose from their perch, diving in and circling Sleep with a furious roar.

Sleep clambered back trying to escape the flock. They felt a tug on their sleeve. Looking back, they found a small galah that stood crouched under the mob pecking at them, pulling them under the birds and towards red soil. Rolling onto their belly, Sleep crawled until they hit dry grass. As soon as they were free from the hoard they jumped up and ran down the gully. Sleep stopped, realising they had lost their little saviour, only to see it and *Crow* fly past their head and disappear toward a vast empty desert. The other birds dared not to follow, retreating to their mother tree.

Sleep caught their breath before trying to trace the path of their guides. Parched dirt cracked under their soles. The air was thick and arid and left a film of ick in Sleep's mouth. The trees here twisted unnaturally into each other, creating a path for them to follow. Sleep's footsteps echoed, and every breath bounced down the desert no matter how they tried to silence themself. Greenery peeked from the deadness in front of them. They quickly started sprinting towards the hope of the lush bush. The numbness trailing up from their feet and fingertips left their body as soon as they stepped onto fresh grass.

The tall grass hummed as Sleep slipped past it. It gradually got taller and taller until Sleep couldn't see over it. Jumping up, they could just make the tops of the stems. The buzz of cicadas echoed around them until it was almost deafening. They kept wandering, getting deeper and deeper, worried they would be forever lost in this ever-growing meadow. They stumbled through the stalks, hope draining with every step, until they fell through the grass and straight into a patch of mud.

Spluttering, they stood up. In front of them was a farmhouse: their aunty's farmhouse. The wooden building stood amongst the towering grassland. Blue-green flickering Christmas beetles wafted around the house, bumping into each other. Stepping closer, Sleep realised the house wasn't man-made from planks of wood, but rather carved out from a single giant gum. The rest of the trunk lay behind the house, flattening the grass around it. Sleep looked back at the sea of wild grass. Uncanny as the farmhouse might be, it had to be better than being lost.

Their rainboots clunked across the wooden porch as they walked toward the front door. Instead of a door, this farmhouse had a fist-sized hole and a perch where the door knocker should be. Sleep tentatively lifted their hand and knocked just beside the perch. Their knocks resounded throughout the farmhouse. Silence.

Sleep shuffled their feet. They felt just as at home here as they did in their aunty's house back in Otherwhere: That is, not much at all. They stepped back just as the familiar galah appeared through the hole with a fluttering of feathers and landed on the perch.

'Oh, um, hello! Thank you, you know, for earlier,' Sleep said, running their fingers through their curls. The galah preened and tweeted, before disappearing back into the hole. A glowing line appeared and travelled from the hole down and around the wood creating the shape of a doorway. Clicking into place, a door appeared and snapped open.

It opened into a living room that mirrored their aunty's, but in place of furniture and clutter sat roots, moss and mushrooms. The galah fluttered in the roots, moving lichen and sapphire flowers around the room. Sleep took it as an invitation and stepped inside, swerving to miss a buzzing beetle. The room was lit up, but Sleep could not find the light source. Everything glowed, soft and warm.

'Why did you help me ... um?' Sleep asked.

'Ohhhh honey, my name's *Galah*!' It fluffed up, bouncing around the room and never taking its eyes off Sleep. 'And I'm sorta a friend of *Crow*, thought it was right to help you out!'

'Sorta? And you live here?' Sleep wandered around. Where their aunty's couch and old box TV normally sat was a snoozing goanna on a bed of moss. Instead of a kitchen there was a patch of blooming lavender and a native bee nest. The bees buzzed around like kitchen clutter. Sitting on a giant toadstool sat *Crow* with a wide smile, one great claw wrapped around a mug made from thick quartz.

'Not going to run away again, huh? You are good at that,' *Crow* teased.

'My human lives here, and *Crow* helped me get my colours! Look at me now!' *Galah* spoke up, ignoring its grinning friend. It lifted its grey and pink wings, twirling around in the air.

'Your human?' Of course, their aunty's family were galah people. 'Why is her house here? Is the whole town here?' Sleep questioned.

'It's here for you, for you to come back home.' *Galah* directed

Sleep to a neighbouring log and they were surprised at how soft it felt. Sleep stiffened up as *Galah* sat on their shoulder and preened their hair. No one had done that since …

'I don't really have a home.' Sleep shook their head, overwhelmed by all the sensations prickling at their skin.

'Home is what you make of it, sweetheart, and it's there waiting for you.' *Galah* darted past them to collect a beakful of river mint and lemon myrtle.

'And you ran so far away from it you fell outta your world, didn't you! Worrying your aunty,' *Crow* laughed. *Galah* swatted at it with their wing as it flew past and returned to Sleep, decorating their hair with the herbs. Sleep leaned down and grazed a tuft of flowering buds. Their aunty was worried? How long had they been here? They tried to count the minutes, but time warped and blurred together. *Galah*'s loving stare matched Aunty's and Sleep felt homesickness well up in their chest.

'I … I should probably get going,' they mumbled, fiddling with their sleeves.

'Oh, of course! Got places to be, I get it,' *Galah* clucked, flying over and snuggling into their neck. Sleep stiffened but raised their hand, and half hugged the waggling bird.

'Hugs are good for ya, ya know!'

Sleep laughed at *Galah*'s disapproving tone.

Crow followed Sleep out of the farmhouse and back onto the porch . Standing there together they watched as the sun began to rise in the east, and the sky brightened to bedazzling pink and yellow. A wave of humid warmth blew past Sleep before they were cooled by a gust of shade covering them — *Crow*'s wing stretched out overhead.

'So, how're you getting home then, fulla?' *Crow* asked, looking away with feigned disinterest.

'Well! I'll …' Sleep jumped down the steps before pausing. Tall grass surrounded them, their shadow coiling at their boots and beckoning them in. 'How should I get home then?' They bashfully looked back, becoming quickly sceptical of *Crow's* widening grin.

'Home! I can get you home, c'mon kid.'

Crow bounced off the patio and behind the house where the wide tree trunk lay. Sleep rushed to keep up, vaulting up behind it. Their boots slipped on the loose bark, and rollie-pollie bugs scuttled out from under it and down the wood into the soil below. *Crow* stood tall and shook their feathers out, fluttering around like *Galah* with its always-blooming flowers. Above them the sky splintered and Sleep swore they saw visions of Otherwhere flash across the sky. *Crow* waved them to join it. A hot flash passed through their body and they felt their face redden.

They closed their eyes and remembered their aunty, their mum and dad, their cousins, their mob. They joined *Crow's* dance, their black raincoat like falling feathers. A thunderous stampede of caws, squawks and shrieks descended from the sky above in a furious melody, rumbling the farmhouse. Sparks of sunlight and rainfall flew from their fingertips. The sky fissured and rain fell hard down where they both stood.

Then, all was silent.

'Why'd you bring me here, why let me run all o'er the place?' Sleep asked, opening their eyes feeling lighter than ever.

'You had your own path to follow.'

Sleep sighed and glanced up. Above, the waterfall whirled

around itself, its language both unknown and familiar to Sleep.

Sleep snorted. 'You're— you're like my mum!' They shot up a brief painful smile, remembering her wonderfully tough love.

'Oh? You're a crow person too, ey? Who says I'm not you?'

Sleep looked back at their strange friend with a soft smile. 'I just know,' they said, before turning back and jumping up through the water. It spun them up with ferocity, flipping them around and around until it felt like they were falling back down. And so they fell.

And fell.

And fell …

And fell …

They found themself back next to their sinkhole. Breathing in the chilled morning air, Sleep looked up to see the wild storm had moved on and a gentle dawn had taken its place. Feeling better rested than in months, relief filled their body. Almost home.

Climbing out, the morning sun hit their back. A *caw* rang out from the trees. Sleep stifled a groan and peeked up to see *Crow* sitting above them, smaller again now. Its black eyes betrayed the smugness behind its seemingly emotionless face. It cocked its head before swooping down and flying up the path toward home.

'Back to following you again, ey?' Sleep huffed. Another *caw* rang out and they sighed. *Fine.*

Sleep followed the black bird as it bounced from branch to branch, quickly gaining enthusiasm. They spun, skipped and laughed past the sign, through the bush, and back onto the highway and into town. *Crow* dipped up and down above them — disappearing into the sky and away from other townsfolk when they approached the main street.

'CHILD! You had me worried sick!' Aunty's voice cried out from behind a group of tottering tourists. She barged through the group and beelined to Sleep. 'Gone all night! Not in bed! Were you lost? What happened?'

'I'm okay, Aunty! I'm sorry,' Sleep said, interrupting her ranting. Aunty caught her breath and held her hand out to stop them. Sleep noticed her slight tremble.

'I don't understand what I need to do. I give you as much space as you need and … and nothing.' She shrugged in defeat.

Sleep tried to explain. 'I'm just lonely, I guess. And sad. And scared and … ' Despite quickly losing steam they seemed to get their point across.

Aunty deflated, sighing. 'Why didn't you tell me, love? I thought you wanted to be alone, after ya mum.'

'I didn't know how to. I felt bad that you had to take me in and come back here, just cause I had no one else.'

'I didn't take you because I had to. I loved your mother, and I love you. I wanted this to be a new start for us both.' She placed her hands on their shoulders, smiling down at them. Her hair was a mess, the lines on her face deep from lack of sleep, but her hands on Sleep's shoulders were warm and strong. They leaned into her.

'Is now when I come out to you too?' they whispered.

Aunty burst out laughing. 'One thing at a time! But of course. I love all of you. This is your home now.'

Crow caught a gust of wind and flew up, joining a familiar galah on the telephone pole above Home. They watched Sleep run down the main road and down the dirt path with a relieved Aunty. She was fuming, but *Galah* could see the joy in her eyes. *Galah* nestled into *Crow*, squawking when *Crow* huffed and kicked *Galah* away with an eye roll and a smile. A stray branch from a nearby tree shot out, throwing *Crow* off the pole with a burst of feathers. *Galah* squawked out a laugh, thanking Earth for having its back.

SALT IN HER POCKETS

Anna Jacobson

Fradel's week was consumed by ritual and superstition. If cats followed her on a Monday afternoon, she made herself walk through the park without sitting on the benches and looked at no one. If the cats journeyed home with her on a Wednesday, she went to bed at four in the afternoon with an amulet around her neck: a bulb of garlic tied in cloth. On Thursday nights, if the cats and their shrieking made her dream of Dybbuks melding with her soul, she would salt the corners of her room, with a little extra left over for the seams of her pockets. One could never have too much salt. Especially on a Friday. Fradel hoarded heavy packets for emergencies — each packet in a different location in the house. But despite her best efforts, she sensed a Dybbuk already possessed her, lodged in her smallest toe.

Fradel's days were shaken. No amount of salt could shift the Dybbuk. Its presence flared two weeks before her period and stayed until a few days after she bled. Then the cycle would begin again. A cyclical Dybbuk. She had never heard of such a thing but knew the Rosh Chodesh Women's Circle would have the answer. Fradel had never heard of Rosh Chodesh before she'd met Natania, the local queer Yiddish match-maker. The group gathered at Natania's place on the night of the new moon to talk about topics related to women. Natania was beautiful in the way that the earth was beautiful. Natania was also powerful. Her fierce blue-black hair spun around her head.

Fradel knocked on Natania's door on the night of the new moon. From behind the door, she could hear a broom sweeping, as though made from one hundred scratchy twigs. She could just make out the sound of muttered Yiddish in time to the sweeping: *Swish shmaltz, swish shmuck, swish shlock, swish-swish gefilte fish.* Already Fradel could smell wood-smoke and something familiar, like cinnamon and cholent. The scent was sweet compared to the sea salt smell of Fradel's own home. The door opened and there was Natania in an emerald velvet dress, hair billowing from her face in the cool night breeze.

'I have a Dybbuk in my toe,' said Fradel.

'Shh! Get inside, quick my darling. We mustn't start until the others arrive.'

A narrow corridor lined with jars of gefilte fish led all the way to the back of Natania's house. Fradel's stomach always shrank at the smell of the minced carp suspended in jelly. Hemmed in by jar upon jar of gefilte fish, a waft of the smell of baking *challah* settled her. Towards the centre of the house was just as Fradel remembered it: a kitchen with chicken feet sticking out of a bubbling soup pot. Five cats lay sleeping or stretching close to the stove to take in its heat; two of which Fradel recognised as the ones who followed her around the streets. Natania brought down a jar, sang three notes into it, then waved the jar under Fradel's nose. The pickle inside the jar was shrivelled.

'Try it, *abisl*. Learning through eating is the Jewish way. It will make you feel better.'

Fradel reached two fingers into the jar and extracted the pickle. Under Natania's eyes she nibbled self-consciously on the end of the pickle and tasted bitter vinegar. But her anxiety lessened, and she felt surer of herself, enough to forget she was still a slave to salt and corners and pockets.

Zelda arrived with Irma. The cats scattered at the disruption of the two large women clamouring to get through the door. A light rain had started to fall outside. When the candles were lit, and they were seated in a circle with coffee and sweets, Natania spoke.

'Dybbuks are hard to shift, Fradel. Especially one linked to the menstrual cycle. But I can offer a suggestion. You must get rid of your superstitions, starting with the salt.'

Fradel looked at Natania, not understanding.

'You must, Fradel! Throw your superstitions to the wind, your rituals to the fire,' said Zelda.

At nineteen, Fradel was the youngest in the group and sometimes felt like the others just didn't get her or the troubles that plagued her. She still could not comprehend what they wanted her to do, but was getting an inkling.

'How many packets of salt do you have in your home?' asked Irma.

'Three,' Fradel lied. Closer to ten.

'No more salt,' said Natania.

Fradel's hands twisted in her lap. Had she known she would be forced to stop her ways, she would have sprinkled salt more liberally in the corners of her room before the packets were confiscated. She only had a few crystals remaining in her pockets.

Fradel vowed to never wash this outfit.

'Nothing bad will happen if you stop the salting — I promise, my darling. Once you believe this, its power will stop haunting you and you will be free from more than just the Dybbuk.'

'It's for the best, Fradel,' said Zelda.

Only Irma looked unsure as she gazed into Fradel's face.

The following two weeks went like this: all her rituals and superstitions were amplified, she became exhausted, low in mood, and high in anxiety. Now there was no salting to be done, Fradel didn't know what to do with herself. She paced in agitation. She knew the logic behind Natania's words: that if she stopped salting, Natania thought she would be free of her woes, have more time to herself, and not be a slave to her rituals. But it was clear that the woman didn't understand. Fradel knew that if it wasn't salt, it would be something else. She lay in bed, unable to get up to make herself a meal. Not that she had any ingredients. The shelves were bare — her paintings for art school had been due a few days ago and she'd had to choose between a tube of dark magenta paint or her grocery list that week. She'd been living off the six eggs she had boiled earlier, chopped up with tinned herring in stale pita breads. Finally, her hunger drove her out of the house — this often happened when she tried to save money on food, she ended up starving and spending even more.

She could smell the bagel shop at the end of her street. She couldn't afford to spend money on a bagel every day, but maybe in these two Dybbuk-toe-haunting-not-allowed-to-salt weeks she could make some sacrifices. Irma was inside the bagel shop. Fradel tried to hide, but Irma spotted her.

'Fradel! My dear, you look terrible.'

'It's the Dybbuk-two-weeks.'

'Here, I'll get you a bagel and we can have lunch at my place.'

Fradel did not know if she had strength to socialise, but knew she had to try. Maybe Irma would be a good distraction. On the way to Irma's, they talked and walked.

'I've been investigating cyclical Dybbuks — I think there's a new treatment available, Fradel.'

Fradel's anger flared. Did Irma think that Fradel had not turned over every possible stone? Doctors and physicians refused to believe her when she spoke of the nature of her depression and mood that she knew was linked to the menstrual cycle. But maybe Irma had found a doctor with empathy, who understood, and specialised in Dybbuks? No, it sounded too good to be true.

'This is off-label, Fradel. I know you've been trying. My cousin's daughter-in-law's sister had the same problem, and they found an alternative answer, but you may not like it.'

'What is the answer, you must tell me.'

'Ok, but you didn't hear it from me.'

Irma opened the side door to the outside patio of her home, and they took out their bagels from the brown paper bags, using the wrapping as plates.

'The instructions are the following—'

'Instructions?'

'Yes — you must walk, Fradel, a long way from home. The journey must be yours alone. And on your way, you will rid yourself of the Dybbuk.'

'Where do I walk to?'

'The instructions don't say, but you need to take yourself through the forest, many forests.'

'Walking? That's it?'

'Yes,' said Irma.

'The Dybbuk will probably die of boredom.'

'That's one theory.'

'What's the other?'

'The Dybbuk will begin to talk to you.'

'Why would I want any more voices in my head than I already have?'

'When the Dybbuk talks to you, you will learn its secrets, and how to get rid of it.'

'I'm not a traveller.'

Irma took a big bite of bagel, crunching red onion between her teeth.

'Listen, Fradel, this came from a highly regarded source.'

'The suggestion came from Natania, didn't it?'

'Perhaps. But I trust Natania with my life. She found me Zelda, didn't she?'

'I suppose. So how long will this take?'

Irma shrugged. 'I don't know. Days? Months? Only way to find out is to start walking.'

Fradel left Irma's feeling worse than before but knew her journey was the only way. When she returned home, she planned what to take. She decided on three things: her sketchbook, special ink pot, and the last of her savings. She planned to stop at inns along the way, order the cheapest meal on the menu, and journey on. Her toe throbbed — she knew the Dybbuk probably had other arrangements for her. She swept all traces of salt from the floors. She ate the last pieces of herring she'd saved in the fridge. She clicked the clips shut on her soft leather backpack, opened the front door, and locked it behind her. At the sight of a cat watching her, she did not reopen the door and retreat inside, but instead turned on her heel and began to walk. The Dybbuk began speaking to Fradel halfway down the street.

'So, Fradel, we meet in Human-speak.'

'Hello, Dybbuk. You've caused me much grief.'

'You call that grief?'

'My mood plummets, I feel like I am rotting in my own bedroom, you stay for weeks and then I'm just meant to pick up my life again. You are a disruptive parasite and I want you gone.'

Fradel decided to buy some food supplies before she ventured into the forest. She bought a loaf of bread and considered what else would last the journey.

'Doughnuts,' the Dybbuk whispered. Remembering what Irma had said about the Dybbuk unknowingly giving her secrets to get rid of it, Fradel crouched down in the aisle to listen further.

'Yes them, sprinkled with cinnamon and sugar and filled with jam. And what are these *latkes* in a packet?'

'Potato chips?'

'Yes, get the ones called crinkle cut — they sound interesting.'

Each time the Dybbuk spoke, Fradel looked around to make sure no one else could hear. But the voice seemed to be for her and her alone. She picked up a bottle of water.

'You are kidding me,' it said.

Fradel's anger at the Dybbuk grew but she found herself reaching for the box of chocolates near the counter before she could be asked. Or perhaps the Dybbuk had asked, and Fradel had thought the voice her own. She feared the longer it learnt her ways, and the quieter it became, the more it was taking over her mind.

On the way to the forest, Fradel did things she wouldn't usually do. She crossed the road half-way down the street and not at the lights. She got the urge to pick the neighbour's flowers. Just little things — nothing to get worked up about, but Fradel worried the Dybbuk's urges might start becoming bigger. She wanted to always be in control and felt an uneasy dread filter through her. The kind of dread that could slowly morph into a full-blown panic attack. Fradel remembered her last panic attack: waking up and not being able to breathe, as though a ghost was sitting on her lungs, holding them tight. She needed to get rid of the Dybbuk, and fast.

The Dybbuk was quiet as Fradel's feet took her to the edge of the town, and she stood at the forest entrance. If she headed into the forest now, she might be able to find the first inn by nightfall. Already she wanted a nice hot bath.

'And cholent no doubt. I believe that's on the menu. I wouldn't mind a good bowl of cholent,' said the Dybbuk.

'I guess you experience what I eat too.'

'What you don't understand, Fradel, is that I feel what you feel. It's no fun being a Dybbuk, I assure you.'

'You inhabit me so you can be miserable and taste cholent? Surely not every Dybbuk has a hankering for slow-cooked beef stew.'

'No, but if you don't mind hurrying up so we can reach the inn, I would appreciate it. All you've been eating is stale bits of pita with herring, which I hate by the way.'

At least the Dybbuk hated something — she'd eat more

herring then and wouldn't touch the supplies it had persuaded her to buy. Fradel hurried along the forest path. She stopped to sketch the trees and could hear the Dybbuk's impatience, but the ink was satisfying as she brought the trees into being on her sketchbook. The water from the bottle she'd bought let her play with the ink's light and shade. Painting in this way was a balm for her — she could almost forget that she was possessed by a Dybbuk. But the sun's warmth was disappearing. Packing her supplies back up, she tightened the lid on the bottle of ink so it wouldn't spill, then continued forward. She heard a crack as she turned. Then the sound of one thousand birds erupting into the sky pierced the forest and she saw a huge old tree's heavy dance as it hit the earth. Its graceful decline. The tree's fall had been too close — right across the path she'd only seconds ago stood on.

'Have you cursed me, Dybbuk?'

'Not intentionally. But it would be nice if you stopped gawping at trees and moved on.'

This beast was dangerous and could end in her death. She became aware of a throbbing blister against her smallest toe. The Dybbuk had no right to her body and mind.

'So, hurry up, Fradel, before I fell another tr—'

Fradel kicked a boulder to shut it up. She was sick of the Dybbuk telling her what to do and how to feel. The pain in her toe was incredible.

'*OY GEVALT — MESHUGGENAH*,' the Dybbuk roared, and it did not speak to her again until they reached the inn. Fradel felt she'd won a small victory, though the blister felt like it had grown to twice its size. The doors to the inn looked welcoming and the innkeeper took her money, showed her to a room upstairs, then left her to settle in. The first thing Fradel noticed was the bath. Fradel undressed and saw the side of her toe was red and puffy. She had an idea that she immediately pushed down into a different level of consciousness so the Dybbuk couldn't hear. She filled the bath with hot water, which wrapped silkily around her as she eased herself in. There was a jar of bath salts — she emptied the whole lot into the tub. Then she propped up her toes on the porcelain edge. Her toe pulsed from where the Dybbuk spoke.

'Do you really want me gone, Fradel? You've used an awful lot of salt in this bath. If your toes weren't propped up on the edge, I'd suffocate.'

Fradel thought about the continuous two-week cycle where she couldn't function. A mood put upon her from outside, that wasn't her true self. The tears and upsetting thoughts that swirled.

'First you must eat the cholent and then I will be on my way. Just don't dip your feet into the water. All that salt will ruin my taste buds.'

Fradel knew that cholent alone would not be enough to shift this Dybbuk. She plunged her foot into the bath.

Fradel was drowning. As though a dome had descended over her, pushing her under the water. The dome was the Dybbuk. It was under the water but it was also smothering her from above, stopping her from breathing. The Dybbuk was doing everything to take her with it. Fradel's eyes stung, and she gripped her toe with her fingernails, clawing at the blister as though trying to force out the Dybbuk-splinter within it. She felt sharp pain and went inside the pain. She could see the Dybbuk's energy in her toe — a dark magenta energy like the colour of the paint she'd used in her art school pieces. Fradel pushed the magenta outside her body as though squeezing out the tube of paint. Then she heaved with all her might against the dome. She did this with her anger against the Dybbuk, and the doctors, and a society that refused to prioritise research into women's issues — periods and all. Resistant at first, the dome gave way as suddenly as it had been suctioned in place. She listened to the shrillness of the glass' music as the tiniest crack in the windowpane splintered and air returned to fill her lungs. Fradel looked down at her toe and saw pus and a small bloom of blood swirling through the water where the Dybbuk had left from the force of her visualisation, her anger, her will.

She inhaled breath after shaky breath, then stepped out of the tub, dried herself with a towel and put her clothes on. She walked into the hall, cats twining themselves around her. She ordered a bowl of the chef's special — not cholent with beans — but schnitzel with peas. After the shock of near drowning wore off with each mouthful of fried schnitzel, Fradel did not get up and rejoice that her good mood had returned to her. She did not cry or yell at the rafters. When a cat jumped into her lap, Fradel did not push it off but stroked the cat's ears and realised her superstitions had left her along with the Dybbuk. She was back to who she recognised she was. She felt settled and at peace. And now her new life could begin. Fradel finished her meal and stared at her reflection held within the spoon. To not have her energy and mood funnelled endlessly downwards, but to feel okay again was a gift. Her world swelled with the sweetness of relief. Tonight, she would sleep better than she had in months.

SURGE

Em Readman

I dodge the bindis on the way over to the shed, keeping my eyes two steps ahead to avoid any prickles sinking into my heels. Jude usually mows, but they have been working a lot lately. I pull the doors open and rummage through the storage containers and toolboxes. I need a hammer. Nails would help, too. The steps leading to the verandah have warped in the cycle of rain and heat this summer, and my thongs always catch on the boards when I run up them. I'm going to fix it before Jude gets home. He keeps mentioning it, but they haven't found the time yet.

It's hot in the shed. My head starts to pound, like my brain is thrumming against my skull. I take myself over to the shade of the mango tree before things in my vision start to get blurry. A few of the mangos have fallen, abandoned in the heat, and the air is sweet and sticky under the tree. I look down at my shirt: the fabric is turning a darker brown from sweat patches and my chest strains to get the breath in. The heat is all anyone can talk about this week. There's a storm coming sometime, and the temperature has been climbing as it gets closer. It's hot and muggy, and the sweat makes my hair cling to my face at the front.

I start to feel a bit better, so I head back over to the shed to keep looking. I click open a tacklebox and find a handful of nails that look long enough to hold the planks down. I find the hammer in the bottom compartment of the box. I stick it through the belt loop of my shorts to keep my hands free and throw the nails in my pocket. I leave the shed doors open and hop back across the yard the way I came.

The old nails in the boards have rusted over time, so I pull them out and try to find a new groove in the timber to replace them. I line up the first nail, closing one eye as I steady the hammer over it. I bring it down over the nail, but my wrist moves the wrong way and the nail comes out of place and pings off into the front yard. I fish another out of my pocket. Jude is better at this than me, but they're good at a lot of things. When Dad taught us about taking care of the house, Jude always got the hang of it so quickly even if he hadn't done the task before. They have strong hands like Dad does. I want strong hands like they both have. My hands are scrawny, with skinny fingers and bitten nails. Jude says our hands compliment each other, but I'd rather be more like him. The next nail goes in easier. I try giving short, clean taps rather than trying to get it in one fell swoop. The board sits flush against the others now. I set to work on the next step, getting rid of the tripping hazard one warped piece of timber at a time.

'Hard at work?'

I look up. Jude's coming in the gate, in their dark green uniform. He's come off shift late. He should have been home a while ago, but they struggle to say no to helping out. I focus on lining up the next nail.

'Getting there,' I say, as I bring the hammer down. I hit it off centre, and it bends the nail at a weird angle. Jude laughs as they reach the steps.

'Here, I'll show you a trick,' Jude says. He tries to take the hammer out of my hand.

'No,' I say, moving the hammer out of his reach. 'I can do it, I've already done a few of the steps. I can do it.'

He pulls back. They push their hair out of their face, and breathe in and out deeply. He seems tired. They rest one foot on the first step.

'I believe you, Sacha,' he says as he moves to step past me. On the step before he reaches me his boot catches on a board and he almost trips into my side. He grabs onto my shoulder to steady himself.

'Watch it,' I say, as I ready another nail.

Jude doesn't reply, he just makes his way inside. He doesn't close the sliding door all the way, so I listen to them moving around the entryway and rifling through the kitchen. This always happens after he finishes work. Jude is in his first year after the graduate paramedic program. Even when he was out on placement, they'd always come back starving after work. I remember what he looked like walking the stage at his graduation, beaming as he looked out across the crowd, sweating bullets in the academic robes. The verandah steps are in the full afternoon sun, and I'm sweating the way Jude did in those robes. I wipe it away, staining my sleeve, and keep on working on the steps. The last nail sinks into the timber — all the steps back in line.

I run up to the sliding door, ready to show off my handiwork. Jude is asleep on the couch, the one we carried home from the kerbside collection down the street a few months back. It's a pine-lime green, with dark wood furnishings. It's disgusting, but Jude loves it. He's still wearing the paramedics get-up. I look at him: his strong frame, strong hands, and light stubble. He's a fair bit older than me, but I can't wait until I can be like him, to be stronger and taller and more masculine. I can't imagine caring about the work I do as much as they do though. I don't even know what I care about beyond the temperature going down again.

'Are we still going to go down to the beach?' I ask, but only quietly.

Jude stirs, half-asleep.

'Yeah, we can still go,' he says, peeling himself off the couch to get changed out of his uniform.

We usually go to the beach after school, once it starts to cool off for the night. I walk ankle-deep along the shoreline, careful to not let the waves nip me and leave my legs itching. Jude walks further up the beach, on the soft sand, his eyes always on the part of the water that drops off from light blue to black. I spot a few ghost crabs scuttling along the shore. I pick one up in my hands, and feel its little legs skitter over me. We used to go mud crab catching, but there's a hold on putting out the crab pots since their numbers started declining. We learnt about it in science. When the crab eggs get too warm in development, it skews their birth sex ratios. The mud crabs mostly come out male now, and it's tanked the population.

'Got a text from Dad,' Jude says, coming over to put his feet in the water.

I let the crab go and it darts off. They hand me their phone and I read it. There's a photo of Dad, sitting in a chair on his verandah. *Hope you're both getting on ok. Not too hot down here, but warmer today. Call soon.*

'A man of many words,' I say.

'Yeah,' Jude says. 'It's never been his strong suit, hey?'

We laugh. Dad lives down in Tasmania; he moved earlier this year. It's too hot for him to stay in Queensland, at home, with us. Tassie is one of the places the oldies flock to and it's packed down there now. We were going to go too, but Dad hasn't found a spot big enough for all of us yet. He says we'll only have to hold out a little longer. Jude doesn't mind staying here with me, he says. One day we'll all get down there together. We haven't put anything in Dad's empty room yet.

'Will we go visit soon?' I ask.

'I hope so,' they reply.

'Do you have work tomorrow?'

'Nah,' Jude says, 'I'm on call, don't think they'll need me unless it's a scorcher.'

He never says no when they call him in. The ambulance service is always busy now and Jude always goes to help. He pulls his shirt off and heads into the water. I sit down in the sand and watch. Jude has swimmer's shoulders, their arms strong as he slicks his hair back and wipes the salt water from his eyes. He has an ear piercing that he made with a fishhook one time. He offered to do mine too, but I said no. They wave to me, calling out.

'Come on!'

I take my shirt off and lay it by my thongs. I step into the waves, wading in until the water reaches my knees. No matter how hot it gets outside, the water is always a relief. Jude is out further, lying on his back. He gently floats over the swell of the waves before they break closer to the shore. The scars on their chest look lived in, faded to white over the years. The scars contrast with the collection of tattoos running down his arms. They breathe in and out deeply, without any struggle on the inhale.

There are a lot of things about Jude that I want. His strong hands, his deep breathing pattern, his flat chest. Jude flips over and dives under, pulling his legs out of the water and into a handstand. It's funny looking at someone who's so serious all the time dicking around. He comes back up for air and swims back to stand with me in the shallows.

'Have you been wearing that all day?' Jude asks, pointing at my binder.

I look out at the waves, bringing my arms up to cover my chest.

'No,' I lie.

'Yes you have, I can see the lines from the fabric digging into your shoulders.'

'Why'd you ask then?'

'You're gonna hurt yourself. It's too hot not to be taking breaks.'

I lift up my arms to stretch and wade back in to put my shirt on. The binder has been hurting since I went over to the backyard shed, but I wasn't going to tell Jude that. I can hear them calling after me.

'If it's cutting into your skin you've got the wrong size,' he says. 'You shouldn't even be wearing a binder for more than eight hours, especially not in this heat. Have you even washed it?'

I ignore him, and make for our beach exit. Jude is impossible to stop when he gets on a medical tangent.

'You're going to get dizzy, or get heatstroke, if you're not being careful,' they say. 'Besides, even if it wasn't this hot you wouldn't want to have it on this long. What about your ribs? One day, I'm going to get a callout and it will be to our house because you've passed out in the front yard—'

'Shut the fuck up, Jude!'

He stops. I haven't ever yelled at him like that.

'There's no need for that,' Jude says.

'There's no need for what you're doing,' I say. 'I know it's not the optimal choice.'

'What you're doing is far from optimal.'

'Well, Jude, what else am I supposed to do?'

He's standing there in his shorts, shaking sand out of his shirt. Looking at his scars just makes me angrier.

'I don't get to have what you have yet,' I say. 'This makes me feel good.'

'Feeling good and being safe are different things.'

'Stop with your paramedic preachy bullshit, Jude!' I feel hot, and my breath is shaking.

'Sacha, I'm trying to help you.'

I turn away and make my way up the dunes.

'Sacha!'

I kick off running. The streets are getting dark. I feel the residual heat of the bitumen radiating into the balls of my feet. The air feels almost liquid, still muggy and heavy even at nighttime. I gulp down breath after breath as I run through the streets, my chin beginning to wobble. I grind my teeth to stop it. My chest burns. Jude doesn't run after me, but he won't be far behind. Our house is only a few streets back from the beach.

I reach the steps and fly up them; the nails have held well. I swing a right and sit on the wicker chair at the end of the verandah. I'm out of breath, and the fabric is chafing my skin and Jude is right and everything hurts. I snake my hands under my shirt and pull the binder away from my chest. The pressure softens and I breathe deeply, throwing my head back.

'Should I leave you alone, or do you want to keep talking with me?' Jude asks, as he comes up the steps, taking a seat on the top one.

'Depends,' I shrug.

'I'm not trying to upset you, Sacha. I just don't want to see you hurting yourself without realising.'

'I have to do this. It doesn't feel right if it's not flat.'

Jude pauses, and looks down at his own chest, just for a moment.

'Safety comes first,' he says.

'Feeling myself comes first. You don't get it,' I say, and I watch Jude's gaze harden as the words hit him.

'I do get it, obviously I get it. I did it. For a lot longer than you have.'

The knot in my stomach surges upward.

'You don't! You didn't bind in these boiling summers we're stuck in, it wasn't as hot then. Your chest wasn't at all like mine, either, and you know it. The waitlists were so much shorter when you were on them. Dad was here when you were going through this, too.'

I'm standing up now. Jude stays sat on the top step, his face turned to stone. It's frustrating how calm he always looks. I watch him for a reaction, for something to snap or waver.

'I'm here for you going through this,' they say, softly. It wasn't the part of what I said I thought he would respond to.

'You don't need to be a part of my decision,' I reply.

'All I want is for you to take breaks, and not wear the binder when you're out in the sun. It's on the instruction card if you don't believe me.'

'I've read the stupid instruction card,' I say. 'Leave me alone.'

'Fine.'

He leaves me on the verandah, heading inside. I hear the shower turn on. I try not to cry but it comes up out of my throat before I can catch it. I sit back down on the chair and pull my legs up to my chest. I use both hands to pull the bottom band of elastic up to create breathing space in my binder. I don't want to take it off yet, even if it hurts. The crickets are out in force tonight, loud and chirping in unison with the cicadas. I pull out my phone to call Dad. It goes through to voicemail. Things are hard without him here.

My breaths shudder in and out. Sometimes I think Jude forgets what it's like, even though he shouldn't. His work comes before anything else; getting through to Jude means getting past the medic in him. It's like he's forgotten how endless this all feels. I go inside my room before the shower stops so I don't have to speak to him.

When I wake up, Jude is gone. It's sweltering, as always. I check the clock: 11:50am. There's a note on the counter.

Called in. It's going to be hot today, be safe. 4.17am left.

His handwriting sounds like he already knew I'd slept in my binder. I don't usually leave it on, but last night I couldn't face up to taking it off. My ribs ache, but I push through it. I fold the note up and throw it in the bin, and think about texting to ask when he'll be back. Jude always says yes when work calls, always. I decide not to text. I am not holding out to see them, and it's almost been the length of a shift since he left. I shake out my shirt to create some air and open the windows to make a cross breeze. Jude's left without his belt: it's still on the arm of the sickly green couch. I think about his uniform, how hot the canvas jumpsuit would be, how he should just worry about himself instead of me. Hypocrite. I sink into the couch, but the fibres catch on my arms and the back of my neck, the velvet making the sweat cling to me. The texture is awful in this heat, so I stand and make my way outside. My eyes are itchy and puffy. Out on the verandah, one of the boards on the top step has sprung back up. It didn't hold overnight, or Jude tripped it up again on the way out. The nails and hammer are still out there, so I nip inside to pull shorts on and head out to fix it, again.

The sun beats down on my back as I sit on the steps. The sweat on my forehead pours out, collecting on the top of my brow. It's so hot it makes me feel sick. I yawn as I line up the nail. I try to focus on it, closing one eye to steady my vision. I think about Jude trying to intervene yesterday, always offering advice when I don't want it. The hammer comes down. I miss. It collides with my thumbnail, making a gruelling *smack* before the nail splits down the middle. I cry out, wrapping my fingers around my thumb to try and stem the shooting pain. I stumble down the steps, spinning around in circles while swearing. The pain thrums from my hand up my arm, and I start trying to breathe through it, long, deep breaths like Jude says to do. I can't manage anything more than shallow and shaky. I swallow to try and get more air down but it doesn't help. My thumb is radiating with pain. I need to breathe.

I pull my oversized shirt off one-handed. With my fingers wrapped around my thumb, I try to use my other hand to get the binder off. It's tight, and hot and sweaty and my eyesight is swelling with pins and needles. Everything burns: my head, my chest, my ribs, my feet on the concrete, my hand. I can't get a good grip to pull it off. I feel myself start to panic, desperate to get the air in. I cannot breathe.

'Sacha!'

Jude's voice carries across the yard, and he jumps the fence. They're back, they can help me. I raise my arms up as he reaches me and yanks the fabric up and off, tossing my shirt at me as he starts to guide me up the stairs. I suck in the air. With the tightness off my chest, the pain contracts into my nail. I pull my shirt on while he tends to my hand, pulling ice out of the freezer and a bandage wrap from the first aid kit. He treats my thumb as I'm gasping for air, coming back to myself as my breathing slows.

'You okay?'

'Yeah,' I heave. 'I'm okay.'

'How do your ribs feel?'

'Not good.'

'I bet,' he laughs gently as he threads a safety pin through the bandage and secures it.

'I'm going to take a break from wearing it until the humidity breaks,' I say.

'You won't want to hear this,' Jude starts, 'but lots of people are getting heat exhaustion in these heat waves. Loads. That's what you have as well.'

I don't reply, I just breathe in and out.

'It's a hard summer this year,' Jude says.

'Nothing's getting any easier,' I say, starting to choke on my words again.

Jude walks up to me, and pulls me in, wrapping me in his arms. I look up and he has his eyes closed, like they're trying not to tear up. The circles under his eyes are more pronounced than usual. He's been crying too. Jude looks just like Dad does when he's tired.

'No. It's not,' he says, 'but I've got you. Listen, I have you some binding tape you can try. I'll help you learn how to put it on. Safely, of course. And I'm sorry for upsetting you yesterday.'

'Thanks, Jude. I'm sorry too.'

'Keep the ice on your thumb.'

Jude gets up and heads over to the couch, collapsing into it like he did yesterday. I can feel my pulse radiating outwards from my nail. My hand is expertly bandaged. His job is to fix these kinds of things, but it doesn't make his skill less impressive. I lie down on the concrete floor to cool my body. They look over, slide down to join me, and we listen to the crickets buzz away outside. I focus on Jude's hands. They're strong because they know how to heal, how to carry me, carry all of this. I just have to let them. Jude knows how to put things back together.

'We could go to the beach later, when it cools down?' I ask.

Jude's face twists then softens as he looks over to me. They nod.

'When it cools down,' they say.

HOSTEL NIGHTS LIKE THESE

Henry Farnan

He could hear it when he pressed his head against the wall. It was faint. Skin slapped against skin with a squelch that melded them together as they moved. Anyone would say that sort of thing doesn't make a sound. But Lon knew what to listen for. That, and the moaning.

Lon had his elbows on his headboard under the stag's head that had been mounted there years ago. As he listened, his rapid breath bounced back against the eggshell walls.

There was a click and the twist of metal on the other side of the room. Lon instinctively leapt away from his headboard to the opposite end of the bed. His bed springs squealed as he landed. He tore open a book. The door creaked.

'Lawrence,' she said, her sharp voice making him cringe.

Lon tried to look as engrossed in his book as possible before looking up at his mother. She was wearing her old nightgown from before his dad had left. Lon was in his pyjamas too.

'Rubbish needs to go out.'

'Uh,' he said, swallowing a little, 'sure.'

She turned to leave before scowling at the wall behind him.

'And try to ignore those men in Room 1, won't you?'

The door creaked to a close and he was left lonely once more. In so many years living with his mother, scowls like that had meant nothing to Lon. All those tiny eyerolls, scoffs and spits — they'd just been part of his life growing up. But now, in the years since his father had fled the hostel, they evolved into something else in his head. The echo of her scoffing words, the glister of her spit on the door of Room 1 — they stirred up something inside him. It wasn't anger or sadness of any kind, but more a curiosity. Especially on nights like this when those images and sounds in his head could dance with the moans reverberating from Room 1.

'Sure, Mum,' Lon replied, even though he guessed his mother was already in her own bedroom. He tossed his book across the bed, which he only now realised he'd been holding upside down. Praying that his mother hadn't noticed the upside-down cover, Lon groaned as he ran his hands through his hair.

Lon had the kind of ginger hair that he constantly defended as strawberry blond. It had been a long time since he'd needed to though; his friends never visited the hostel anymore. He pulled his freckled hands down his face. Their last visit was nearly two years ago now, and the woods had been off limits long before then, ever since his uncle had been eaten. Lon spent his waning adolescent days and nights reading the same books he'd read ten years ago and trying to get the hostel's shitty wi-fi working. Lon combed through his curls with his hands again and headed for the door. As the door creaked shut behind him, a clump of pale flesh from Lon's fingers clung to his wiring curls. It had come from one of his fingers.

The neon sign outside Oasler Hostel was always on. Day and night. A pale blue beacon on that lonely, winding road that snaked through the dense woods. It signalled humans to a refuge and snarled at the other things in the woods to leave it alone — forced them to stay in the dark.

Tonight, there were two cars in the carpark. A red car that Lon had seen many times before and a black car he didn't recognise. He knew they belonged to the two men in Room 1.

Lon lugged two black garbage bags behind him, their colour straining to grey with effort. Cans, jars and his mother's bottles scraped against the uneven ground. It was the only sound Lon could hear in the sign's sunken halo of light. Lon couldn't say the same for what lay beyond the light, in the woods. It wasn't anything he could hear, but he knew they were out there.

The rhythmic scraping of Lon's lugging was broken by a loud clatter. Cans spilled out onto the concrete from a tear in one of the bags. It had caught on a loose rock.

'Perfect,' muttered Lon. He left the torn bag and dragged the other two to the bins where, with an ungraceful cacophony, he tossed them in. The bins sat directly beneath the neon sign. Lon tried to rub his shoulders lax from the weight, staring out at the woods beyond the neon veil. Like every other time, he could've sworn there were eyes staring back at him. He scurried back after the torn bag.

As he collected the cans in his arms, a square of yellow light hit his face. Lon's head flicked up on instinct. His mother was watching him from the kitchen window.

He slipped the cans back into the hole of the bag and carried it by the opening to the bins. All this, illuminated in the blue light of the sign. It stayed on. That was the rule. His mother had made it the night his uncle was eaten.

'An extra safeguard against those things,' she'd said to Lon. The way she'd cradled his head in her arms had been hindering Lon's persistent gaze at the red switchbox on the wall.

'But uncle will be back, won't he?' Lon had asked. 'Back with a body?'

'Not if we keep the sign on.'

Neither of them, not Lon or his mother, knew that her curse would only keep out the creatures. And she would never know the truth, for Lon's uncle would never return.

When Lon closed the bin lids and turned back to the hostel, his mother had abandoned the kitchen window and the square of yellow light was gone from the carpark. The sky was morphing between purple and navy — Lon's cue to head back inside.

He walked briskly back to the door of the hostel before he noticed the window of Room 1 and its curtain slightly ajar. He crouched by it, listening. There it was again. The sound of skin melding with skin, and the moaning that always accompanied.

He pushed against the balls of his feet and met the sill of the window with the freckled bridge of his nose. It wasn't anything he hadn't seen before. The man with the moustache, who now knelt over the other, brought lots of men to Lon's mother's hostel. As they touched and pulled their bodies apart, their skin stretched against each other like warm, melted cheese.

A wave of guilt washed over Lon. He knew his mother didn't approve of him watching what the man with the moustache did in his room, but Lon's pang of guilt wasn't about what his mother may think. The shame that roiled in his stomach was more a product of having to lurk in the shadows in the first place.

Something grinded against the concrete of the car park, and headlights flashed against Lon's crouching figure. An old, white car pulled into a space, and raucous, lively voices spilled out from the open windows. Lon bounced from his crouch and darted for the door into reception.

A tiny strand of skin from Lon's nose hung like an icicle from the windowsill. He didn't notice. He was too busy trying to cool his burning ears as he slipped through the door into the light. Hopefully they hadn't noticed him crouching there in his pyjamas.

Lon came out of his room again when he heard his mother call from reception. There were three people around Lon's age standing across the desk from her.

'And no loud music past midnight either,' she said, her head buried in the top drawer. She'd make any excuse to avert her gaze from kids like this. Lon could've sworn he'd seen two of them before.

One was a girl with a messy, blonde mullet. Lon knew she was a girl because she had a patch on her black denim jacket in the shape of a middle finger that read, I'm A Fucking Girl. Then there was the other familiar face. Their dark, calloused fingers played with the tarot card they'd pegged to the spokes of their wheelchair. Their hair faded into tight, thick curls that were tinted with a pale silver. This person had stayed here at least once before. Lon was sure of it. Part of that was because Lon could see their body. It was a new body. The kind people got from the woods. The other person he didn't recognise; they had black nail polish flaking from their small fingers. They were staring aimlessly at their ripped canvas sneakers.

'Lawrence.' His attention darted to his mother at her insistent tone. She was staring at him, waiting. His eyes widened, heart thumping. He was supposed to have heard something she'd said. He swallowed and tried to force his heart rate back down with his saliva.

'Sorry?' he asked slowly, angling for his mother to be merciful and repeat her instruction. From the corner of his eye, he could've sworn he'd seen the girl with the mullet smile.

'Show them to their room,' his mother repeated, sliding a key across the counter at him. 'I'm going to bed.'

Lon leant against the door of Room 3 and grunted as he elbowed it open. The three guests filed in, and Lon brought their cases in after them, setting them down by the first bed. Room 3 had pink walls and there was a stag's head mounted above each bed.

The person with the silver hair gawked at one of the heads. 'That's not them, is it?' they asked, turning to Lon.

He was taken aback. Not even his father or his uncle had talked about the creatures of the woods so brazenly.

Lon blinked. 'No, they're just normal stags.'

'That's kinda gross,' the girl with the blonde mullet remarked.

'It was my dad and my uncle. They used to go hunting all the time, but they stopped.'

'After the perytons found this place?' The person with the silver hair looked at Lon with excitement in their eyes.

Lon gave a wary nod.

'Hello?' The deep voice behind Lon made him jump.

A man stood at the door of Room 3. He was holding his shoes in his hand and his skin was pouring over the scuffed leather. He breathed heavily and his forehead glossed with sweat. It shone in the pink walls' bouncing light. Lon recognised him. He'd just been in Room 1 with the man with the moustache.

'Can I help you?' Lon instinctively stood up straighter and his tone changed as though he was working behind reception.

'Your toilets are locked,' he said, jerking a thumb down the other end of the hostel where the communal bathrooms were.

'Yeah, sorry,' said Lon. 'My mother has me lock them after 10pm. She doesn't like it when things get in there.'

The man turned back out into the parking lot and swore loudly. He dropped his shoes and started towards the woods.

'Should we …' the one with the ripped sneakers finally piped up, 'should we stop him?'

'Did you see his skin, Arty?' The girl with the blonde mullet looked at them.

'It was dripping,' said Arty. 'Like mine.' They put their thumb to their index finger and pulled them apart. The tips stayed connected like slime.

Lon stared at the guests, unsure of what to say. He only then realised that the girl's ear lobes were slightly longer than they should've been, and her cheekbones were throbbing beneath her golden skin — she had a peryton waiting as well. A hand of dark, calloused fingers brushed warm against Lon's forearm.

'I'm helping these two get their bodies,' they said, like it would calm Lon down. 'Arty's been wanting his for years now, and we met Sarahlee a few months back.'

They'd said it so normally. Everything these three spoke about — their bodies, the perytons — it was as though they weren't afraid of what people thought. They weren't hiding from anyone.

'And this,' Sarahlee bent down, patting them on the shoulders, 'is Lyric.'

Lyric looked up at Lon and smiled, before settling their hand back on the tarot card in their wheel. Sarahlee had a look on her face like she knew something Lon didn't. In fact, now that he looked around, it seems like they all did.

A scream ripped through the silence of the car park. The four of them piled out the small doorway, but there was nothing to see. Lon darted across the verandah and peeked through the curtain of Room 1. The man with the moustache was asleep, alone.

'There!' Lyric's arm shot out, pointing beyond the blue light of the sign. Lon strained his eyes with everyone else. A silhouetted figure took shape in the darkness as his eyes adjusted — four legs and winged. It was bent down, eating something. Eating the writhing man.

'He must've gone to pee in the woods.' Sarahlee flicked her mullet from her collar as she spoke.

'At least he'll get his body now,' said Arty. 'He needed it.'

Lon watched as Arty and Sarahlee examined their own dripping fingers, before his eyes and ears were drawn back to those shapes and screams just beyond the sign's light. A hand tugged at his sleeve. It was Lyric again.

'We're going to turn in for the night,' they said, starting to turn their wheelchair back to Room 3. 'Thank you for being so welcoming, Lawrence.' They winked at him before turning fully and wheeling back to the room. It took a moment for Arty and

Sarahlee to follow their friend.

'You can call me Lon,' he called after them. 'If you want.'

'Great!' Lyric called back over their shoulder, before wheeling through the door. 'I will.'

Arty hung back at the door with a grin stretched across his face. 'And you can call them if you want!'

Sarahlee's hand smacked Arty from inside the door before pulling the grinning boy into Room 3 with her.

Lon struggled to wipe the smile off his face before he turned back to the woods. Beyond the threshold of the blue neon, the peryton and the man with his new body both stood and calmly walked into the woods together. Lon sighed. He'd have to call someone in the morning to tow the man's car.

There was a small wooden clock that sat atop the big red switch-box on the wall in reception. As it struck 9am, Lon was already knee-deep in the day's work. The ticking of the little clock on the switch box bore into Lon's head as he sorted the keys onto their hooks. He tried to shake off last night's dream.

The dream had been mostly the same as every other time. In it, he was standing on his toes watching the car park through the kitchen window, and his mother stood out in the dusk, shaking his father's rifle at two creatures. This was before his mother had made the rule about the sign. It was a dream about the night she made it.

Lon's subconscious never remembered exactly what she'd been screaming. The only sequence of images that he had retained was the sight of his uncle lying, all bones and muscles, on the concrete. He'd just been mauled by the larger of the two perytons standing silently beneath the unlit sign.

A peryton was a bloodthirsty creature. A winged stag with antlers like gnarled branches, rows of fangs, and talons that could crush stone. The larger of these two had a shadow that wasn't its own. Not the shadow of a winged stag, but an exact copy of his uncle's.

Lon had watched as his uncle stood up. A new body seeped through the breaks between his exposed innards and bubbled forth from the fang-made cavities in his skeleton. To Lon, his uncle looked exactly the same, if even a little nonchalant.

The shadow of the peryton writhed and was no longer his uncle's but its own. A beautiful, dark reflection of the creature. Lon's uncle twisted his head towards Lon's mother and spoke.

'There is nothing here for me now.' His voice was muffled by the bubbling of fresh flesh. 'You stay away from us.' Lon was never sure if they were the real words his uncle had said, or if his subconscious was just making up for his faulty memory.

Like every other time in this dream, his uncle's peryton folded its wings and beckoned to his uncle to follow it into the woods until they were gone from view, gone from Lon's wailing mother.

Like every other time in this dream, the smaller peryton would stand staring blankly at Lon's mother as she screamed at it, rifle cocked.

'If your kind ever come under the light of this sign again,' she waved the rifle at the small creature, 'I will make sure you don't make it back into those woods.' Her curse was veiled in neon blue as, for the final time, the sign automatically blinked on. She'd never turn it off again.

Lon could remember the way the small peryton cowered and

fled, but in all the times he'd relived this memory he could never see the beast's shadow. He'd awoken sweaty many times wishing it might have been his own.

The only thing that was different about the dream last night, was something Lon noticed before his mother had cursed the perytons to leave them alone. It was before the sign had blinked on and before his uncle had entered the woods in his new flesh. When his uncle had turned to speak to his mother, his uncle's face was not his own, as it had been so many times. The ginger curls, the pale complexion: this time, his uncle had worn Lon's face.

The ticking of the little clock perched on the switchbox was so loud in Lon's ears that morning, he almost didn't hear his mother walking into reception with the laundry basket.

'Here's the new sheets for Room 3,' his mother said, hauling the basket up onto the counter. 'Are they still out?'

This was his mother's way of telling him to go change their sheets for her. He knew better than to try and say no.

'I think so,' he said, sliding the basket over the counter and into his arms. The key jangled around his finger as he walked out of reception and pulled the door shut with his foot. His only company on the walk down the short, concrete verandah was their white car that watched him like a creature stalking its prey. Lon wondered to himself, as he pushed against the door of Room 3, if it was the only thing out there that was watching him.

Lyric and their friends had clothes and books and bags strewn across the orange carpet. When he closed the door, Lon expected to feel lonely in the empty room. But as he escaped the watchful eyes of the car, he didn't feel lonely nor did the room feel empty. He pushed aside some clothes to make space for himself and the basket beside the first bed and knelt down. The eyes of the dead head on the wall above were watching him. Lon could feel it.

So many times, Lon had wished he could climb up onto the bed and peel back its stiff mouth with his fingers. Then he could feel the sharp, serrated fangs of a peryton on his skin. If they were even there. The truth was, Lon had no idea if this was the head of a peryton or just a regular stag. He wished it was a peryton though.

As he pulled the fresh white sheets over their beds, Lon imagined that, were the creature's blood still fresh, it might drip down onto them and stain the pure white sheets with crimson. Then the perytons — its family — might tear out of the tree line to retrieve their fallen kin. That is, if scent was even how they tracked. Maybe then they might take its body back with them. To wherever it is they live.

There had been many times he'd considered wandering into the woods, to see if there really was a peryton with his shadow out there waiting for him. But he knew the wrath of his mother and he didn't want to face it again.

As Lon finished up with the sheets, he picked up the basket again and headed for the door. A wave of shock jolted up his body as his foot caught on an upturned book, and the basket fell back to the carpet.

Like the silk of a spider's web, long strands of pale pink skin stretched up from the wicker to Lon's fingers and palms. Lon's stomach turned and his heart began to beat like desperate wings. The further he pulled back his fingers, the more skin would trail down the strains, making them thicker and thicker. He shook his hands furiously to try and detach them, but he only ended up tangling his melting flesh into a complex web. Lon's head was clouding with anxiety and anticipation all at once. He wanted to scream, cry, laugh — anything! There was nothing in his throat.

Moments became minutes became who-knows-how-long. He knew there was no hiding this from his mother. With one last look at the stag's mounted head on the pink wall, he knew he had to meet the real thing.

Lon's search for his mother's hiding place for the switchbox key had been in vain, so he'd had to break it open. It was the banging of his fists against the glass that drew her out to reception at 8:25pm.

His fists left behind chunks of flesh as he pounded against the rusty red door of the switch box. It didn't hurt the way Lon had expected it to. The bloodless holes in his hands were melded over by his liquefying skin.

'What do you think you're doing?' Lon's mother screeched at him over the sound of him breaking the metal hinges.

Lon winced at her words. He dared not look at her, only realising she was right next to him when he saw her hand recoil from his fists.

'No,' she uttered, her breath shorting — hyperventilating. 'No, it can't be you as well.'

There were so many things Lon wished he had the strength to say to that. So many things for himself, for his uncle, for everyone who's had their shadow cast by a peryton.

'I want this.' That was all Lon could think to say. The little red door to the switchbox came free, sticking to the flesh of his hand.

His mother was saying things, he could hear the sobs in her voice, but Lon wasn't paying attention. He flicked the little switch and the blue neon from the parking lot died. The first time he had experienced pitch black in years. He felt his way to the door and could feel his flesh leaving behind sticky traces on every surface he touched to get there.

His mother's grasping fingers found his melting forearm — they disappeared fast. As the fresh night air hit Lon out of reception, he heard his mother gag and retch at him. He slammed the door shut on her sobbing objections. She screeched at him as he locked it behind himself and wedged the little red door of the switchbox against the handle, making it impossible for her to open. Impossible for her to get to him, ever again.

'Lon?'

A voice came from behind him. Lon turned to see it was Lyric. The only light out in the parking lot now was the moon's glow on the concrete. In the silver spotlight, Lyric was wheeling themself ahead of their friends towards him.

'Sorry we were out all day,' they said. 'We wanted to try and find the perytons to get Sarahlee and Arty their new bodies.'

Lon looked over to them. 'Any luck?'

Arty looked dejected being comforted by Sarahlee. But despite the concern she wore for Arty, Sarahlee's eyes gave away an extreme euphoria. Lon noted to himself that she didn't look any different with her new body, but maybe that wasn't the point.

'Did the sign go out?' Lyric asked, pulling Lon's focus back. Their question drew Lon's ear to his mother's wailing in the hostel behind them. He pushed her from his mind.

'I turned it off,' he said. He flexed his hands and a nervous laugh bubbled up from his stomach. It was then that the three of them seemed to collectively notice Lon's melting flesh.

'I knew it!' Sarahlee said, jumping in excitement.

Lon grinned and stared up at the dead sign.

There was something extra on its rim, clinging to the letters with its taloned grip. It spread its wings before its lunar halo, and it was gone. A dark shape flitted through the night. Arty smacked against the concrete and screamed at the beast that had landed on top of him. It tore at Arty's shirt, bringing his melting skin with it as the peryton feasted.

Lon circled the feasting creature and watched its shadow in the moonlight. It was next to Arty's and it was the same as Arty's.

'It's so trippy,' Sarahlee whispered under Arty's cries, 'seeing a creature with the same shadow as yours.'

Lon's instinct was to run to his aid, but the one thing he knew about perytons was that once it had found its fated prey, there was no intervening. Besides, this was why Arty was here in the first place. Without being stripped of his melting flesh, how would he ever acquire his new body?

'Lon.' Lyric wasn't looking at Arty's peryton. Their gaze was cast out across the carpark. Lon followed it and saw what they were staring at. Its antlers were perfectly symmetrical, meeting at the crown of a body whose fur was a rich brown. He'd never seen one standing so peacefully. It probably knew that Lon wouldn't put up a fight. Deep down, Lon knew it too.

The peryton walked slowly, its wings folded against its back. It had no need to fly. Its antlers shone like fresh bone as it entered the moon's spotlight. Lon looked down at his own shadow to confirm.

'You're right,' he said to Sarahlee, 'it is weird seeing your own shadow on something else.'

His mother's pounding on the door broke through Arty's muffled cries and the sound of his heart in his head.

'You can ignore her,' Lyric said, their voice measured against the cacophony of sounds that battered the cool air of that night. 'There's nothing to be scared of.'

'I know,' he muttered, swallowing a lump in his throat.

Lon's eardrums scratched as the peryton strode, clawing its talons against the tarmac. His eyes stayed fixed on the peryton, and it stared back at him.

'I want this,' he said.

Lon's peryton bared its teeth and closed the space between them with a swift glide through the night air. Its breath was warm against his forehead.

An involuntary laugh leapt from Lon's throat. A sign of nerves, he figured. He wished it hadn't shown, not in front of Lyric and their friends. He closed his eyes and let the air out of his lungs. A peryton only gets one human shadow. However long his mother had tried to delay, he knew this was always meant to happen.

A hand slipped between Lon's melting fingers, and a warm voice met his ears. It was Lyric's.

'Good luck, Lon.'

He heard the peryton's fangs part, and they were cold on his melting flesh. Lon's skin left his bones behind. He was about to be more whole than ever.

THE VAMPIRE AND THE AUNTY

Lin Blythe

The mind is like a garden,
Where mycelium sprouts, garlic flowers,
Chilli blooms and pepperberry flourishes.
Its fragrance draws outsiders,
Who uproot and poison our bowers—
How our pride impoverishes.
A roof of cloudy glass keeps warmth in
And keeps white robes out at all hours
Why risk the stars if your child perishes?

A song of the Jerlipiur people
(author unknown)

'But garlic is good for your health!'

The short human stood with their hands on their hips, eyes blazing through their visual aids.

Kif checked her translator. Two hundred hours until it completed a dialect scan and could generate her foolproof responses. So much for Arehi implants being hi-tech. 'I do not,' she repeated, which seemed to be the best option of the lot. 'Bad for my immunity.'

'What? Who told you that, your aunty? You come to my table, take Aunty Diya's seat, eat me out of my yum cha dinner and now I bring you to my home, what? You spit on my cooking?'

Back on the Suraci, the crew had had the occasional argument or heated moment, but it never lasted long — well, not more than a few days — but this felt different. This 'Aunty' mortal, in their little jumpsuit, standing in their kitchen, was already impatient and expecting a resolution. Kif consulted the guidebook again. *Median life expectancy is one hundred and twenty years.* Right, so they would die before long.

'Aunty, I mean no harm,' she said.

'Mm-hmm. Eat up.'

Perhaps this was the only resolution.

As Kif gobbled down her second bowl, she wondered what would kill her first. Would it be the garlic, which might counteract her solar meds? Would it be her gravity meds? Prolonged disconnection from the hive? Did she care? The soft slippery noodles were to die for, soaked in kecap manis, ground peanut, birds-eye chilli, crushed fresh ginger and garlic.

Before she had ended up in the Aunty's flat, Kif had expected to spend her first 296 hours on the Jerlipiur northern station, at a minimum, laying low and letting her guidebook catch up. The view of the cloudy planet below and the black above took her breath away but she had mimicked the disinterested expression of the stationers, just in case. All of them looked unhappy at all times — their expressions were all in their voices — as they threatened and pleaded with hangar operators, merchants and hawkers, waving purple discs in their hands. Not wanting to make a scene, she'd paid thrice the listed price and left the hangar operator snickering.

Everything had been going to plan. She and her comrades had spaced themselves, swindled an emergency shuttle and landed here. They'd spent the 102 hours of transit talking, and then Kif had napped while the others had sexual relations. Then, they parted ways: the random number generator selected her as the one to take Space Station A. The three planet-bound comrades were grim as they took their fair share of the high-gravity meds. They had the lowest chance of survival.

How was she, a rookie stowaway, meant to know that taking the one spare seat in the galley (correction: for-profit eatery), would make a local stick to her like carbon scoring?

'Oi. Can't sit here, daughter,' the mortal snapped. They tended to a plate of rice spilling out of an aromatic brown leaf.

Kif got up immediately. 'Please take my sorry ...' her translator whirring, she snatched a phrase she'd heard used when addressing a superior, '... Aunty. I—'

'My son must've stood me up again. Why does he book lunch when his business meetings always run overtime. Must be wool in his ears. Where you going?'

'I—'

'Can't any young people make time for their elders anymore? When I was your age, I made dinner for my mother and grandmother every night. What say to that, huh?'

Kif thought about her answer long and hard. 'Please take my sorry, Aunty—'

'Enough, sit down before the staff bother us. What you want?'

Blood. 'Hungry.'

'Yes yes, you want order for you? Ah, you don't know this place. Hey! Hey!' Aunty waved her hand in the air and glared around the room until a silver four-wheeled creature lurched up to them.

'*Ha gow, xiao long bao, cha siu bao, siu mai,*' it beeped.

'*Haiyoh*, one of each but not the *ha gow*. No one wants your frozen prawn. They say it's been frozen for centuries hah, think anyone would eat it they knew that?'

'*Of course, valued customer.*'

'Hah! Stupid waiter. Can't even stay loyal to your boss.'

'*Enjoy your meal, valued customer.*'

Over the next hour, Kif gained a lot of intel and would need many more hours to sift through it and record what was valuable. Aunty Ovee Zh was ninety-two, of average weight and height for Jerlipos, widow of Aunty Diya Zh. They had three adult children, and Woolly Son Epun she saw regularly as he often came up to the station to meet clients, but Woolly-headed Epun didn't show up half the time due to said meetings going overtime. 'Stupid boy could take the spare room at my place instead of up and down to the planet. Then he could at least have tea with his mother.' Aunty Ovee had five children in-law and nine grandchildren with a tenth on the way, at which point 'the babies stop or Diya's inheritance won't be enough to give everyone gifts. That woolly son of mine says he'll pay for lunch then doesn't show up, so what happens? Does he think I can walk out without eating or paying? Give me that bill, silly girl.'

Aunty handed over an awful lot of those purple discs. Kif understood that stationers performed labour in exchange for these ration tokens. What she didn't understand was why nobody questioned her. If only she had finished downloading the guidebook from the Arehi mother corporate, then she might understand, but there had been no time. And now she was being taken back to the mortal's flat, which made her heart pound. This was also clearly a local custom and so refusing came with more risks.

While Kif slurped away at her second free meal, Aunty studied her with interest.

'You used to working for food?'

Her mind went back to the yum cha bill. 'Yes, Aunty, I—'

'Good. You start tomorrow. Where you from?'

'Areh. Migrant. Worked repairs on ships for money.' That had been her assigned cover story. Her comrades would deliver their own variations when questioned. It was risky mentioning Areh, but their mother empire had ensured that no civilisation other than hers would be able to travel between galaxies. It was only realistic.

'*Haiyoh*, long way to here. You bring vampires with you again? Not much people left after last time Arehi were here, thousand years ago.'

'No, Aunty, no vampires.'

Aunty pressed a small bowl of yellow liquid into her hand. 'Drink up, it helps you heal. Go rest. Spare room all ready for the son that never comes.'

Before she could construct another sentence, the little mortal-woman left her, singing something mellow under her breath.

Deep in the galley of emissary-class rover Suraci, many years ago, Kif drew the tube away from her mouth, licking her lips of residual blood … the feeder tank, a hulking silver beast that exposed its underbelly of nipples to the room.

'… We approach a Green Solar System with eleven planets, two of them habitable and nine of a gaseous, icy composition. Our rock harvester colleagues will be pleased to hear this, and so they will be here in a few decades …'

'Praise be to our mother corporate Areh …'

… Her comrades erased their names from her RAM so they could not incriminate each other …

One of them with short white hair spoke with their hands … next shift, we go.

Kif woke to her stomach churning. Objects blurred in and out of her vision until she located something that looked enough like a waste channel. She hobbled over, little needles of pain filling her knees, a feeling that was numbed by hot pulp that forced itself past her teeth and down the brown pipe. She heaved, dribbling down her neck and onto her clothes: she'd need to clean that. How many hours of sleep had passed? It felt like a moment ago she had set herself down. More pulp, there goes the rice—

'—child? Is it the garlic allergy?'

'Not a child, I'm centuries older than you,' Kif grumbled to herself.

Light filled the room as Aunty Ovee marched through the doorway, drawing herself to a full height at Kif's elbow. Between belches, as Aunty held her by the shoulder, Kif decided that this little mortal was her shift leader. It was unorthodox, but all the principles of the Arehi mother corporate applied.

When she was finished, she followed orders: down ginger tea

and congee, change into Ovee's son's old clothes, press a heated stone to her stomach and lie on her side in a foetal position. Twenty-one hours later, she was woken, fed more ginger tea and congee, emptied her bowels and told that she had had enough sleep. Following detailed and sometimes shouted instructions, she reset the waste cycle, reorganised the contents of the dresser into eight outfits, fixed the inventory tracker and synced it with the supply schedule of the station, seasonal availability of produce, and Aunty's calendar. Notifications would now go to Kif's implant, allowing her to screen them before sending on the relevant items to Aunty's visual aids.

Once Aunty understood that she slept once every 128 hours, she began to let her sleep for at least twenty hours. Too much, according to Aunty Ovee, too little according to Kif, but it was a good enough compromise. In those peaceful twenty hours of slumber, Kif learned what it was like to dream. She dreamed of the events leading up to her desertion of the Suraci ship; sometimes she dreamed even further back, unlocking memories she shouldn't have. She saw herself on a white table, surrounded by white robed medic officers who plugged needles into her wrists, her belly, her skull, changing her. It was painful to see, so she decided best not to think about it for now.

Aunty Ovee watched every spoonful of chicken rice enter and leave Kif's mouth. Kif hoped she thought her clumsiness could be attributed to her poor health, not a lack of practice with cutlery.

'So, no garlic for you, hah?'

'We will try again some time,' Kif said. Her implant told her that her digestive system was acclimatising to this new diet.

'Hmm. You speak better now. Any food you want?'

Kif thought about her answer. 'Just blood,' she said, then, when Aunty's thin eyebrows rose, she added, 'blood-rich foods.'

'Ah, you from one of those crowds that worships the vampires?'

Kif coughed, sending the rice the wrong way.

'*Haiyoh*, concentrate on eating. We hear about the vampires, the ones your Arehi mother corporate made. I was a teacher, you know, so I knew all the stories of mother demons, plague bearers, dead babies; all of them stories been around since the Blood and Cloaks, since those Areh ships did it. My wife, your Aunty Diya, she got sick, you know. Now you take this old person shopping.'

Did mortals always transition conversation topics this fast? Kif shoved more rice into her mouth, hoping her guidebook would catch up. 'Do we have enough rations, Aunty?'

'No, but you say you work for more rations. I explain it to the blood sausage hawker — they understand. Then I go to family dinner at the yum cha, take a nap, and come back for you.'

'Yes, Aunty.'

Clouds of ash billowed through the atmosphere before Kif's eyes, like a hand smoothing gunpowder over its glassy surface. Who knew which planet this was or when it was …

'… least one of the species will dominate an ecosystem and reduce its diversity …'

… on the infovis holo display … the yellow dot, flashing with warning.

'A hidden trove, waiting to be found by an unintelligent people,' the shift leader's lover mused. 'Is it the absence of knowledge that turns technology into magic?'

'... *blow to the food production, combined with disease, means population will be set back by around 870 years from their current position. Casualties are ... about 29% of the population.*'

... Her colleagues board the shuttles, hooded in pristine white cloaks, cloaks that were deep with pockets of concealed Arehi tech. The fabric was sewn to their skin, for it could not be removed. They had 300 hours to spread awe and fear for the Arehi mother corporation: to invade dreams, drink blood and liberate temples. To fuel allegiance to the corporation when it came knocking for bodies, rocks, blood. And then they would be consumed by the robes and their shuttles would burn, for 300 hours was considered the safe window in which an Arehi could not be turned. The robes would linger until they were imprinted in the minds of the locals, uploaded to their stories.

... Three more spaced themselves, one of her comrades signed, *their hands punctuating the sentence firmly.*

Have you deleted the shuttle?

Yes, *Kif signed.*

And we know our destination?

Yes. The ship will pass through the system but not stop. The last visit was recent and still inspires fear.

The third time Aunty Ovee brought Kif to family dinner, the children and grandchildren stopped asking Aunty questions about Kif and started asking Kif about Kif. As Kif served Aunty the plumpest, fluffiest *cha siu bao*, then served the rest of the table, the eldest daughter-in-law, Sutant, took issue with the wait-droid. At least this routine was comfortingly familiar.

'... and don't give me the soggy ones that have been sitting in your trolley all day like you did last time.'

'*We pride ourselves on serving only the freshest food made by expert hands.*'

'Well this wasn't fresh or professional, you hunk of metal. We don't need you down at home you know, and I wonder how your manufacturer convinced the station dwellers to pay for you. You can't even hold a conversation!'

'*Yes, valued customer.*'

'The rise in wait-droids can be attributed to low labour costs and the professionalisation of the human workforce,' Kif said.

'According to who?'

'Jerli zine, Stationer variant, volume 886, issue 9412. Humans are simply too qualified to want the same jobs as droids, the study would suggest.' Now that her guidebook had spent enough time processing local content, she didn't hesitate to use this knowledge.

'*Please take a seat, valued customer.*'

'*Haiyoh*, no fight in them anymore. No fun.'

Although she'd never admit it, to Kif, Sutant was beautiful. It was never the features that mattered: it was the way she paired fitted shorts with stiff blazers, or soft boleros with sweeping a-line skirts, and brought it all together with her copper piercings and eyeliner. Everything she wore shone, like she wanted to be confused for the droids she hated so much. All these observations Kif kept to herself, knowing that few would understand her appreciation was purely aesthetic, and devoid of attraction.

The family let Sutant continue griping until the Woolly Son arrived. This was the first time he'd made it to a lunch with Kif in attendance. A shiny brooch was fastened to his teal skort, right above the knee: the shape of an eye made from black stones, signalling his allegiance to a popular worship franchise, The Limited Sky.

'Sorry I'm late, Ma.' Epun patted Aunty Ovee on the cheek and the wait-droid assembled a chair for him next to Aunty. He looked around the circular table and the faces that rose from its top, winking and smiling at the little ones, a few nods at the older ones. His eyes stopped on Kif, then he smiled. 'New clothes today!'

Kif glanced down at herself: on Aunty's instructions, she wore a loose red tunic with gold and black geometric patterns stamped around the neckline, waist and hem. A gold belt delineated the deep pockets, and matched her gold stockings. She'd bought boots that were well worn, then replaced the frayed laces with stiff red ones, and bought a more expensive pair and multicoloured stockings for Aunty.

Slowly, uncertainly, Kif smiled back. 'Thank you for letting me borrow your clothes. I am eager to return them to you—'

'Keep them. Don't fit me anymore.'

'She bought Ma new clothes, too.' A grandchild had spoken, xeir eyes fixed on Aunty's.

'Little one, how do you know these things?' Aunty Ovee patted the grandchild's hair.

'You never buy yourself new things. Too expensive you say, not worth it for old lady like you.'

Kif choked on her *bao,* the tang of pepperberry sliding down her throat. Epun stood suddenly.

'Eh, another meeting?' Aunty Ovee asked.

'Kif, please accompany me to the waste-cycles.'

One look from Aunty told her that this action had her approval. She followed the flapping tails of his jacket to the most expensive part of the yum cha: a boardwalk with a glass floor, revealing the inky blackness of space below. Embedded in the railings were thin tanks made of glass. Tiny air vents and strategic moving blue lights gave the illusion of water, at least in an abstract way. Little metal creatures with sharp ribs, diamond-shaped fins and heads with eyeless sockets zigzagged back and forth, like they were swimming.

'Are you boinking my mother?'

Kif's guidebook went into overdrive.

'Look,' he continued, 'you may not be from around here so I'll break it down for you. In Jerlipiur, a family is an elder feeding milk to an infant. You get what your family gives. You may come from some cushy foreign government that spoon feeds you from the moment you feel hunger, but you can't have her. She has lived on Ma Diya's inheritance in this plush station for years and to what avail? And now you come along and — explain yourself, tell me that I'm wrong.'

She sighed. 'I am aware that you lost your Ma Diya recently, and that—'

'Oh, you think you know about my mum? It was seven years ago. Don't talk to me about her. I work in system security, do you know? I could have you spaced, or worse, sent back to whatever hole you came from.'

Kif processed his words. He had probably worked out that she was Arehi, but perhaps his job allowed him to investigate her further. 'I earn rations for the both of us, two-thirds of which go to her children—'

'Of course you do, how else do you get into her bed without her feeling she owed you, you—'

'She gave me sanctuary, that is all. We have separate rooms. I take no personal gratification from sexual relations — at best, it is like exercise to me, and at worst, it makes me regurgitate a full stomach — is that what you wanted to know?'

She returned to studying the metal fish, until Aunty Ovee came to fetch her. '*Haiyoh*, Kif, no need to scare him like that. Introduce new ideas to a mind and how can he say he is the same person? Come, we must go before the hawkers leave.'

Steering her out of the restaurant by her wizened arm, Aunty Ovee laughed and laughed, repeating the things said between Epun and Kif for her own amusement.

'That boy couldn't understand love if it hit him in the throat. Your Aunty Diya may be dead, but my heart is still in her mouth.' Her eyes twinkled. 'They say back before Blood and Cloaks, Jerlipiur culture was predominantly aromantic. Different time, then. Diya and I would be the strange ones.'

The Suraci share-bed, the five vampires crammed together on it, sucking and enjoying their last drops of blood … Speaking of the crewmates they would never see again, never sleep with … Kif wondered not for the first time how some lived their lives driven by these desires, these distinctions between one peer and another. To her, many individuals were beautiful, like an elegantly built ship, gleaming amongst the stars. That was all.

'Oh, that reminds me — could anyone find out anything more about Areh?'

Everyone shook their heads. Their mother corporate was too

much to process, which was probably why so many vampires
spaced themselves after learning the truth. She was grateful she'd
found her comrades, even if she would never see them again.

After that encounter with Epun, Kif saw a lot more of the children, who now insisted on taking Aunty out to meals and shopping, even paying for her on occasion. Kif had more time to do cleaning and technical repair work in return for rations, as well as time to herself.

Aunty Ovee was 'over the moon', as the locals liked to say. 'You see, another grandchild comes into my life, what. Now my children must take me shopping, pay for my lunch, for they think they must fight for their inheritance! Works every time.'

'Every time?'

'Did you think all those grandchildren belong to my kids? Some look nothing like! *Haiyoh*, thought you were polite not to say so.'

'You adopted some?'

'They feel threatened then they get over it. Then it's time for another.'

Eventually, Aunty Ovee extended her newfound influence to have Kif minding a grandchild once every few cycles. She would tutor xem in computer languages, physics and history — hopefully enough to get xem into any professional workforce so xey wouldn't be stuck in 'volunteering'. Xeir mother, Sutant, suddenly had a heightened awareness of labour issues. Besides, who would say no to unpaid services?

The child played with xeir hair, staring off into the distance.

'Little one, tell me about something in your planet's history.'

'My name is Trepzi,' xey huffed. Trepzi drew xemselves up to xeir full height, which was not much. 'Are you a you-know-what?'

'A what?'

'A vampire. Is that why you like blood sausage so much?'

'No, it's because I've got a blood condition.'

'Yeah. Like a vampire. Do you have a reflection?'

'Let's talk about vampires.'

The child took the bait. 'I know they say vampires came from Areh and then the Blood and Cloaks happened. Or they came after. But actually, I *know* the Areh made the Blood and Cloaks happen.'

'Really?'

'Yeah. They sucked all the blood out of my great great great great great great great great Aunty.'

Kif started to calculate the generations, then decided against it. 'How do you know?'

'Ma and Mama and Ma Mee told me, obviously. And they say if you don't know how far back your ancestor is then just say great times eight.'

'So what happened?'

'They sucked everyone's blood. Then they gave everyone a cough. Maybe they gave it when they were sucking the blood. Then they killed everyone with the cough and the blood and since then we have,' xey dropped to a whisper, 'demons.'

'Demons? What do they do?'

'Everyone knows. How come you don't know?'

'I'm not from around here.'

'Whatever. They're in my dreams — but I'm not scared. When I told Mama and Ma and Ma Mee about my nightmares — I mean my dreams — they told me and my siblings these scary stories about them. To protect us or something. If we know what demons look like then we can ... we can not die.'

'The demons, does everyone see them?'

'They say that everyone sees them when they're little.'

'What about adults?'

'You're not supposed to talk about them! Do you not have any where you're from?'

'Maybe,' Kif shrugged. 'I heard Aunty singing something the other day — are there songs about the—'

'Everyone knows the songs.'

'Can you sing one for me?'

Trepzi pouted, but began to sing almost immediately:

> The mind is like a garden,
> Where mycelium sprouts, garlic flowers,
> Chilli blooms and pepperberry flourishes.
> Its fragrance draws outsiders,
> Who uproot and poison our bowers—
> How our pride impoverishes.
> A roof of cloudy glass keeps warmth in
> And keeps white robes out at all hours
> Why risk the stars if your child perishes?

Kif stamped her feet in approval, as was the custom here. The child beamed, then frowned when Kif's eyes went glassy. A message had appeared in her peripheral vision — not from Aunty but a blocked number. A comrade.

Areh is gone.

Several cycles (or 'months') later, Kif decided she was ready. She waited until Aunty Ovee had settled onto the mat with her tea, before beginning her rehearsed questions.

'Why do you live as a stationer?' she asked.

'Eh?'

'This is for Trepzi's tuition. Trust me.'

'Mm-hmm. Your Aunty Diya's place, this place, was left to me.'

'Why not move downstairs with your children and grandchildren?'

Aunty Ovee snorted. 'The children might complain but they don't want me down there — not with the sickness.'

'What sickness?'

'Ah, I forget sometimes you are from Areh, and don't know these things.' Kif highly doubted that Aunty ever forgot that. 'Your mother corporate Areh only tells you nice things. Since the Night of Thin Blood and White Cloaks — young people call it Blood and Cloaks now, too lazy to say the whole thing — there's blood sickness, very contagious. My grandmother used to say it was because they drank so many people's blood back then and then those people made babies, that it probably gets passed down. Other sicknesses, too. White spots, insects that infect instead of just pollinating like they meant to.'

'What else do they say about the Arehi, about the mother corporate empire?'

Aunty looked down at her tea for a while. 'Are you upset?'

'Why?'

'Your planet. Gone. I heard the news but hid it from you.'

'No, I already knew.' Kif took a deep breath, deeper than

usual. 'I have contacts. I told you I'm Arehi, but it's a bit more complicated than that.'

'You're a vampire, lah.'

Kif gave herself several moments to process this. 'How did you know?'

'Obvious. You used to want blood and told me when sick you were alive for centuries. You don't sleep then you sleep for hours. My children never did that.'

'Then why haven't — why haven't you panicked? Or told Epun? Or had me killed?'

Aunty Ovee beamed and sipped her tea. 'You're weak, lah. Not like vampire stories.'

'How did Aunty Diya die?'

'*Haiyoh*, why you bringing that up?'

'It's important.'

'She was helping rebuild telecoms for Jerlipiur-8. They say a thousand years ago, before Blood and Cloaks, we could talk to other planets.'

'And?'

Tears shone in Aunty's eyes. 'She got sick. Not sick like they do downstairs — mind sick. She saw the white cloaks in her dreams, in her congee — drove her crazy. Dead.'

Kif put a hand over hers, hoping this would communicate her condolences. Spoken words didn't seem to be enough.

'Your hands are so cold. That gave it away too, you know. I thought vampires were strong and fast. Are the others like that or they all weak like you?'

'All weak like me,' Kif laughed. 'We're designed to survive intergalactic space travel. That not superhuman enough for you?'

The dreams of being on operating tables, the patriotism of the Areh ship culture, which were all she could remember — although they never felt *right*. The Night of the Thin Blood and White Cloaks. Areh, the mighty empire that lay galaxies away: gone. Now that she had had thousands of hours to think, it all made sense.

Kif had come to this station hoping to hide and dissociate herself from the Areh mission, free herself from the myth. She and her comrades had separated in the interest of their survival, when the opposite was true.

By her estimations, she was about 734 years old, though she looked like a teenager to the people of Jerlipiur. That gave her approximately a millennia to live. That wasn't much, but as she had learned from the ways mortals packed everything into a single cycle, it was enough time to make a start. She would train to be a neurological researcher, as her Aunty Diya had been. 'That way you can stay here with me,' Aunty Ovee had reasoned. She and her comrades would learn all they could about the white cloak virus that Arehi had created, the one that lay dormant in every mind until the slightest scientific progress was made. Thoughts of reaching the stars, contacting other planets, probably even some medical advancements — all seemed to trigger the white cloaks, which would haunt the host mind until their death.

She had centuries to live. That was enough time to learn how to remove the virus. Then, if there was time to spare after the viruses were removed, with the local's minds no longer blocked, they would move onto planetary defence systems, hacking Arehi ships, liberating more vampires with the truth: the truth that

Areh was gone and they were lone ships, serving a dead mistress that had presumably destroyed herself.

When she presented this Thousand Year Plan to Aunty Ovee, she was instructed to make several changes, which included a myriad of ways that her children and grandchildren could be employed out of this, however tenuous the link between the mission and their skills.

'Also, child?'

'You know I'm older. You should call *me* Aunty,' Kif countered.

'Ha ha. Very funny. You spend too much time with Trepzi, that cheeky one. When your friends coming for dinner?'

'In two cycles, Aunty. I have scheduled the shopping already.'

'Mm-hmm. Child, you should make some of those surgeries that make you vampire, give them to me so I can supervise you, lah. Otherwise you'll be stuck with my children forever.'

Kif opened her mouth to remind Aunty Ovee that being a vampire was excruciating, when she saw the glint in Aunty's eyes.

'*Haiyoh*, thought you never learn a sense of humour.'

Kif laughed back. 'Yes, Aunty.'

ABOUT THE CONTRIBUTORS

L.E. Austin has a Bachelor of Arts from Edith Cowan University, and currently resides in Perth, where she works in a library by day and spends her evenings reading, drinking tea, and procrastinating writing. On weekends she creates content for her various social media platforms (and spends far too much time scrolling Instagram looking at other people's bookshelves). Austin has always had a passion for YA stories. She especially loves getting stuck into a good fantasy novel equipped with sword-fighting, ale-drinking and, of course, a morally grey villain with a redemption arc.

Shaeden Berry is a writer with a BA in English Literature, and is currently midway through her Masters of Creative Writing. She has written for *Refinery29*, *Fashion Journal* and *Aniko Press* and has upcoming pieces with *Kill Your Darlings* and *soft stir*. She lives in Boorloo, Western Australia with her partner and their two cats, Frumpkin and George.

Lin Blythe is a proud spec-fic writer, a Eurasian/ABC and asexual woman. Her writing has been published in *Overland* online magazine, *Left Turn on Red Permitted After Stopping: UTS Writers' Anthology 2022*, *Moon Orchard* and the *Heroines Anthology: Vol. 4*. Since completing her Bachelor of Creative Writing at the University of Technology Sydney, Lin has written about her Malaysian Chinese family's intergenerational trauma, as it seems to help her heal. She hopes her stories tear down the wall of complacency, crush othering and encourage readers to fight for justice and peace. Lin is a socialist, feminist and antiracist activist who lives on the unceded land of First Nations people. Always was always will be Aboriginal land.

Elizabeth Bourke (she/her) is a young writer living on unceded Dharawal land. Her writing tangles nature, technology and queerness. She was highly commended for Express Media's 2022 Catalyse Nonfiction Prize. Her work has been featured in *Island*, *Newcomers Journal*, and won third place in the 2022 Honi Soit Fiction Writing Competition. She is an alumnus of Express Media's ToolkitsLITE: Fiction program. You can find her on Instagram @ elizabethbourkewriter

Aidan Demmers is a freelance editor and creative writer living on Jagera and Turrbul Country, who has recently graduated from QUT with a Bachelor of Fine Arts in Creative Writing. He loves queer romance, genre fiction, and the Oxford comma, and hopes to someday publish a book featuring all three. Currently, they are working as Commissioning Editor of the queer sci-fi anthology *Celestial Bodies*, which will be published by Tiny Owl Workshop in 2023. Their poetry can be found in *Baby Teeth Journal* and *Scratch That Magazine*.

Emma Di Bernardo is a queer cisgender writer and educator from Meanjin/Brisbane. She was listed in the 2021 Richell Prize for Emerging Writers Longlist. Her non-fiction work has been featured in the 2021 Black Inc anthology *Growing Up Disabled in Australia* and *ABC Everyday*. You can find her on social media at @ emmadiwriter.

Henry Farnan grew up on unceded Whadjuk Noongar boodja, constantly moving between suburbia and the south-west. They have a BA (Hons) in Creative Writing from Curtin University. Their prose, poetry and non-fiction writing has appeared in a variety of journals and magazines including *Blue Bottle Journal*, *Pulch Mag* and *Aurealis* among others.

Jesse Galea (they/he) is a transmasc writer living and creating in Boorloo. They're a future librarian and spreadsheet enthusiast who has recently graduated with a Bachelor of Arts in Creative Writing from Curtin University. When he's not writing, he can be found cycling through several crafty hobbies (most recently, bookbinding) or unashamedly listening to Midwest emo. As a teenager, he didn't have access to LGBTQIA+ YA and so didn't know these stories existed. Since discovering them in adulthood and devouring as many as he could get his hands on (something they've never stopped doing), he's proud to be able to add his voice to the ever-growing sea of LGBTQIA+ YA writers. Their writing has appeared in *Pulch Mag*, *#EnbyLife*, and *just femme & dandy*, among others. They're also on Twitter and Instagram @JesseGalea_.

A.R. Henderson is a writer, editor, and researcher working on Ngunnawal country. They completed a PhD in Creative Writing at the University of Canberra, where they studied LGBTQIA+ representation in young adult literature. Way back in 2012 they were a finalist in the *Sydney Morning Herald*'s Young Writer of the Year competition. Their short stories have appeared in literary magazines such as *SWAMP* and *#EnbyLife*. You can find all their work in a nice, neat pile at arhendersonwrites.com.

Anna Jacobson is an award-winning writer and artist from Meanjin (Brisbane). *Amnesia Findings* (UQP, 2019) is her first illustrated poetry collection, which won the 2018 Thomas Shapcott Poetry Prize. A second collection, *Anxious in a Sweet Store*, is forthcoming with Upswell in 2023. Anna is the recipient of the Nillumbik Prize for Contemporary Writing, a Queensland Writers Fellowship, and the Queensland Premier's Young Publishers and Writers Award. Her website is www.annajacobson.com.au

Clover Lake is a queer transgender author and university student looking forward to continuing her English studies at a postgraduate level. She is interested in magical realism, new materialism, and a currently unexplored field she knows as the 'odd & unremarkable'. These interests, along with gardening, spaces of reclamation and decay, gay stuff, reconciliation towards the natural world, liminality, and a little bit of horror are what informs her work.

Jes Layton (he/him, she/her) is a writer, illustrator and arts worker living and working on Wurundjeri Land. He is the current co-CEO and Executive Director of the Emerging Writers' Festival. Jes' written and illustrative work can be found at *SBS, Junkee, Voiceworks, Kill Your Darlings, Archer, The Big Issue* and scattered elsewhere online and in print. She also has work published with Black Inc, Fremantle Press and Nero Books among others. His tweets have been written about in *Teen Vogue, the Daily Mail, Screen Rant, Buzzfeed* and more. Exposure was apparently payment. Find him online at @ageekwithahat

Lian Low (she/they) is a Kuala Lumpur born writer of Peranakan-Chinese-Malaysian heritage, currently based in Footscray on the unceded lands of the Kulin Nation. Lian has work published in *Growing Up Asian in Australia, Kill Your Darlings, The Lifted Brow,* a story podcasted on Queerstories and was a previous editor of *Peril.* They created site-specific spoken word pieces for the Melaka Art and Performance Festival, Malaysia from 2013-2015. Lian has been a recipient of a Wheeler Centre Hot Desk Fellowship and of their inaugural Next Chapter scheme to work on a young adult speculative fiction novel that is a paranormal romantic twist on a migrant coming-of-age story that traverses Footscray, Melbourne and Malaysia.

Seth Malacari (he/they) is an award-winning writer and member of the LGBTQIA+ community. Their work has appeared in *Underdog: LoveOzYA Short Stories* (2019). He is the founder of Get YA Words Out, has a Master of Arts (Writing and Literature) from Deakin University specialising in Queer YA and was the former chair of LoveOzYA.

Alistair Ott (they/he) is a Wiradjuri Queer artist. Born on Gundungurra and raised on Ngunnawal Land, they were taught Dreamtime stories and their family's language and culture from their Ngama and Mudyigang. These stories, his time on country with mob and family, and his queer community inspire his writing; these are the spaces where his spirit resides. When they aren't writing, Alistair spends their time working in LGBTIQA+ community services and on their PhD at the Australian National University. He hopes to continue writing stories that spark joy for queer blakfullas like himself. Dyiramadilinya badhu Wiradjuri!

Em Readman is a nonbinary writer hailing from Meanjin (Brisbane) and residing in Boorloo (Perth). Their work has been published by The Suburban Review, Bowen Street Press, Aniko Press and others. They often write about family, memory, and queerness, with a focus on the transient natures of all three. In 2022, Em won the Hunter Writer's Centre Blue Knot Award.

Lukah Roser is a twenty-six-year-old self-taught writer living and working out of the Goldfields region of Western Australia. If not writing or watching anime, Lukah can be found sneaking in reading time at work, running his small business or spending time in Boorloo with his found-family. When home, his best company are his friends, father, his two dogs and his two hairless cats. As a transgender, bisexual man, Lukah is passionate about using his writing to bring light to the subjects of gender identity, sexuality, and strong platonic forms of love. His favourite genres are magical realism and horror.

Ash Taylor is a man of transgender experience, born and raised on Gumbaynggirr country on the mid-north coast of Australia. From a young age he was always telling and reading stories, and this fascination with words and tales has followed him throughout his life. Ash is currently living on Anaiwan country in Armidale, New South Wales, where he is pursuing a Bachelor of Media and Communications at the University of New England, majoring in Writing and Publishing.

Alexander Te Pohe is a Māori trans man living on Whadjuk Noongar Land. His prose and poetry can be found in the collections *Australian Poetry Anthology* (Volume 9, 2021-2022) and *To Hold The Clouds* (2020, Centre For Stories), as well as publications such as *Djed Press*, *Portside Review*, and *Strange Horizons*.